The Cottage on Pumpkin and Vine

The Cottage on Pumpkin and Vine

Kate Angell
Jennifer Dawson
Sharla Lovelace

KENSINGTON PUBLISHING CORP.
http://www.kensingtonbooks.com

KENSINGTON BOOKS are published by

Kensington Publishing Corp.
119 West 40th Street
New York, NY 10018

All Kensington Titles, Imprints, and Distributed Lines are available at special quantity discounts for bulk purchases for sales promotions, premiums, fund-raising, educational, or institutional use. Special book excerpts or customized printings can also be created to fit specific needs. For details, write or phone the office of the Kensington special sales manager: Kensington Publishing Corp., 119 West 40th Street, New York, NY 10018, attn: Special Sales Department, Phone: 1-800-221-2647.

Kensington and the K logo Reg. U.S. Pat. & TM Off.

eISBN-13: 978-1-4967-0689-8
eISBN-10: 1-4967-0689-7
First Kensington Trade Edition: September 2016
First Kensington Mass Market Edition: September 2017

eISBN-13: 978-1-4967-0690-4
eISBN-10: 1-4967-0690-0

10 9 8 7 6 5 4 3 2 1

Printed in the United States of America

Contents

Charmed by You

KATE ANGELL

To my readers who celebrate Halloween:

Ghosts and Goblins
Spooks Galore
Scary Witches
At Your Door
Jack-O-Lanterns
Smiling Bright
Wishing You A
Haunting Night

Boo!

Acknowledgment

Alicia Condon, editorial director,
once again, and always,
thanks for everything!

Chapter 1

"**D**on't roll the pumpkins, haul them on the industrial dollies. The pumpkins are carved. They bruise and dent easily. You're squinting eyes and breaking teeth. Be more careful," cautioned Grace Alden, the local party planner and owner of Charade, "A costume shop for all reasons and seasons." She'd been hired by her godmother, Amelia Rose, to decorate her B&B, Rose Cottage, for Halloween. She tapped the face on her watch, reminding the workers for the hundredth time of her tight two-day schedule. "Work faster, please. The exterior isn't close to being finished. The interior is next. There's a lot of furniture to rearrange. Decorations to be displayed."

Work the fuck faster? Cade Maxwell straightened from rolling his pumpkin. He stretched his arms over his head, cracked his back. Then his knuckles. The woman was a ballbuster. No slack. She'd hired his moving company and muscle to drive to a local pumpkin patch at dawn to pick up an order for twenty 100-pound, professionally carved pumpkins. Orange and round would line the cobblestone sidewalk leading to the bed-and-breakfast, lit from the inside by flameless candles. Each pumpkin was unique. Some smiled; others smirked. One looked downright evil. Then there was Cinderella's pumpkin, set closest to the porch stairs. Ready to be transformed into a carriage with a pair of glass slippers at the base.

Three Men and a Truck were doing their job, as instructed. Still Grace hovered. She didn't trust anyone. Not him or his two cousins. She had to be on top of every little detail. Pointing out minor mistakes as if they were major. She wanted things done with the snap of her fingers. Lady had done a lot of snapping. His men responded by slowing down. He didn't blame them. There'd been no breaks, and it was nearly noon. Hunger made men grumpy. Clumsy. Cade caught their side-glares and grumbles from the south side of the lawn.

"Lunch," he announced. He didn't have to tell them twice. Kyle and Jake stopped what they were doing and headed for their trucks, parked at the curb. They couldn't get away fast enough.

"One hour," he called, as they burned rubber.

He hoped they'd both return. Kyle was debatable. The younger man often got distracted by the cute waitress at the Kopper Kettle, his regular lunch spot. He ate his way through the afternoon. Left a big tip. He needed to ask her out soon. His shyness had packed on fifteen pounds. Jake only worked enough hours each week to pay his rent and stock his refrigerator. He wasn't out to get rich. He bordered on lazy.

His cousins were good guys. They came together and completed most jobs. Grace, however, rode their last nerve. They didn't like being bossed around by a woman, not even an attractive one.

Cade set his back teeth, tightened his jaw. He wasn't into Halloween. He never had been. Never would be. He found it ridiculous. A total waste of time. He could do without the costumes, gauzy spiderwebs, and rubber black bats. He would tolerate the nonsense for two days. No more. His contract with Grace was lucrative. He'd purposely jacked up the price to discourage her. She hadn't blinked an eye. She'd written him a check on the spot. He was in the transport business, although loading and delivering pumpkins was a first for him. A decorating addendum was included in the charge. One he'd anticipated, but hadn't realized would become so complicated. No amount of money was worth what he faced right now. Sadly, his signature was binding.

Grace came down the stone sidewalk toward him, her steps quick and precise. He'd known her a long time. She hadn't changed. Much. She walked the same way now as she had in first grade. In control and going about her business. Even on the playground she'd planned activities. Timed to when the bell rang. He'd often teased her. She always blew him off.

He took a moment and checked her out now. Not as a business contact, but as a man would eye a woman. She was a brunette with blue eyes, arching eyebrows, and high cheekbones. Full lips. It was fifty-five degrees, and her curves hid beneath a bulky knit sweater and baggy wool slacks. Short-heeled boots lifted her to five-two, if she was lucky, standing next to his six-four.

She was pretty. Also pushy. He could think of better uses for her mouth than ordering him around. He liked his women patient, tolerant, and able to exhale. Not jacked up on Halloween.

She momentarily stood beside him, deep in thought. Worrying her bottom lip. A light breeze rustled the leaves on the trees, the scent of fall heavy on the air. A hint of her perfume drifted his way. He breathed her in. Vanilla and linen. Clean. Subtle. Memorable. He wanted no memories of this day. He turned his head away from her. Inhaled the faint wafting smoke from across the street, as a neighbor burned a pile of fallen leaves.

She clasped her hands before her, thoughtful. "Every year Amelia throws the biggest and best Halloween party in town. It starts at five and goes to the witching hour. Both locals and guests at the inn show up in costume. It's an incredible night."

Cade listened, but didn't comment. What she thought incredible, he found idiotic. There'd be no changing his mind.

She closed her eyes for a beat, then opened them slowly, envisioning the decorations. "I want the front yard creatively spooky, but tasteful," she said. "The pumpkins are in place, once you coordinate the final one. A few more feet, move it gently. Turn the dent away from the sidewalk."

Dent? Hardly. It was barely a dimple. He was cautious. Treating the freakin' pumpkin like porcelain. He settled it in line. Made sure it was perfectly spaced. Then stood back, and rubbed his hands together. Checked out his handiwork.

Despite his dislike of Halloween, he had to admit the sidewalk looked good. The carved pumpkins would come alive at night. Lit up and glowing, they'd make a nice entry to the party. Guests would be impressed.

She tapped her finger against her chin. Short nails, clear polish. "We have otherworldly figures with glowing eyes and haunting faceless specters. Graveyard tombstones. Zombies crawling out of the ground for the yard.

We'll wrap mini–orange twinkle lights about the trees. A gigantic inflatable spider will hang from a gauze cobweb off the porch." She paused, cut him a look. "Perhaps a witch or hellhound. I'll fill you in as we go."

Fill him in? The corners of his mouth tightened. She had sufficient creepy and spooky—how much more did she want? He ran one hand through his hair. Halloween had taken on a life of its own. He could already hear ghostly boos and cackling witches. The howl of a demon black dog. He needed to clear his head.

Stepping back, he said, "We'll discuss this further after lunch."

Her eyes rounded. "You're stopping? Now?"

Damn straight. "I'm not working while holding a sandwich."

"Amelia will fix you something. That way you won't have to go far."

Far sounded good to him. Clear across town worked best. Truth be told, he didn't want to impose on Amelia. The Kopper Kettle had a New Englander's fish and chips special that couldn't be beat. The clam chowder was thick, creamy, and stuck to his ribs. The blueberry pie was homemade. He turned slightly, not wanting to offend Grace, yet needing to make like a ghost and disappear for an hour. "I've got other plans."

Or so he thought. The front door opened, and Amelia called to them from the porch, "Grace, Cade, join me for lunch. Lobster rolls."

He sucked air. He hadn't made his escape fast enough. He could walk away from Grace, but not Amelia. Declining her offer would appear rude. He was fond of the older woman, despite her eccentricities. She was known about town for her fortune-telling. Reading tarot cards and gazing into a crystal ball. Some people scoffed at her abilities. Others believed her every word. Especially when the unexplained and undefined became reality. Her predictions gave him goose bumps.

Still, he liked lobster. And Amelia served generous portions. He waved to her. "Be right there." He glanced at Grace. "You coming?"

She blew out a breath, debated. "I should keep working."

"The yard isn't going anywhere," he stated. "Time to recharge."

She pointed to a ladder leaning against a red maple. "I could have the twinkle lights up before you're done eating."

How much did she think he ate? "You're not using my ladder," he said firmly. "It's too dangerous. You might fall."

Her hands settled on her hips. Her chin lifted. Stubbornly. "I've climbed many ladders. I've decorated two-story roofs. Hung banners and streamers from municipal streetlights. A tree is nothing to me."

It was something to him. "Think about the inn and not yourself," he pointed out. "An accident, a broken leg, a hospital stay, and decorating comes to a halt. Amelia would be stuck with no more than a pumpkin walkway."

Concern creased her brow. "You wouldn't finish the job for me?"

He didn't have to think twice. "Contract terminated. Your fault. No refund."

"I don't like you much."

"Feeling's mutual, babe."

She huffed, turned toward the inn. Power walked. The heels on her boots clicked on the cobblestones, providing a soundtrack to her mood. He didn't care whether she was angry or not. They both needed a break. He more than her. She would go nonstop if he let her. He put his foot down.

He followed Grace, but his thoughts were on the Thirsty Raven, a small, cramped, and tucked-away tavern off Haystack Lane. It catered to blue-collar workers. Some called it a dive. Others, happy hour's finest. Quarter drafts, half-pound burgers, and a sexy bartender drew Cade. He dated Dakota on occasion. Nothing serious. Just sex. They both enjoyed a good time.

His thoughts shifted from the bar to the B&B. He scuffed his work boots on the bristled welcome mat, so as not to track in dirt. Then stomped his feet. One step inside Rose Cottage, and he traveled back in time. The place reminded him of a museum with its priceless antiques and Victorian ambience. In his experience, these kinds of rooms were labeled, *Look, but don't touch.* He jammed his hands in his jean pockets. Stood off to the side.

Grace's own thoughts touched on Amelia and her welcoming warmth as she ushered them inside. "How's my goddaughter?" she asked Grace, extending a hug and kiss on her cheek.

"Fine," Grace responded. "We've gotten a good start on prepping for the Halloween party. I have lots of ideas."

"Lots," Cade muttered behind her.

"I'm sure you do, dear." Amelia sounded pleased.

Cade offered his hand, and Amelia held it between both her own. Amelia was *reading* him, Grace realized. Her godmother was intuitive, picking up vibes through touch. Interesting.

Grace adored Amelia. The older woman was a close friend of her grandmother and mother, and a constant in Grace's life. She visited Amelia often. The inn was her second home.

As a child she'd always raced up the stairs and raided Amelia's bedroom closet, and Amelia had encouraged her unconventional behavior. Grace had loved dressing up in vintage clothing. Attempting to walk in a pair of high button shoes. Amelia was the first to recognize Grace's love of costume. Her enjoyment of tea parties. She'd supported Grace's dream of opening her business, Charade, when Grace sought a career. From birthdays to holidays, the costume shop was popular and successful. Grace couldn't have been happier.

She admired Amelia now. Her long, braided hair was the same soft gray as her eyes. Years accumulated, but never seemed to touch her. She appeared youthful, ageless, in a sage-green tunic, belted over a paisley gauze skirt in shades of cranberry, green, and gold. Elaborate gold hoops hung at her ears, ones designed with silver beads and tiny gold bells. The thin metal chains on her three-tiered necklace sparkled with lavender rhinestones and reflective mirror discs. Bangles of charms looped her wrist. A thick, hammered-silver bracelet curved near her right elbow. A triple gold ring with three pearls arched from her index finger to her fourth. She sparkled.

Her cottage was spectacular. The décor merged the past and present, and brought out the best in both. Grace couldn't wait to decorate. Cade was big and strong, all wide-shouldered and solid. He could easily rearrange the furniture into small social circles all by himself, if it came down to One Man and a Truck.

She wasn't sure his cousins would return after lunch. They hadn't seemed taken with the project. Or with her, for that matter. She'd seen them frown. Heard their grumbles. Maybe she had snapped her fingers one too many times. No matter; she wanted Halloween perfect for Amelia. She'd keep her eye on Cade. Wouldn't let him stray far. Definitely nowhere near his vehicle.

"This way." Amelia motioned them toward the kitchen.

Grace cut across an Oriental rug done in a plum, navy, and cream geometric pattern. The colors in the carpet pulled the richness of the furniture together. She noticed that Cade walked the perimeter of the room, sticking to the hardwood floor.

Off to the right, a glassed-in sunroom caught the first rays of sunshine from the overcast day. The forest-green wicker furniture, abundant greenery, and a small bookcase with monthly magazines and mystery novels offered peace and solitude.

Reception was a vintage rolltop desk. A 1900s-era candlestick telephone took calls. Grace had been fascinated by the phone as a kid. It featured a mouthpiece mounted at the top of the stand, and a receiver that was held to the ear during conversation. When the telephone was not in use, the receiver rested in the fork of the switch hook protruding to the side of the stand. Grace had run to answer the phone each time it rang whenever she'd visited.

They passed the lower-level stair landing and the innkeeper's office and found themselves in the kitchen. Cade walked closely behind her. His heat and maleness closed in. He wasn't her type. She preferred business-men in tailored suits and stylish ties. Not tall, dark-haired, unshaven, muscular guys. He overpowered her. She walked a little faster, and he matched her stride. Her awareness of him intensified.

The moment they reached the kitchen, she hurried to the far side of the oval table, distancing herself from him. He eyed her strangely before pulling himself to-gether. He ran his hands through his hair, pushing it back off his face. Then went on to tuck the navy T-shirt emblazoned with a moving truck into jeans nearly as old as Amelia's antiques. His leather work boots were worn, broken in. He didn't move or discourage Archibald from kneading and clawing his right boot when the enormous Maine coon strolled in from the pantry. The animal was like black smoke with gold eyes. A furry mystic with large, tufted paws and ears. Legend and lore surrounded the cat. Some stories were amusing, some mere fantastic flights of fantasy, and others actually plausible.

Cade hunkered down and stroked Archie. "You're one big boy."

Amelia glanced at him from the counter, where she was filling gourmet rolls with lobster salad. "He's close to thirty-five pounds and sturdy," she said of the long-haired cat with the bushy tail. "He's very social, at times even intrusive. No door stands in his way. He greets everyone as a friend, and believes they all love him. He'll be joining us for lunch."

Amelia located the cat's food dish, added dry kibble, along with several diced pieces of lobster. She set the dish on the floor next to a large bowl of water. "He has a fondness for water," she explained. "Archibald washes his food in it or just plain plays in it. He splashes, so watch for puddles. I don't want you to slip."

The cat finished his food, then rubbed and wound about Amelia's legs, head butting her calf, purring, charming her into giving him seconds. "He's bottomless." She passed the Maine coon a few more choice pieces of lobster. Archie's *meow* was loud with gratitude.

"Have a seat," Amelia suggested.

The table was small, and, no matter where Grace chose to sit, she'd be rubbing elbows with the moving man. She was suddenly aware of his lingering summer tan, his earthy, outdoor male scent, and the long look he gave her. Surprisingly formal, he pulled out a ladder-back chair and waited for her to be seated. The gesture was completely unexpected. For reasons unknown, he put her on edge.

Her nerves got the better of her. Her mind was on him and not her chair when she lowered herself onto the cushioned seat. Distracted, she slipped off the side. Had it not been for Cade catching her by the arm, she would have landed on the floor. And in a puddle, made from Archie's splashing.

Cade's grip was strong, but gentle. He gave a significant squeeze before he released her. His expression was polite, yet his gaze amused when he said, "Careful. No need for a wet butt."

Wet butt. She hadn't brought a change of clothes, and it would have taken time for her wool slacks to dry. Normally she was cautious. Unduly so. Strangely, Cade's closeness undid her. She didn't have time to evaluate the situation or her feelings. She would eat lunch and return to the yard without further mishap. The grounds were far larger than the kitchen. She'd put space between them.

"Oh, Archibald," Amelia sighed. She snagged several paper towel sheets from a roll and bent to wipe up the spill. "No swimming." The Maine coon had both front paws in his water dish.

Archie compromised. He removed one paw, only to flick water with the other. Amelia shook her head. "Silly boy."

The older woman tossed the damp paper towels into a trash can under the sink. She then set out fine china place settings. Sterling-silver flatware. Linen napkins. A plate of lobster rolls came next, followed by a romaine lettuce salad in a cut-glass bowl topped with fresh pear slices, walnuts, cranberries, and blue cheese crumbles. Glasses of sparkling water.

"Apple dumplings for dessert," said Amelia, as she settled on the chair Cade held for her. She gave him a soft smile, patted his hand. "Help yourselves."

Cade made conversation, ate slowly, and drew out his meal. Grace swore he chewed each bite twenty times. Obviously, he was procrastinating. There'd been no sign of his cousins' return. The job would go much faster with three people. Unfortunately, she might have to settle for Cade alone. He'd be responsible for climbing on the rooftop, stringing the outside lights, and anchoring the zombies, tombstones, and everything else that went bump in the night.

Rearranging the indoor furniture would put him into overtime. Fortunately their contract had set a fixed rate. He'd be forced to work around the clock if necessary. But then, so would she.

"How many guests are in residence?" she asked Amelia.

"All twelve rooms will be filled on Halloween," Amelia told her. "I even have a waiting list this year."

"Everyone in town is aware of your party," said Cade. "You'll have a packed house."

"How about you, son?" Amelia inquired. "Will you join me for a batwing cup of bubbling potion punch?"

"Bubbling?" She'd surprised him.

"Dry ice under the cauldron," Grace said, giving away the secret.

Cade eyed Amelia. "Your party sounds fun. But I don't do Halloween. Not since—" His voice dropped off.

Amelia finished her salad, dabbed the linen napkin to her lips, and completed his sentence. "Not since mischief night, seventeen years ago. I remember costumed skeletons and pre-Halloween tricks."

He raised his eyes to the ceiling. "Good memory."

"You pranked me."

He blew out a breath. "That we did."

Grace's eyes rounded. She huffed. "What did you do to my godmother? To the inn?"

Cade's jaw worked. "Six junior high school boys raised early Halloween hell. Minor vandalism. Two a.m., we toilet-papered Rose Cottage, used soap to write on the windows, and egged cars in the side lot."

Amelia pursed her lips. "All to impress girls, I believe."

"Thirteen-year-old mentality, and the girls got upset we chose the inn. They adored you, Amelia, and hated us afterward."

"I slept through it all," Amelia recalled. "The neighbors phoned in the disturbance. Marlene Litton swore she saw skeletons and heard bones rattle."

Cade ran one hand down his face, admitted, "The six of us were known for mischief making. The cops caught up to us in under an hour at Billie Murdock's house. Our costumes gave us away. We confessed, returned to the scene of the crime, and had the area cleaned up before first light."

Grace was stunned. "Why didn't I hear about this?"

"Nothing was made public," said Amelia. "No formal police report, no juvenile arrest."

"No punishment?" asked Grace.

"Not by law enforcement—only from Amelia," said Cade. "She requested we each serve twenty community-service hours at the inn. We did odd jobs, two hours a day for ten days."

Amelia smiled fondly at the delinquent skeleton. "Cade returned long after his sentence was completed. He raked leaves in the fall, shoveled snow off the front walk during winter, and mowed the grass, spring and summer. He even took up guard on the front porch every mischief night throughout high school, protecting the cottage from pranksters."

"No more skeleton costumes," assumed Grace.

"No more costumes, period."

"I can understand your aversion," Amelia said. "However, your buddy Billie Murdock doesn't feel the same. He and his pregnant wife plan to join the fun. They're dressing up."

"I rented them costumes," said Grace. "A pirate and his sidekick green parrot. The parrot suit was stretchy. Sue is in her sixth month."

"Should you change your mind, there's always room for one more," Amelia told Cade. "People come and go, a rotation of Disney characters, superheroes, ghostbusters, mad scientists, and evildoers."

"What costume did you finally choose?" Grace asked Amelia. She'd selected three choices for the older woman: a fairy godmother's gauze and glitter gown, a good fortune gypsy, and a fringed and boa flapper. Amelia would shine in whatever she wore.

"Gypsy," Amelia said. "I'll play the part, setting out the crystal ball and reading tarot cards throughout the evening."

"Always a highlight," said Grace. She could already picture Amelia in the black off-the-shoulder blouse, wide gold-and-red-metallic embroidered belt, and full, multilayered skirt with fringe and lace accents. Amelia would sparkle in a sequin knit headband and her own jewelry.

Amelia glanced at Cade as she pushed back from the table. "Last lobster roll?" she offered before clearing away the dishes.

"I've already had two."

"You'd be doing me a favor, no leftovers."

"One of your guests might enjoy it."

"They ate earlier and are all away for the day." She placed the lobster roll onto his plate. "Some planned to shop while others were headed to the World's Biggest Pumpkin Patch, south of town."

"Quite an attraction," Grace agreed. "Customers walk the acreage, hunting for the perfect pumpkin."

"I was there last week," mentioned Cade. "With my niece. It took Sara over an hour to make her selections. A big one for the family porch and a smaller one for her teacher's desk at school."

"I've met Sara," Amelia commented. "What is she now, six or seven?"

"Six," he confirmed.

"Did you carve the pumpkins?" Grace was curious.

"I did the eyes and noses and Sara did the goofy smiles."

"Goofy?" from Grace.

"I wouldn't let her hold the knife by herself—too sharp," he explained. "We carved with my hand over hers, which got her laughing. Her fingers shook with each tooth. One side of the big pumpkin's mouth was higher than the other. Almost reached an ear."

"Sounds perfect to me," said Amelia as she warmed the apple dumplings in the oven. "A pumpkin with personality."

"Lots of character," he agreed.

"Whipped or ice cream on your dumplings?" she asked them, once the crust browned and the filling bubbled. She sprinkled additional cinnamon sugar on top.

Grace and Cade responded as one, "Ice cream."

Cade leaned his elbows on the table, cut her a curious look. "I didn't think we had a thing in common."

She gave him a repressive look. "Ice cream doesn't make us friends."

Amelia scooped vanilla bean into the bowls with the dumplings. Her smile was small, secret, when she served their dessert, and she commented, "Friendships are born of likes and dislikes. Ice cream is binding."

Not as far as Grace was concerned.

Cade dug in to his dessert.

Amelia kept the conversation going. "I bet you're more alike than you realize."

Why would that matter? Grace thought. She had no interest in this man.

A simultaneous "doubtful" surprised them both.

Amelia kept after them, Grace noted, pointing out, "You were both born, grew up, and never left Moonbright."

"It's a great town," Cade said. "Family and friends are here."

"*You're* here," Grace emphasized.

Amelia patted her arm. "I'm very glad you've stayed. Cade, too. You're equally civic-minded."

Grace blinked. *We are?*

"The city council initiated Beautify Moonbright this spring, and you both volunteered."

We did? Grace was surprised.

Cade scratched his stubbled chin, said, "Mondays, I transport trees and mulch from Wholesale Gardens to grassy medians between roadways. Flower beds were planted along the nature trails in the public park."

Grace hadn't realized he was part of the community effort. "I help with the planting. Most Wednesdays."

Amelia was thoughtful. "You're both active at the senior center."

Cade acknowledged, "I've thrown evening horseshoes against the Benson brothers. Lost. Turned around and beat them at cards."

"I've never seen you there," Grace puzzled. "I stop by in the afternoons, drop off large-print library books and set up audio cassettes for those unable to read because of poor eyesight."

"There's also Build a Future," Amelia went on to say. "Cade recently hauled scaffolding and worked on the roof at the latest home for single parents. Grace painted the bedrooms in record time."

"The Sutter house," they said together. Once again.

"Like minds," Amelia mused, as she sipped her sparkling water. Casually, she asked Cade, "Single or seeing someone?"

Grace widened her eyes at Amelia. The personal question didn't faze Cade. He shrugged it off. "More single than seeing someone seriously." He glanced at Grace. "You?"

Men in her life were practically nonexistent. She had a close male friend she invited to a movie on occasion. He reciprocated, taking her to dinner. They shared mutual respect. No sex.

She realized in that moment most of her recent relationships were imaginary. She spent far too much time with her costumes. Batman, Prince Charming, Darth Vader, the Mad Hatter. She hadn't been with a real man for a very long time. Not since Greg Dorsey. He'd sold advertising for a radio station, and, as she learned too late, had only dated her as long as she bought airtime for her shop. He'd moved on when she hadn't renewed her contract, looking for a more lucrative hookup.

Amelia and Cade were both looking at her now. Awaiting her answer on dating. She couldn't lie. Amelia knew her status. Dateless. She hated to admit as much to the moving man. He was too good-looking to sit home. He had to be sexually active.

"I date when I have time," she finally hedged.

"Time gets away from her," Amelia added.

"Work can take over, if you let it," said Cade.

Enough said. They returned to their apple dumplings, and compliments flowed. "Killer dumpling," Cade said.

"Delicious dessert," came simultaneously from Grace.

"Seconds here, please," requested Cade.

Grace debated. "No more dumpling for me, but a little more ice cream would be nice."

Amelia rose, smiled innocently. "Food and sex, there's always room for seconds."

Grace blushed, and her ears burned.

Cade blew off any embarrassment he might feel. He leaned back in his chair, said, "I like the way you think, Amelia. Philosophy for all occasions."

"Old and wise and words to live by." Amelia returned to the table. She set down their second round of desserts.

When Grace finished first, her thoughts returned to the decorations, and all they still needed to accomplish. The list was long. She nudged her godmother with her elbow. "One major item of importance, your crystal ball. In it futures are told and unfold in the blink of an eye."

"I've never seen your crystal ball," Cade commented.

"You've never attended her Halloween party," Grace reminded him.

"Touché."

"The ball is in my suite. I'll gladly give you a glimpse into the future once we've finished lunch," Amelia said.

"Almost done." He stretched out his long legs under the table, settled on his tailbone. He shook his foot, rotated his ankle, as if he'd sat too long. The movement caught the cat's attention. Archie's back arched, his tail swung, ready to pounce. A long lunge, and Cade stiffened. "Dude, I'm not a scratching post."

"*Archibald Reginald Rose*," Amelia called him by his full name. She clapped her hands. "*No!*"

Grace tipped on her chair, caught the action under the table. This was no sweet kneading from the Maine coon. He bared his claws on Cade's thigh, close to the man's groin. Cade inched back, avoided kicking the cat. His jeans were white-seamed and laddered. Archie swatted, then latched on to the loose, swaying threads. He tugged. Denim split, shredded, leaving a sizable hole.

No underwear for this man. A shift of his weight, and Cade flashed Grace. Not purposely, yet she got an eyeful. In that moment, she learned more about him than she ever needed to know. He tucked left. His sex, substantial.

She jerked, and hit her head on the edge of the table. She rubbed her forehead as she straightened. Archie had done his worst and now lay passively at Amelia's feet. The older woman hopped up, packed a Ziploc with ice. Hurriedly handed it to Grace. "Minor bump, but we don't want it to swell," she said. "Did you see stars?"

"No . . . not stars." Just Cade's package.

"Cade, I'm so sorry," Amelia apologized. "Archie's usually so sweet. He loves string, ribbon, and, in your case, loose threads. Did he break the skin? I have antiseptic. A Band-Aid? I'll mend your jeans."

Cade flattened his big hands over his groin and thigh and covered the tear. "No mending, no problem. My jeans are old and can be tossed. I have extra work clothes in my truck. I'll go get them and change."

"The powder room on the first floor is private and available," Amelia said.

"Thanks." He stood, drew the shredded fabric over his thigh. Shifted his stance. His groin was level with the table.

Grace looked. She couldn't help herself. Visible skin, but no sign of his dick. She breathed easier, up until the moment Cade smiled. A sexy, knowing smile. He'd witnessed her curiosity, and found humor in her blush.

He leaned toward Grace as he passed her chair, and kept his voice low. "Now you see it, now you don't."

He left the kitchen.

Chapter 2

Cade had changed his jeans by the time Grace joined him in the living room. A relaxed fit, his work Wranglers were in slightly better shape than the previous pair, but not by much. No threads, however. He was safe around Archibald. The Maine coon trailed Grace, his ears twitching and his tail flicking. Amelia was close behind Archie.

Grace glanced Cade's way, met his gaze for a heartbeat, and then lowered her eyes to his groin, where she stared for a moment too long. Pink-cheeked, she looked away. She seemed more embarrassed over his torn jeans than he was. He hadn't planned for her to see his privates. But she had, and now she continued to check him out. She licked her lips. Full and moist. The action got to him. He could feel her taking him in her mouth. His jaw tightened.

They both swallowed self-consciously.

Both drew a breath.

Both moved on.

He crossed to the fireplace and admired the stonework

while she concentrated on the vintage sofas and chai[r]
He listened as she spoke to Amelia. He was part of t[he]
decorating team. Whatever Grace said affected hi[m]
too. Miserable as that might·be.

"I plan to push your furniture against the wall, the[n]
cover and protect each piece with thin, clear plasti[c]
Grace explained. "I don't want your antiques to [be]
damaged by spilled food or drink. And I don't wa[nt]
people to just sit, I'd prefer they mingle. I'll strate[gi]
cally seat life-size scarecrows and skeletons around t[he]
room. Great decorations to start conversations."

Amelia nodded her approval. "The crowd will [be]
larger than last year. The cottage will be bursting at t[he]
seams."

"I've hired Butch Barnes for crowd control," sa[id]
Grace.

Cade looked at her questioningly. "The bouncer [at]
the Thirsty Raven?" The man was built like a brick. Y[et]
when he stood in the shadows, still and silent, h[e]
seemed invisible.

"Just as a precaution," Grace said. "There won't [be]
any liquor served at the party. Still, it will be nice [to]
have him here in case someone gets rowdy. You don['t]
always know who's who in costume. He separated Zor[ro]
and Kool-Aid Man last year when both wanted to wa[lk]
Dorothy down the yellow brick road."

"Butch circulated, talked to everyone," Amelia sai[d]
"He had a good time. He was dressed as Yogi Bear, an[d]
few recognized him."

One corner of Cade's mouth curved. "What w[ill]
Butch wear this year?"

Grace touched her lips with her fingertip, as if sha[r]
ing a secret. "A gingerbread man outfit. That's con[fi]
dential."

Cade chuckled. "Not a word, swear." It would almo[st]

be worth attending the party to see Butch as a big decorated cookie.

Grace began pacing the room. Pausing, contemplating. "My store assistant, Kayla, will stand just inside the
front door dressed as a cowgirl. She'll greet your party
guests and hand out chocolate marshmallow ghosts to
young trick-or-treaters."

"What about Archie?" Cade was concerned for the
cat. The Maine coon now wound about Grace's ankles,
back arched, seeking attention.

Grace bent and ran her fingers along the cat's back.
Cade had the unexpected sensation of her running her
fingers over him. Along his shoulders. Across his chest.
Down his zipper. A smooth, steady stroke. An arousing
squeeze. His sex stirred, subtle yet significant.

Damn. Up until now, they'd been cordial, but distant. Just passing acquaintances. Today, his dick wanted
to know her better. He shifted, turned away from the
women. Then leaned against the antique upright piano.
The sheet music for "Shine On, Harvest Moon" was
propped on the music rack next to a vintage metronome.

He felt Grace's eyes on him as he looked everywhere
but at her.

"Amelia and I have decided that Archibald should stay
in her bedroom during the party," said Grace, straightening. "He'll have a guest, too. Dooley, the neighbor's kitten. They'll keep each other company."

"Archie's good with kittens?" Cade was surprised.
Thirty-five pounds of Maine coon could squish a tiny
kitty.

"He's very gentle with Dooley," Grace assured him.
She pointed to the fireplace mantel. "Third framed picture on the right, you'll see them together."

Cade scanned the photo gallery. He immediately
smiled. A gray kitten was draped over Archibald's neck,

all playful with pinprick-sharp teeth, biting the big cat's ear. Archie lay there, passive, unaffected. "A very patient guy," he praised.

Archibald's purr was deep and loud, as if he understood. He sprawled across Grace's feet. Her boots were completely hidden beneath him. She wasn't going anywhere for the moment.

Grace didn't seem to care. The party was foremost on her mind. "The caterer would like to use your sideboard buffet for the skull platters, raven plates, and broomstick-style forks. The florist will provide a bouquet of black roses. The cauldron punch and batwing cups will go on the dining room table."

"Menu?" Amelia requested. "We'd discussed finger food last week. What did you finally decide?"

Grace ticked off the items. "All the food is easy to eat while standing," she assured Amelia. "Chicken-witch fingers, miniature goblin burgers, chocolate crescent witch hats, ghost sugar cookies, pumpkin Bundt cake, sliced caramel apples, small popcorn balls, and a big bowl of candy corn."

Amelia nodded. "Great choices. Something for everyone. Works perfectly for me."

Cade silently agreed. He was well aware of Grace's talents. She'd thrown a discounted Snow White–themed birthday party for his niece in June. Spring had been tough on his brother. Raydan had lost his job to downsizing. Despite his dwindling finances, he hadn't wanted to disappoint his daughter. Grace cut Ray a deal. She hadn't skimped on much, from what he'd seen.

Cade had promised to stop by toward the end of the festivities, and he had kept his word. Sara was dressed as Snow White. Seven of her friends were costumed as dwarfs. Grace was the evil witch. A touch of theatrical putty shaped her pointed nose and chin. She cackled, offering shiny red apples to the small guests. Shrieks and giggles rose around her as the kids scattered. There'd been games, prizes, and backyard amusements.

Sara had taken Cade's hand and led him outside as the party wound down. "Heigh-Ho," the dwarves' marching song to and from work, played on tape. The two crawled into the castle bounce house. A snug fit for him. He'd tucked his head to his chest, bounced. He'd gone on to eat a big piece of confetti cake. Sara had had the time of her life.

Grace at work was a sight to behold. He presently witnessed her eye for detail firsthand. She threw herself into her job, and was good at it. His heart, on the other hand, hadn't been in the work. He'd been dragging his feet. Wishing to be anywhere but at the cottage. He sucked it up, and forced himself to be nicer. He gave her his undivided attention.

Grace turned to her godmother, said, "The crystal ball and tarot cards? Where had you planned to sit while you tell fortunes? Someplace visible, yet safe."

Amelia's gaze swept the room. "Let's set up a table at the corner of the sideboard buffet. Everyone will pass by the food. That gives me a chance to greet them and offer a glimpse into their future, should they show interest."

"Perfect. We'll use the small marble-top table and cover it with a lacy cloth," Grace suggested. "Should a line form for readings, it can wind down the hallway toward the kitchen, out of the way. I'll keep an eye out so the caterer has room to replenish the food."

"You'll be as busy during the party as you are setting up beforehand," Cade noted of Grace.

Amelia gazed fondly on her goddaughter. "She runs on anticipation and adrenaline."

Grace's lips pursed. "Somehow it all comes together. Even last minute. Afterward, guests have had such a good time, they hurry to reserve their costumes for next year."

"I'd like to show Cade the crystal ball, since he won't be at the party," said Amelia.

Cade shifted uneasily. "Don't go to any trouble." He wasn't into Halloween. The metaphysical creeped him out.

"It will only take a minute." The older woman walked quickly to the back of the cottage, to her innkeeper suite, returning moments later with a square velvet box and an ornate silver stand. She set the box on the marble-top table, opened the lid, and revealed a flawless crystal sphere. She removed the ball and placed it on the stand. It sparkled, casting rainbow prisms onto the Oriental rug. She took a step back and motioned Cade forward. "Take a peek, if you like," she invited.

He hesitated, not wanting to offend Amelia. "I, uh—"

"Are afraid to see your future?" Grace asked.

He shook his head. "Not afraid."

"Don't believe in visions?" Grace again.

He shrugged. "I doubt I'd see anything."

"You won't know if you don't look." Pushy Grace.

There'd be no looking, not on his part anyway.

Amelia took pity on him. "The crystal ball is a novelty to some, while others seek answers. Perhaps you'll take a look later?"

Cade made no promises. "We'll see," he said, keeping his response open-ended.

"I'll take a look now," said Grace. She wiggled her toes, and Archibald rolled off her feet. The cat beat her to the table. His back arched, his ears flicked, and his tail swished. He gave Cade a Cheshire cat smile. Archie was full of mischief.

Cade watched as Grace tucked her hair back, then gazed into the crystal ball. He blew a short breath. He could care less what she saw. Minutes passed, and nothing happened. He was ready to suggest they return to work, when the sphere misted, clouded, turned a swirling gray. *What the—?*

He blinked, certain his eyes played tricks on him. Grace was a believer. She stared intently. Her gaze soon widened and her lips parted. Her breath hitched. *What did she see?* he wondered. His curiosity got the better of him. He angled for a better look. The gray mist disappeared before he could glimpse the image. The sphere was again clear and sparkling.

Grace and Amelia now shared a look. Amelia arched an eyebrow, and Grace shrugged. "A man's hands," she said so softly Cade barely heard her. "I'm not sure I understand."

Amelia's smile was slow and sage. "Interpretation comes with time. It's often unexpected."

"I'm in no hurry," said Grace. She turned toward Cade and asked, "Back to the yard?"

He nodded. He was more than ready to return outside. Unable to resist, his gaze was drawn to the crystal ball one final time. A hint of gray beckoned him to look deeper. He refused. Should he happen by the table later in the day, perhaps he'd take a peek. Just not right now, with Grace and Amelia looking on. He rolled his tongue inside his cheek and wondered if everyone who stared into the ball received a vision.

Amelia read his mind, which left him uneasy. "Images materialize when change is imminent or important decisions must be made."

Neither concerned him. His life was steady, secure, on track. He assessed and concluded on his own, and hadn't faced a major decision for a long time. He was his own man, and didn't need a quartz sphere to guide him.

He reached the door, held it for Grace. She passed ahead of him. Pausing on the porch, she noted, "Your crew deserted you."

They damn sure had. Not a surprise, but still disappointing. He'd have a word with his cousins tonight. They'd show tomorrow, if he needed them.

Grace assumed, "They didn't like taking orders from a woman."

"We've worked for women over the years. Not an issue."

"It was me, then." She'd figured it out on her own. "I pushed too hard, didn't I?"

He was honest with her. "We're good at moving. Ask us once, and it's done. Ask us twice, we slow down. You rode our asses. My crew quit for the day."

"You stayed."

"For Amelia."

"I'm guessing you would have left, too, if she hadn't invited you to lunch."

"I'd have returned. We have a contract."

"Amelia said you'd keep your word."

"She did, huh?"

"I sought her advice on a moving company. She recommended you."

"I'll have to thank her." There were other movers in town. He appreciated the work, even though it involved Halloween. He could tolerate Grace for thirty-six hours. She had decorating down to a science. The sooner they got back to work, the sooner he'd wrap up. "What's next?" he asked her.

"My apology."

That surprised him. "Accepted."

She sighed. "I'll try not to be bossy."

"I won't roll my eyes."

She held out her hand. "Deal."

They shook. Her hand was small, soft, and got lost in his larger one. He held it a beat too long. Until she pulled back, confusion in her eyes. He raised both hands in question. "Something wrong?"

A man's hands. Her vision in the crystal ball. Grace eyed his palms. Big and rough. A scar ran the length of his right thumb. A flick of his wrist, and she saw the broken and bruised nail on his left index finger. She worried her lower lip. Surely she was mistaken. He wasn't the only man she knew with work-worn hands. She refused to read more into his palms than was actually there.

She found her voice, assured him, "Everything's fine."

"Let's do it then."

She startled. Shivered. "Do what?" Her thoughts were unexpectedly sexual. A first for her.

He side-eyed her. "Tree lights, spiderweb, what did you think I meant?"

Her cheeks heated. She spun away from him, nearly missing the top step in her escape. Cade grabbed her upper arm, saving her from a nosedive. "Stay where you are," he said. "I'll get the roll of gauze." He hopped off the porch and headed for her Town and Country minivan, packed with the majority of the decorations.

Moments later he'd accomplished his task. He hitched a hip on the porch railing, asked, "Best position?"

"Position?" She licked her lips. Her mouth was suddenly dry. Cade referred to the spider, yet her mind was on him. She could imagine him in bed. His chest would be wide, muscled, and his abdomen lean. She'd already seen his sex. The image stayed with her. She was out of her element with this man.

Cade reached out his hand, tipped her chin toward him. "What's going on, Grace? You've lost focus."

He'd been her focus. She cleared her throat, collected herself, and continued with, "Gauze first. We'll stretch the roll across the entire porch, then anchor the spider off the front drainpipe."

She held one end of the roll while Cade unwrapped. He was surprisingly creative, weaving the gauzy web under and over the porch rockers and covering the front windows, then climbing on a step stool and draping the webbing from the lantern lights.

"I have two-sided tape if you need it," she offered as he worked his way back toward her.

"I'll tape along the drainpipe and edges of the roof," he told her. "Once I anchor the spider, I'll tuck gauze under its legs."

"Thank you," she softly said once he reached her.

One corner of his mouth tipped. "Gratitude?"

"I appreciate all you're doing."

"We'll get it done."

His words reassured her. The job had begun with four people, and now they were down to two. She and Cade. They'd be forced to double their efforts. She pushed forward. "Let's unfold Ignacio."

He eyed her strangely. "What's Ignacio?"

"The spider."

"You named the blowup?"

"Inflatable," she corrected him. "He's boxed in my van next to the small air pump and hose. We'll also need a long extension cord. There should be an outdoor outlet at the corner of the cottage."

They collected what they needed. Cord in hand, he

stretched it to the outlet, then tossed the remaining length onto the roof while she unboxed the spider. He next leaned a ladder against the porch roof. Then, hoisting the small pump and coiled hose under one arm, he held out his hand for Ignacio, which, folded, was momentarily no more than a three-foot square of heavy nylon fabric. She passed it to him.

"Full of air, how big is the spider?" he asked from halfway up the ladder.

"Five feet wide and eight feet long."

"A Godzilla spider."

"He's visible from the road."

"Visible from space."

She cuffed her pant legs and started up after him, only to hear Cade say, "I have it covered. No need for both of us on the roof."

"I have the gauze and anchor stakes."

"You can toss them up to me."

"I don't throw well."

Once on the roof, he set down the air pump and inflatable. He held out his hands, said, "I can catch most anything." He'd played football in high school and college. Wide receiver.

She winged the roll of gauze at him. Purposely hard. It flew over his head. "Maybe not everything," he mumbled, as he went to retrieve the roll.

Grace stuffed the double-sided tape in the drawstring bag with the stakes and rope that was wrapped about her wrist. She was up the ladder in seconds. She swung her foot onto the roof, gained her balance, just as Cade returned.

His face darkened. "You don't listen well, do you?" he grumbled.

"I hear what's important," she said. "Besides, two people can position the spider faster than one."

His stance was wide, his feet firmly planted, when he asked, "You'll continue to argue with me, no matter what I say? Even if it's for your own safety?"

"My business, I always have the last word."

"Last words could land you flat on your back."

Flat on my back? On the roof? On the ground? In his bed? The latter shook her. She was out of her mind to even go there. Still, her heart tripped. Warily, she took a step back, a bit too close to the edge for Cade's liking.

He caught her by the shoulder. His big hand curved, squeezed, as he drew her close to him. "There's nothing to break your fall, Grace. Cobblestone sidewalk, lawn. You could even land on Cinderella's pumpkin. *Splat.*"

"*Splat*" stuck with her. "I promise to be careful."

He released her then. "The roof slopes. Stand above me."

"So if I slip, I take us both out?"

"I'm big enough to take your weight and stop you from going over."

That was reassuring. Cade was built. A human protective barrier between her and the ground. However, she had no intention of falling. The sooner they set up Ignacio, the quicker she'd be back on the ground.

Together, they knelt on the shingles and unfolded the inflatable. They bumped shoulders and hips. At one point, his large hand covered her own as they both reached for the same section of the heavy nylon fabric. He lifted his hand slowly, yet the feel of him lingered. Her fingers tingled. She was very aware of him.

Enormous and black, Ignacio was a customized inflatable with orange eyes and eight hairy posable legs. Cade hooked up the hose and air pump. They leaned back on their heels while it expanded. Twenty minutes later, she removed the hose and pushed in the plug.

She then stood and walked around the spooky arachnid, listening for leaks. Fortunately, there were none.

Cade pushed himself up and said, "Spooky spider. He looks ready to jump on trick-or-treaters."

"Ignacio will draw squeals and giggles." She retrieved the bag of stakes and rope. "Let's get him anchored."

Once the spider was secure, she retrieved the roll of gauze and began a web pattern over and under his legs. Cade then took the double-sided tape and attached the webbing to the drainpipe.

The perfectionist in her wanted to be sure he'd done it correctly, so she took a cautious step toward the edge of the roof, only to get her foot caught in the gauze. Cade jerked up on the roll, just as she stepped down. The fabric slipped between her legs. Up her thighs, all the way to her crotch. She froze. Her eyes went wide. Embarrassment colored her cheeks.

"Grace?" Cade's voice was deep, amused, questioning. He gave the webbing a tug, attempting to pull it free. Instead it rubbed intimately, at the crease between her sex and thigh. His gaze on her groin, he gave a second slow pull. His eyes darkened. A muscle jerked in his jaw. His nostrils flared. He rolled his shoulders and released the tautness of the gauze. The clearing of his throat cut the tension, the silence. "Snared in a spider's web," he joked, lightening the moment. "Take two giant steps backward."

She did so. The webbing slid down her leg, gathered at her ankles. She kicked it aside, and barely avoided tripping in her retreat. She felt stupid and uncoordinated. She breathed deeply, collecting herself.

Cade rose, stretched his arms over his head. Cracked his back. "What's next?"

"More ladder work," she decided. "I want to fill the trees with orange twinkling lights."

He cut his gaze over the yard. "How many trees?"

There were many. "All of them."

"That's going to take hours."

"Or less," she defended. "You'll go high with the strands, and I'll come behind you and cover the lower branches."

He closed his eyes, his expression pained. She awaited an argument, but he didn't raise his voice. Opening his eyes, he began cleaning up. He collected the empty cardboard roll from the gauze, the two-sided tape, and the drawstring bag. He nodded to the ladder. "I'll go down first, you follow."

She huffed. "Still afraid I'm going to fall?"

"Just being cautious, Grace."

"You honestly think you could catch me, if I slipped?"

"I'd try, but if I couldn't, I'd wave as you went by." He clutched the top of the ladder, swung one leg off the roof, and stepped onto the top rung. "See you on the ground."

She wasn't afraid of heights, but suddenly the idea of following Cade down the ladder made her stomach flutter. Should he glance up to check on her, he'd see her butt. Should she slip, she'd be sitting on his head. Her knees nearly buckled.

He paused halfway down. She nearly stepped on his hand. "*What?*" she asked.

"Making sure you're getting down okay."

"I'm fine."

He stared at her a moment longer. His grin was amused, sexy. He'd never looked at her *sexy*. A misstep, and her heel caught on the rung. She nearly lost her footing. He reached for her. His big hand caught her leg just above her knee. Crept higher up her thigh.

Continued upward. "What are you doing?" she croaked when his palm fully cupped her bottom.

"Supporting you. You seem shaky."

She clutched the sides of the ladder more tightly. Pulled herself together. "Not shaky."

He released her. Chuckled. "If you say so."

Cocky man. "I know so."

He and his smirk continued down the ladder.

She and her nerves followed.

Her last step landed her against him. He stood so close. His arms were raised above her head, ready to move the ladder to the next location. She ducked under his arm, and their bodies brushed. Her shoulder skimmed his chest; her hip tapped his groin.

His intake of breath drew her gaze. He released a short pant. Widened his stance. His zipper no longer lay flat. It bulged. Largely.

Her lips parted on her own indrawn breath. They'd touched, and he'd gotten an erection. Her breasts grew heavy. Her panties dampened. Embarrassingly so.

Recovering, he asked, "Which tree?"

"We'll start with the white pine. I'll get the twinkle lights. They're boxed in my van." She made it to her vehicle and back before he reached the tree.

He carried the ladder across his body, walking slowly, stiffly. She couldn't help herself, she glanced at his groin. Pronounced zipper. He was still hard.

Cade secured the ladder. Cleared his throat. "How high on the lights?" he asked her.

"As high as you can reach. I'll start at the base. We'll meet in the middle, and plug the cord into the power strip."

She bent, opened the box, and withdrew a thirty-foot coiled strand. She handed it to him. He hooked it over his shoulder, headed up the ladder. Her gaze followed him up. He looked good climbing. Tight butt. Lean hips. Strong legs. She wet her lips, just as he happened to glance down.

"Checking the sky for rain?" he asked.

"None forecast."

"I know."

Chapter 3

Cade managed to wind the lights around the tops of the maples and pines without mishap. The evergreen fought him. There was depth to the branches and the needles were prickly. He got poked in the eye, the ear. A pinecone scratched his cheek. He'd had enough. The tree was toward the back of the property. No one would notice a few missing twinklers. He tossed the remaining length of lights over a branch, and let it hang. He was done.

Grace continued to work, spacing the rows on a sugar maple evenly, effortlessly. Perfect, just like her. Some of her perfection slipped when she looked at him. She did so often. Each time he felt her eyes on him, he stared back. Their gazes locked and lingered. He was surprised any work had gotten done.

He watched her now as she plugged her last cord into the commercial power outlet. She stood back and admired their handiwork. In the cloudy midafternoon gloom, the orange lights twinkled brightly. Grace went from tree to tree, assessing the decorations.

She stopped at the evergreen, looked up. Pulled a face. "Not your best work. The distance between the strands is uneven. You didn't test the lights before they went up. Several are burned out."

He climbed down the ladder, brushed needles from his T-shirt. Grunted, "The tree and I battled."

"So I see." She closed in on him, finger-brushed the scratch on his cheek. "I have antiseptic in my van."

"I'll live." Her touch got to him, light with concern. He turned his face away. "No one's going to care if the strands aren't wrapped exactly a foot apart"—he'd seen her measuring with a ruler—"or if one or two tiny lights don't sparkle."

"I care." Her voice was soft, yet firm. "I counted at least ten dark bulbs toward the top."

The top. He groaned.

"I have replacements at my shop. We'll go get them."

We? She was dragging him with her. The lady had trust issues. Did she honestly think he'd disappear the moment she drove off? He rolled his tongue inside his cheek, said, "You don't need to keep an eye on me. I've every intention of finishing the job."

"I never thought you wouldn't," she said evenly. "I need your muscle in the storeroom. There are several heavy boxes blocking the spare light bulbs. I'll need them moved."

He'd misjudged her. "Let's do it."

He rode with her to Charade. She was a cautious driver, slowing and stopping when streetlights turned yellow. Coming to a complete halt at stop signs, and not rolling through. Their windows were down, and a light breeze played with her hair, as would a man's hands. Gently flipping the ends. Brushing her bangs off her forehead. He liked her mussed. Sexy and approachable.

He'd become as curious about her as she had about

him. According to Amelia, they had a lot in common, more than he'd imagined. She was different from other women he knew. Aloof heat, he thought. Uptight. She needed to replace her need for perfection with an orgasm. Sex would relax her.

"We're here." Grace nudged him with her elbow.

Cade blinked. His concentration had been on her and not their destination. She'd already parked in the alley between her shop and the local drugstore. He rolled his shoulders, unbuckled his seat belt, and exited the minivan.

He'd never been inside Charade. Never had a reason. He wasn't into costumes. He'd once dated a woman who got off on role-playing. She'd dressed up as a slutty nurse, and he'd been her naked, bedridden patient. She played jungle archaeologist, and discovered him, a naked tribesman, heavily tattooed with edible body paint. She'd licked dark chocolate from his chest. Tasted caramel at his groin. He did naked well.

He followed Grace now, as she entered through the side door that led to the storeroom. He stopped just inside the door. Where to go? A maze of paths wound between big boxes, stacked from floor to ceiling. He scanned several labels: dragon inflatable, bounce house, Fourth of July parade costumes, dollhouse, *Star Wars* lightsabers. *Adults Only* raised his eyebrow. Apparently she was prepared for any request.

"Over here, Cade," Grace called from the far corner. He maneuvered toward her. She stood before six stacked boxes. "Second from the top, please, marked bulbs. It's not terribly heavy. Just don't drop it. All glass."

He gazed upward. "How'd you get the box up there in the first place?" he asked.

"Four women and a ladder."

"Only one man to get it down?"

"I thought you capable."

He was. He only needed a ladder. She produced a rolling ladder on a ceiling track. She locked the bottom wheels. He climbed, shifted the top box, and easily secured the carton of bulbs under his arm. Once back on the floor, he asked, "Want me to put the box in your van?"

"Thanks. Let me check with Kayla, my store manager, and I'll be right with you."

"*Right with him*" ran twenty minutes. He watched as a steady stream of customers came and went. All carried garment bags to their cars. Costume rentals were going strong. Cade ran one hand down his face. He debated going after Grace. Three hours of daylight remained. There'd be no decorating after dark. A bar stool at The Thirsty Raven had his name on it. He deserved a tall, cold Sea Dog after rolling pumpkins, stringing twinklers, and dealing with Grace.

He slapped his palms against his thighs, sought her. He reentered the shop. Maneuvering the storeroom, he pushed through Western saloon–styled batwing doors, and found himself amid racks of hanging costumes and shelved accessories. Make-believe stared him in the face. He took it all in.

He soon located Grace behind the checkout counter. He headed toward her, only to be stopped by Mrs. Wayford, a surgical nurse from the local hospital. She was a rather large woman, who fit better in scrubs than her present velvet and lace ball gown. She stood before the outer dressing room mirror, straightening her powdered wig.

She lightly touched his arm. "Marie Antoinette, what do you think, Cade?"

History had been his favorite subject in high school

and college. "Very . . . French," wasn't much of a compliment, but it was all he had.

The woman swirled her skirt, beamed. "I feel like the queen of France. There'll be no 'off with my head' on Halloween."

He'd nearly made it past the row of dressing rooms, when Gina Avery, a longtime friend and day-care provider, requested his opinion. An aviator cap covered her short hair. She eyed him through a pair of goggles. "Steampunk, I'm a sky-pirate. You like?"

He liked a lot. He was seeing Gina in a whole new light. Gone were her T-shirt, jeans, and tennis shoes, replaced by a brown leather, wide-belted corset and tight, black leather pants. Several zippers ran down the sides of her hips as decoration, and buttoned straps ornamented the front of each shin. Spike-heeled, knee-high boots were banded with brass straps and buckles across the ankle and calf.

She wouldn't be changing diapers, bottle-feeding, or chasing rug rats in that outfit. He half-expected her to captain an airship, and sail over sea and sky.

"Hot," covered her new look.

She winked at him. "If you're in the mood for exploration, I'll be at Rose Cottage on Halloween."

"I'll keep that in mind."

A costumed sheriff swaggered out of the last dressing room he passed. He was a man of moderate height, wearing a cowboy hat low on his forehead, a fake handlebar mustache, red bandanna at his neck, white shirt, brown suede vest with a silver badge, jeans, a holster with two gray plastic guns slung low on his hips, and boots. The man tipped back his hat, pulled a gun, and grinned at Cade. "Stick 'em up, dude."

Jim Kramer, police officer, had stepped back in time.

Instead of controlling small-town crime, he was out to tame the Wild West. "Amelia's Halloween party," Cade guessed.

"The wife and I take the kids trick-or-treating first, then we hire a babysitter for our night out. Rose Cottage is a good time. You going?"

"No immediate plans."

"It's kick-ass. You get your spooky on."

"I'm not really into spooky."

"It's open house, you walk in, walk out."

"In costume."

"Charade has lots of options, man," Jim encouraged him. "There's even a black T-shirt with orange lettering that says *This Is My Costume*."

The shirt Cade could manage, if he was planning to attend. He wasn't. So he passed with, "Watch out for bank robbers and gunslingers at the party."

Jim twirled the plastic gun on his index finger. "I'm ready to make an arrest."

Cade needed to find Grace. "The boss lady?"

Jim knew exactly where he could find her. "See that line of kids at the front counter?"

Cade nodded. Ten or more youngsters stood patiently. Grace addressed each one. "What's going on?"

"They're bartering for costumes. Grace has a big heart. She lends costumes to those who can't afford the full rental price. Kids repay her with candy, after they've been trick-or-treating."

Bartering? This he had to see. He walked toward them, only to stop by a rack of capes. He squinted between hangers, staying hidden. He recognized the children. Each of them lived with single parents or in a foster home. For all of them, money would be tight. Most couldn't afford a cool costume.

He listened as Tommy Olson, a fifth grader, spoke intently to Grace. "How much for Batman?" He clenched his hands and held his breath.

Grace was thoughtful. "That's a popular costume, Tommy. Worth three bite-size Butterfingers."

"I can go four," the boy replied.

"We have a deal."

The boy released his breath, whooped. He pumped his arm. Bounced on his toes. Ecstatic.

Cade swallowed hard. Grace was generous. Tommy kept his pride.

"Return the costume on Monday," Grace reminded the boy. "Not too dirty."

"Dirty wasn't my fault last year," Tommy defended. "It rained, I slipped—"

"Slipped?" Grace called him on it. "That's not quite how I heard it. You jumped in puddles and kicked mud. You added a lot of spots to the Dalmatian costume."

He pulled a face. "Who squealed on me?"

"The ghost of Halloween past."

"I'll do better this year, promise."

Grace nodded. "I'm sure you will. Go get your costume, and Kayla will pack it up for you. Do you need a treat bag?"

"Too small," the boy said. "I'm going with a grocery sack. I'm expecting a haul."

Cade edged closer, not ready to make himself known. He wanted to catch the exchange between Grace and Libby Talbot. Seven and shy, Libby talked to the floor. Eye contact would come when she got older, he figured. She came from a big family. Her mother had suddenly passed away, and her dad worked two jobs. Her older brothers and sisters talked over and around her. Libby couldn't have gotten a word in edgewise, even if she'd tried.

Grace took her time with the girl. Her voice was soft,

encouraging, when she questioned, "Which costume, Libby?"

Libby dipped her head, shrugged her tiny shoulders.

Grace rounded the end of the counter, knelt down beside the girl. "Mermaid, Supergirl, princess?" she suggested.

Libby shook her head. She tucked her chin against her chest.

"A pink bunny, Minnie Mouse?"

"Yoda," the boy behind her said. "She's short."

The galactic Jedi master? Cade silently disagreed. Not a good fit. Libby was too delicate. Too girly.

Grace passed on Yoda, too. "Ballerina, then? I have a new rainbow tutu."

"No," was barely audible from Libby.

Grace grew thoughtful. Tapping one finger against her chin, she proposed, "You like candy, right?"

Libby raised her head slightly. Nodded.

"I like sweets, too," admitted Grace. "You could wear the same costume I did when I was your age."

The girl's eyes rounded in interest.

"A roll of Life Savers."

Libby giggled, a tight, raspy sound.

"It's one piece, designed with all five flavors, and easy to wear," Grace assured her. "The costume comes with a plastic pumpkin candy bucket."

Libby's lips moved, but Cade couldn't hear what she'd asked or said. He presumed she'd asked the cost, given Grace's response.

"Two Pixy Stix and a hug."

Another giggle, pure happiness as Libby launched herself into Grace's arms. Libby rested her head on Grace's shoulder and her whole body sighed. She was slow in letting go.

Afterward, Grace stood. She called to another of her assistants. "Cheryl, one roll of Life Savers to go. Extra-small."

Cheryl joined them. She held out her hand to Libby, and the girl grabbed hold. They headed for the children's section. Libby's steps were light.

Cade waited for Grace to speak to one final boy before he reminded her of the time. Over an hour had passed. Last came thirteen-year-old Ricky Riley. He was rough and tumble. All boy. His father was a janitor, and it was rumored the old man took Ricky to work with him at night, and had him cleaning. Ricky didn't do well in school, and absenteeism had forced him to repeat the sixth grade. He was basically a good kid, chewing bubble gum, and hopped up on Halloween.

"Vampire, zombie, mummy, or flying monkey?" he asked Grace. "I want the scariest costume."

Grace focused on the teen, as if he were the only customer in the store. Ricky ate up her attention. "Vampire comes with a set of fake teeth and a neat cape. You could dab ketchup on your lip for blood," she said. "I have a skeleton zombie that's gruesome and grungy. Great detail, with bones sticking through the fabric. The mummy is a classic monster from a horror movie. Full body wrap with tears and tatters. Flying monkeys take you to the dark side of *The Wizard of Oz*. Wicked monkey mask and wide wings."

Ricky's brow creased. He was slow to make up his mind. He scrunched his nose and scuffed his beat-up sneakers on the hardwood floor. "Which one do you like best?" he asked Grace.

"I'm not the one wearing the costume."

"I'm, uh, attending a party."

Grace caught on. "A boy-girl party?"

Color crept up his neck. "Yeah."

"Wouldn't you rather protect the girls, than have them running scared?" she suggested.

"Maybe . . ." he was reluctant to admit.

"How about a superhero?"

"Lots of guys are going as Spiderman, Superman, and Captain America."

Grace lowered her voice. Cade strained to hear her. "I have a special costume that's not on the rack," she told Ricky. "I've been saving it for the right young person. A Guardian of the Galaxy Star-Lord outfit."

Ricky's jaw dropped. "Wow!"

"It's one-of-a-kind," she confided. "You'd be the only human-alien-cyborg hybrid. The costume has padded muscle arms and torso and comes with battle gear."

"A quad blaster?"

"Plastic, but it looks realistic."

Ricky puffed out his chest. "Can I see it?"

She pointed to the back of the store. "Boxed in the storeroom. Let's go."

Ricky darted ahead of her. Grace passed the rack of capes. She surprised Cade by separating two hangers and saying, "Batman, Superman, Zorro? One-size cape fits all."

"You knew I was here all along?"

"I know where everyone is in my store at any given time," she said. "Your work boots beneath the hem of the capes initially gave you away. I saw your feet before I caught your reflection in the security mirrors mounted at all four corners."

He glanced up, spotted the two of them. They looked good standing there together. He circled the rack, tapped his watch. "We're losing afternoon light."

"Getting the kids in costumes is as important as our decorating. Amelia would understand."

"Do they all repay you in candy?"

"Sometimes people give out nickels and dimes, and the children share. I'm quite rich after Halloween."

Rich not only in sweets and pocket change, but in knowing she'd given the kids a chance to participate in the night's activities. Priceless.

"Let me get Ricky his costume and I'll be ready to go."

Cade followed her to the back. They found Ricky seated on a cardboard box, his legs swinging. She crossed to a low shelf, removed a rectangular package. She handed it to the boy. He tucked it under his arm, but didn't run off.

Instead, he bartered. "How much?"

Grace took a moment, contemplated. "Star-Lord is a brand-new costume and worth three Milky Ways and a box of Junior Mints."

"I'll toss in a popcorn ball," he offered, upping the payment. He grew momentarily serious. "You're a nice lady, Miss Alden. Thanks."

"You're a good guy," Grace returned the compliment. "Save the galaxy and have a good time at your party."

"See ya," and the boy pushed through the swinging Western-style doors. He walked as quickly as he could without running out of the store.

"Costumes are big business," Cade commented.

"Not only for Halloween, but year-round. Anonymity. People like that fantasy element of being someone they're not." She grinned at him then. "Did you see anything you liked, other than Gina Avery?"

So she'd seen him eyeing Gina. "She asked my opinion on her steampunk outfit, and I gave it. She looked hot. As for me?" He shrugged. "Not going there."

"We have tons of choices." She eyed him up and

down. Her gaze held a second too long on his groin. "I could see you as the Stay Puft Marshmallow Man, Pillsbury Doughboy, or a sugar cookie."

Say what? She saw him round, white, puffy? That didn't set well. "Not quite how I pictured myself."

"Oh?" She was all innocence. "We all see ourselves differently, don't we?"

"Apparently so. I'm more man than foodstuff."

Grace saw him as all man, too. She wouldn't admit it, though. She was having fun with him. She'd gotten him to *talk* costumes. After talking came wearing one. She was getting closer. He'd have fun if he'd just let himself go. For some unknown reason, she wanted him to attend the Halloween party at Rose Cottage, just not as a skeleton. The memory of his childhood misdoings would fade into the night.

"Tarzan, Hercules, and a gladiator are still available," she nudged.

He shook his head. "Not now, not ever."

"A football player, Popeye, *Top Gun,* knight in shining armor?"

"Not happening."

"Astronaut, fireman, mile-high airline pilot."

His eyes darkened. He waved her off. "No more," sounded like a warning. "I don't like Halloween."

So he'd said, over and over again. She loved the craziness of costumes, candy, and creepy decorations. She knew she should drop the subject, but something inside her wouldn't let go. She snapped her fingers, couldn't resist. "You could go as a moving man."

"Damn, woman." He was on her before she had a chance to step back. He slid his big hands into her hair, none too gently. Held her still. "What's with you? I've asked you nicely to stop. Let up or I'll—"

"*What?*" She moved beyond common sense.

He kissed her.

His punishment was sexual, unexpected, yet effective. He was all hotness, hardness, and sensual appeal. Sparked by anger, he bit her bottom lip. Sensation puckered her nipples. Her belly pulled tight. Her groin pressed his. Their thighs rubbed.

The kiss lasted. She had no desire for it to end. His firm mouth softened. He slipped his tongue between her lips with sexy finesse. The man could kiss. He made her want him.

Fully into him, she rose on tiptoe and clutched his biceps. His hands rubbed down her back, cupped her butt, and lifted her slightly, until they were sexually aligned. He pushed against her. She pressed back. Her knees buckled. Her mind blanked. She couldn't name another costume if her life depended on it.

The Western-style doors swung open, and the startled gasp from her assistant broke them apart. Grace jumped, expecting Cade to release her. He did not. He kept his arm about her waist, securing her to him. They appeared a couple, she thought. Sneaking a kiss in her storeroom.

Kayla blinked. "Sorry, I didn't mean to interrupt."

"No interruption." Her voice was unsteady.

Cade's grin tipped. "Grace was just persuading me to wear a Halloween costume."

"Was she successful?" from Kayla.

"Still under debate. I need more convincing."

"Keep after him." Kayla winked at Grace. "Let me grab a lightsaber for a *Star Wars* Stormtrooper, and I'll leave you two alone."

"We're on our way out." Grace managed to sound less breathy. "Lots of decorating still to do at Rose Cottage."

"I can stop by once the store closes and lend a hand," offered Kayla.

"I'll call you if I need you."

Her assistant located the lightsaber and returned to the main shop. Cade released her slowly, running his hand over her hip, and patting her on the butt.

Her cheeks heated. She owed him an apology. She cleared her throat, and with difficulty managed, "I can be pushy—"

"You think?" He cut her no slack.

"I came on too strong. I'm sorry."

"I'm not."

"You're not?"

"We kissed."

"A good enough kiss for you to wear a costume?"

"You could kiss my entire body, and I'd still pass."

His entire body. She'd never considered *naked* a costume, but it might work for him. She looked him up and down. Licked her lips. Her blush deepened at the thought.

She heard Cade swallow. His gaze was hot and dark; his voice, deep and husky. "I've never taken a woman in a storeroom before, but there's always a first time."

His words got her moving. He held the door for her, and she passed ahead of him. Awareness rode with them back to Rose Cottage. Her palms were sweaty on the steering wheel. Cade shifted several times on the passenger seat. The air grew heavy, sticking in her lungs. She exhaled once they reached the B&B. Cade climbed out of the minivan before she could lift her own door handle. He collected the box from the back, seemingly as relieved as she was to put space between them.

She tugged a container of plastic tombstones from behind the driver's seat, and dragged the box to the side of the house, all the while keeping one eye on

Cade. He changed out one light on the red maple and two on the white pine without issue. Then he again tackled the evergreen. The tree showed him no mercy. Needles stabbed, and he repeatedly shook out his fingers. He shoved several branches aside, only to have them snap back and slap him. He swore at the tree. She heard one branch break, then a second, and realized it was at his hands. Because of him, the evergreen had lost its symmetry. She held back mentioning that fact. Cade was in no mood for criticism.

Back on the ground, he came toward her. The tree had quilled him like a porcupine. He brushed needles from his hair and off his shirt. He lowered his head, growled, "Little help here."

Where to touch? The worst of the waxy spikes were stuck from waist to groin. She swiped at his hip, managed to knock off a few. She made a wider sweep on his outer thigh, and cleared a few more. Her hand hovered over his zipper. Shook.

Cade was still picking needles off his abdomen. He widened his stance. "Don't be shy." There was challenge in his tone.

He was getting even with her. She'd forced him to replace the bulbs. His request for her to remove the prickles seemed a fair exchange.

Her heart gave an unfamiliar flutter. Her stomach knotted. They presently stood between the tall box of headstones and a privacy hedge. They weren't visible from the road.

She decided to pick off the needles individually instead of making a palm-wide sweep. There'd be less touching. In her hurry, her knuckles bumped his sex. He sucked air. Enlarged. The tab on the zipper slid down an inch. He made the adjustment.

"Good enough." He pushed her hand away.

She sighed her relief.

He twisted, struggled with the prickles on his back, stretching to brush those between his shoulder blades. Frustrated by those he couldn't reach, he snagged the hem on his T-shirt and tugged it over his head. Shook it out. Grace's eyes rounded and her mouth went dry. He had a magnificent chest.

Broad and bare, his chest tempted her. Her fingers itched to touch him. Even for a second. This was so unlike her. The need to satisfy her curiosity outweighed the consequences. She went with the urge. She traced his flat stomach and six-pack abs. His jeans hung low. Sharp hip bones, man dents, and sexy lick lines. The man was sculpted.

Cade clutched his shirt to his thigh. Stood still. She felt his gaze on her, but couldn't meet his eyes. Not after she flattened her hand over his abdomen, and his heat suffused her palm. His stomach contracted. Her fingers flexed. She scratched him. He groaned.

The slam of the front door indicated someone was close by. Heavy footsteps, the *creak* of a rocker, indicated the person was here to stay. Grace's thoughts snapped to the gauzy spider web woven on the porch. She hoped whoever it was wouldn't disrupt the decorations.

She eased back, their contact broken. A breeze cooled the air between them. Shadows claimed the late afternoon. Touching Cade had stolen precious decorating minutes. It was worth it. A once-in-a-lifetime for her. She would make up the loss later in the evening. The man was hot.

He drew his shirt over his head, hand-smoothed the cotton down his chest. No pine needles remained. She looked up, as he looked down. His eyes were dark, his expression unreadable. "The tombstones won't set themselves," he said. He went to work.

She stuck beside him. Opening the box, they with-drew the thick plastic grave markers. His lips twitched as he scanned the epitaphs: R.I.P. Van Winkle, Dee Cayed, I.M. Gone, and Barry R. Bones. "Dracula, *Fangs for the Memories*," he read aloud and, chuckled.

Grace held up her favorite. "Rigger Mortys. *Death Grips and Holds Me Tight, But I Shall Return on Halloween Night*."

Tongue-in-cheek, he asked her, "What would your headstone say?"

"*She Threw a Great Party*," came to mind. "How about yours?"

"*Death by Decorating*."

Chapter 4

Cade staked and anchored the tombstones. Zombies came next. White-faced and gruesome, they crawled from the ground. Once the undead were secured, he scanned the graveyard. It looked scarily supernatural. He located Grace, working nearby on the Gates of Hell. Wide metal gateposts supported an arch with a gargoyle perched on top. The gate was partially unhinged. Hanging eerily. Chained to the entry, a big skeleton hellhound with spiked ears, long snout, and teeth like a crocodile, stood guard. He stepped closer for a better look, and the hound gave an unexpected howl. A guttural baying at the moon. Realistic as hell. His skin crawled.

"Battery-sensor behind his ear picks up movement," Grace told Cade. "Anyone approaching the arch will be turned away."

The guests staying at Rose Cottage returned for dinner. Several carried shopping bags with the Charade logo. Each one stopped on the cobblestone path and surveyed the yard. Their eyes were wide; their mouths parted. Amazement in their expressions.

"A real haunted house," one man exclaimed, expressing his wonder. With his iPhone in hand, he snapped a few photos. "Souvenirs."

"You have an eye for detail," complimented another visitor.

"We're here from Bangor," the wife of a middle-aged couple said as she and her husband stepped onto the porch. "Word of mouth speaks highly of Amelia's Halloween party."

"You'll have a great time," Grace assured them. "Be sure to have Amelia tell your fortune."

"Do her predictions come true?" The woman sounded expectant.

"I'm a believer." Grace had faith in her godmother.

"How about you?" the woman called to Cade.

He hadn't had a reading, and had no plans to get one. Still, there was no reason to discourage the woman. His comment—"Check out the crystal ball"— was neutral.

Grace seemed relieved by his answer. He would never out-and-out deny the paranormal. Astonishingly enough, she'd seen a man's hands in the sphere, or so she said. He had too much respect for Amelia to debunk her reputation. The guests would get the full Halloween experience.

Cade waited for the out-of-towners to enter the cottage before asking, "Can we stop for today, pick up where we left off tomorrow?" His contract with Grace stated eight-to-five. It was after six. He was in the mood for a beer.

"You can go anytime," she allowed.

"What about you?"

"I'm here for a while yet."

"What's 'a while'?"

She shrugged. "An hour or two, give or take. I want to unload my van. Unbox the rest of the decorations. Hang the crow-and-bat wreath on the front door. Roll up the Oriental carpet. Begin moving furniture. Cover the sofas with plastic."

She'll be here all night, Cade thought. Why that should bother him, he had no idea. But it did. "You still have another day to pull it together."

"I hate last minute," she said. "I don't want anything to go wrong."

"You're in charge. Everything will be perfect." Grace would have it no other way.

"I go overboard on perfection," she admitted. "But it's all worth it. Amelia is special to me."

The older woman had been good to Cade, too. He would give Grace another hour. "I'll deal with your van, and get the boxes inside. Take care of the carpet."

She was visibly relieved. "That would be helpful."

He could be supportive when he wanted to. He still didn't like Halloween, but Grace was rubbing off on him. He admired her dedication. She was loyal to her friends. Liked kids. Was easy on the eyes. He side-eyed her often, and found her looking at him, too. She'd blush. He'd smile to himself. They made a good team.

They worked side by side now. He did the heavy lifting, arranging the sofas and settees in a crescent, which opened the center of the room for circulating and conversation. She added smaller decorations. She dimmed the lights for atmosphere. He thought about kissing her in a dark corner, but never got the chance. Guests came and went. Amelia and Archibald passed through the room. The Maine coon lifted his head, looked around and purred loudly. He settled beneath the marble-top table, guardian of the crystal ball, his furry tail twitching. Amelia put her arm about her goddaughter and hugged her. No words were exchanged. There was no need. Silent communication said it all.

Ninety minutes later, Grace dusted off her hands, said, "Place the blue velvet wingback armchair between the china cabinet and table, and call it a night. Be careful of the crystal ball."

He was aware of the ball. It had been on his mind all evening. The lady from Bangor had come downstairs for a cup of tea, and gazed upon it for a good twenty minutes before returning upstairs. She'd left disappointed. No image.

The man who'd taken souvenir iPhone photos of the yard also peered deeply into the crystal sphere. His eyes rounded. "A baby," he murmured. "My wife and I have been trying to have children. Maybe there is a little one in our future." He walked off in a daze.

Cade hefted the armchair near the sunroom and carried it across the hardwood floor. He was about to set it down when Archie popped up, got underfoot. Cade tripped, set the chair down hard. He accidentally bumped the marble-top table with his hip. The crystal ball tipped on its stand.

He and Grace simultaneously lunged for the ball. He touched it first, saving it from rolling onto the table. From dropping to the floor. As he held it on his palm the ball felt weighty. Warmth seemed to emanate from it, and a gray mist swirled in its depths. He couldn't tear his gaze away. What he saw then, he soon wished he hadn't. It made no sense. An unidentifiable dark-haired woman, her back to him, a small black cat tattoo on the side of her neck. The image was gone as quickly as it had formed. He carefully returned the ball to its stand. Archie rubbed against his ankles.

"Crazy cat," he mumbled, "jumping out at me."

"His way of getting you to look into the crystal ball."

"It was intentional, really?" He didn't believe for a second the big cat had timed that move. It was pure coincidence.

"Maine coons are mystical."

He considered Archibald more of a menace. The big boy scratched the toe of his boot. Leaving claw marks.

Grace was expectant. "You received a message." She waited for him to share.

A message that made no sense. He tucked it away, kept it to himself. No need for Grace or Amelia to read more into the woman and her tattoo than was there. "Nothing of importance."

She pursed her lips, and he awaited her argument. None was forthcoming. Instead, she nudged him toward the door. "You were on your way out."

That he was. "Later."

He had no doubt he'd be back again bright and early. He departed then. Outside, and the yard came alive. The air seemed to breathe Halloween. The orange twinkle lights cast an eerie glow. The spider, zombies, and gargoyles had him looking over his shoulder, twice, on his way to the moving van. He climbed in, drove home. Went on to shower and change his clothes. Then headed for The Thirsty Raven.

He entered the tavern long past happy hour. The place was packed. He knew everyone, and everyone knew him. Orange and black streamers hung from the rafters. Hinged cutouts of ghosts and skeletons were tacked to the walls. Halloween dogged him like a hellhound.

He took his reserved seat at one corner of the bar. He winked at Dakota, communicating a request for his usual. A Sea Dog and loaded burger. She passed his order to the fry cook. Brought him his beer.

Leaning over the counter, she awaited his kiss. A ritual between them for as long as he could remember. Instead of locking lips, he eyed her neck. She wore a V-neck sweater, her skin visible. "Have you gotten a recent cat tattoo?" he asked her.

She scrunched her nose. "No ink."

That eliminated Dakota as the woman in the crystal ball. Then who? he wondered. Time would tell. Or not. He still wasn't convinced he hadn't imagined the whole thing. He kissed her lightly, more cheek than mouth. Dakota eased back, surprised, yet smiling.

"Who is she?" She feigned jealousy.

"She, who?" He skirted the real issue.

"The woman you want to kiss more than me."

He and Dakota had always been honest. They were friends with benefits. Sex was sex, with no future promises. He took a long pull on his beer, shrugged, "There's not much to tell."

"Too early in the relationship," she assumed. "You're getting to know each other."

He'd known Grace all his life. He'd always seen her as perfect and standoffish. Today she'd worked as hard as any man. He'd witnessed her kindness to children and her loyalty to Amelia. They shared an attraction. Her kisses turned him on.

Dakota left him, moving along the bar, mixing cocktails, replenishing beer. Cade noticed she flirted overly long with Josh Hanson, a local carpenter. He'd recently added shelving in the small kitchen and updated paneling behind the bar. He was the strong, silent type. Yet Dakota had him talking. Laughing. Enjoying himself.

Distracted by Josh, she forgot about Cade's food

order. The fry cook delivered his burger. Wally shook his head at Dakota. "She's looking to get lathed." A carpenter pun.

Dakota was obvious in her intentions. Josh was slow on the uptake. They'd connect eventually, Cade figured. Dakota was persistent. Clearly, she'd chosen her next lover. But then, so had he. He wanted Grace Alden.

He bit into his burger. The cook awaited his thumbs-up. Cade chewed, swallowed, approved. "Medium-rare. Perfect, dude."

The cook snagged him another Sea Dog, on the house, before returning to the kitchen. Cade glanced about the bar between bites. The booths were crammed with single women. Steampunk Gina Avery blew him a kiss. Couples took over the tables. Friends waved, inviting him to join them. He didn't have much conversation in him. His thoughts were on Grace. Was she still at Rose Cottage or had she gone home for the night? He'd bet she was still working. He might have to swing by the inn later. Make sure she'd eaten dinner and wasn't overdoing it.

He decided to drop off a burger and fries, as an excuse for checking on her. Despite the fact that Amelia had a well-stocked kitchen, and Grace could cook whatever she liked. He was being thoughtful. That should earn him points with her.

He flagged down Dakota, added a second burger to his tab. Then stared into his beer, so lost in thought, he didn't immediately hear the bone-rattling tapping noise, followed by rubbery fingers touching his hand. He glanced down, started. What the hell?

Halloween reached out to him in a pair of crawling monster hands. A bar prank. Battery-operated, the undead-colored limbs were severed at the wrist, and walked on their own. Those seated at the bar had leaned back, as Dakota aimed the hands in his direction. She'd gotten him. Good. He rubbed the back of his neck, chuckled along with the crowd.

The guy beside him turned one hand over and flipped off the switch. The fingers stiffened. Cade stopped the second hand from climbing up his arm. It gave him the willies.

"Where'd you get the hands?" he asked Dakota when she delivered his take-out order. He didn't appreciate them, but he knew a party planner who would.

"Someone left those on the bar last night at closing, clutching a beer mug. Real funny. I know how much you love Halloween," she said, tongue-in-cheek, "and I wanted to prank you."

"I have someone I'd like to prank, too," he told her.

Dakota was generous. "Take them. All yours."

He finished off his beer, paid his bill, and left a big tip. He balanced the monster hands on the Styrofoam container, and cleared the door in seconds. He was anxious to see Grace.

Grace was eager to wrap up the decorating. She was close to finishing. She rolled her shoulders, shook out her hands. Went on to dim the sconces for atmosphere and effect. She surveyed the living room. Appreciated every little detail.

She'd added a haunted clock with a skewed view of time to the sideboard buffet. The numbers were on backward and went up to thirteen. On the hour, the hands spun.

Next to the timepiece was an animated mirror. It showed no real reflection; instead, a ghoulish girl hold-

ing a lighted candle appeared. She moaned, blew out
the flame, and vanished. Then the mirror went dark.
Freaky.

A five-foot chrome skeleton with a black top hat sat
on the mauve satin settee. His legs were crossed, and
one elbow was bent on the armrest. His jaw was set in a
gaping smile.

A faceless specter in tattered fabric set a spindle-back
rocking chair in motion. The creak echoed in the silence.

A battery-operated ghost family cloaked in illumi-
nated layers of flowing white fabric floated on plastic
stands near the staircase. They drifted and swayed.

Six black witches' brooms leaned against the carved
newel post. It appeared their owners had retired upstairs for the night.

Grace was tired, too. She yawned, and gave in to the
lure of the antique sofa and the temptation of closing
her eyes. For a few minutes. Just until she caught her
second wind. She slipped off her boots. Wiggled her
toes in her socks. She breathed in, smelled French fries.
Impossible. She swore she heard a noise, a *click-clacking*,
but knew she was alone. She felt something touch her
foot. Crawl around her ankle. She reacted, stomping
whatever touched her to pulp.

"You've destroyed my monster hands!" The voice
held more amusement than accusation. Cade? When
had he returned? He hadn't made his presence known.

She spun around and found him leaning against the
front door. A Styrofoam container in hand. He looked
too comfortable. One ankle crossed the other. He twisted
the dimmer switch on the wall, and it became daylight
bright.

Grace lowered her gaze, stared at the bent and broken fingers and loose batteries. "Monster hands?" she
repeated.

"You should've seen them crawl." He sounded proud. "Straight across the hardwood, right to you."

"They were . . . unexpected."

"Scared you, didn't they?" Her answer seemed important to him.

"Maybe . . . a little."

"A lot, Grace." He grinned then. "You jumped a foot off the ground. Came down hard on those fingers."

"Where did you get them?" She couldn't imagine him shopping for anything Halloween.

"The Thirsty Raven. Someone tricked Dakota last night. She got me tonight, and I came after you."

"Lucky me." They were pretty cool. She only wished she'd seen them in action, and hadn't freaked out. Too late now. She inhaled deeply, asked, "Do I smell French fries?"

"Fries and a burger. I figured if you were still working, you might be hungry."

"You guessed right." She nodded toward the sunroom, which was free of decorations. "Join me?"

"If you want company."

"I do."

She sat on a short wicker sofa, and he joined her. Their shoulders brushed. Their hips bumped. Their thighs aligned. He heightened her awareness. Stimulated her senses. Made her smile.

She liked to cook, and didn't eat takeout often. The loaded burger was the best she'd ever tasted. The fries were farmer cut, thick and crisp. She ate with gusto. Not until she was almost finished did she look up to find Cade watching her.

She wiped her mouth with a paper napkin. Closed the lid on the container. Set it aside. "I really packed it away."

"Work hard, eat hearty."

She had. She leaned back, patted her stomach, and sighed. "I'm so full."

"How full?" He settled his hand over hers on her belly.

"Gut-busting." The waistband on her slacks pulled tight.

His palm centered over her navel. He stretched his fingers. Touching her hip bone. Stroking high on her thigh, then back toward her sex. She tensed. She liked having him touch her, but not here, at her godmother's bed-and-breakfast.

He kept things light by saying, "You know what those monster hands were meant for?"

She was too distracted by the pressure of his palm to answer. She shook her head. She didn't have a clue.

"Touching, squeezing . . . tickling."

He ran his hand along her side; his fingers prodded lightly, causing her to twitch. Her skin was sensitive. She was crazy ticklish. "Cade . . . no," she pleaded, serious, until a giggle escaped.

He grinned, deviously slow. He'd gotten the reaction he sought, and went with it. Both hands now joined in the tickle torture. He soon had her wiggling, squirming, and biting her tongue to control her laughter. She didn't want Amelia or the guests to hear her. To find her and Cade in the sunroom in a compromising position.

How had she gotten on his lap? She sat sideways. Her shoulder leaned against his chest. Her bottom sat square on his groin. He was fully aroused. One of his hands ducked under her sweater, his thumb flicked her nipple through her demi-bra. Her legs were spread. His fingers on her inner thigh no longer tickled, they stroked. Sensually slow. The tip of one reached her sex. She was hot for him.

Control. She drew herself up, swallowed, and met his gaze, jet-dark and dilated. Hot. His skin pulled tight over his prominent cheekbones. His breathing was rough. He wanted her. She wanted him. Unfortunately now was not the time. There'd be no sneaking a quickie on the wicker sofa at Rose Cottage. Uncomfortable, crossed her mind. The idea of getting caught scared her off his thighs. He squeezed her shoulder when she settled back beside him. Then worked his hands into his jean pockets and made a discreet adjustment.

"You get to me, Grace," he admitted, his voice husky.

He got to her, as well. She ran her fingers through her hair, mussed from his tickling and her struggle to get free. She next straightened her sweater. Her breasts felt tender. She secured the top button on her slacks. Her stomach softened. Every place he'd touched her still tingled.

"Come home with me," he tempted her.

She might have agreed, had the decorating been complete. But the sunroom still awaited its own scarecrow, witch, and goblin. She planned to set up a sound system to play scary music. A background of wailing ghosts and cackling witches would add to the mood.

"Come to Amelia's party with me," she said without thinking, and immediately wished she could take back her words. She knew how he felt about Halloween. He'd made it perfectly clear.

He leaned forward, rested his elbows on his knees, and steepled his fingers beneath his chin. "You're still pushing me, long after I've passed on the party. Halloween is you, not me, Grace. Accept it."

She could, and she couldn't. She believed with all her heart if he attended, he'd have fun. She would make sure he did. She'd seen his hands in the crystal ball, of that she was certain. They were symbolic of his place in her life. He'd helped her get ready for the party. Had brought her a burger and fries. He'd tickled her senseless. A part of her wanted to apologize and hold his hand forever. But stubbornness had her saying, "Nothing wrong with compromise."

His jaw clenched as he slowly stood. "Nothing wrong with live and let live."

Stalemate. She exhaled, deflated, too tired to argue with him further. "We're done here."

"What about our contract? I still owe you a day's work."

"Consider it honored."

His gaze hardened, his tone turned flat. "If that's the way you want it."

"That's the way it needs to be." She couldn't face him tomorrow, knowing he wouldn't participate in the party. No matter how much it meant to her. Her heart, soul, and party-planning skills went into Halloween. That's who she was.

She let him go. "See you around."

"Around."

She listened to his footsteps walking away.

She heard the door open and *click* closed.

The silence in the sunroom had her realizing how alone she was at that moment. And how much she already missed Cade.

Chapter 5

Cade and his cousins picked up an odd job the next morning. One not scheduled. They moved a newly married couple from an apartment to their first home. It took them only four hours. He had the afternoon free. Free to do what? He had choices. He could stop by the senior center, pick up a game of horseshoes with the Benson brothers. Lose ten dollars. Play cards. Win it back. Drywall needed to be delivered to Build a Future, the construction site for single parent housing.

But when was the last time he'd done something for himself? He thought about working out, going to a movie, stopping to visit his brother. Nothing replaced Grace. She was foremost on his mind. He couldn't shake her. He'd tried.

One way or another, he needed to see her again. She meant more to him than his dislike of Halloween. Maybe it was time to man up. He could make things right by wearing a costume and attending the party. His presence would make Grace happy. Wasn't that his ultimate goal? Her happiness.

He always had an out, he told himself. Should the party get to him, he could hang with Archibald and Dooley in Amelia's suite. The cats wouldn't mind. The Maine coon was wily and wise. He might find it amusing that Cade had compromised.

His mind made up, he felt an immediate need to see Grace. The feeling hit him hard, hounding him to find her. But where? He hopped in his truck, and cruised by Rose Cottage. The inn looked amazing, all lit up and spooky on this overcast afternoon. Adult guests had already gathered on the cobblestone sidewalk. They were costumed, chatting with each other, claiming their place in line. Cowgirl Kayla hitched her giddy-up to the porch railing. She was ready and waiting for early trick-or-treaters with a smile and trays of marshmallow ghosts.

Cade craned his neck and scanned the cars in the side lot. No sign of Grace's minivan. He circled the block and headed downtown. He drove by her shop. Her vehicle was parked in the alley. He drew in behind her, climbed out, and strode around to the front door.

The long window shade was pulled down. The CLOSED sign faced out. A slim space along one side of the shade allowed him to peer in. The shop lights were dim. No activity, until a slender shadow on the wall shifted and came toward him. Cheryl cracked the door, eyed him. "Costumes are all rented," she said. "Can I help you otherwise?"

"I'm looking for Grace."

"Is she expecting you?" He sensed that she was stalling him.

Did he need an appointment? "I only need a minute."

She hesitantly moved aside, and let him enter. She was dressed as a flapper, with red boa and swinging fringe. Her expression was serious. "Keep it short. Grace hasn't been herself today. She's running late. Charm her, don't harm her."

He would never hurt Grace. He had, however, disappointed her, he knew. He was there to smooth things over. To make amends.

"I'm leaving." Cheryl had one foot out the door. "Lock up behind me."

Cade set the dead bolt. Spooky and pretend had long since left the store. He stood alone, amid a graveyard of empty racks and cleared shelves. A splash of light snuck beneath a dressing room door. He heard a groan. A shuffle. A bump. A heavy sigh.

"Uh, too tight."

He walked toward the back, stopping outside the dressing room. The door was cracked a fraction. He rested a shoulder against the wall, and glanced inside. Grace as Catwoman blew his mind. A feline fantasy.

The three-way mirror tripled his pleasure. He viewed her from every angle. Hot, sleek, fierce. The lady could fight Batman in her skintight black leather catsuit and come out the winner.

After a moment she scrunched her nose, slapped her palms against her thighs. Stuck out her tongue at her reflection in the mirrors. He saw what had her so frustrated. Sympathized with her disappointment. Her costume didn't fit. The front zipper hadn't fully cleared her cleavage, which was deep and visible. She wore no bra. She gave a little hop, and her breasts bounced. Full and plump. He felt a tug at his groin. Superhero lust.

He cleared his throat and made his presence known. She caught his image in the corner of the glass, and reached for the fitting room chair, positioning it between them.

Like that would keep him from her. He should've looked away, but couldn't. He sensed her embarrassment. Her panic. Flight? She had nowhere to go. He blocked the door. He wasn't leaving until they'd talked.

"Archibald's going to love your costume," he initiated.

She didn't find him funny. Her gaze narrowed behind the molded cat-eye mask with attached ears. Her fingers clenched in her elbow-length gloves. Inspired by the movie *The Dark Knight,* she'd added a whip and a gun holster. Her thigh-high stiletto boots were killer, adding five inches to her height. Her image would stick with him forever.

She backed against the center mirror, and nervously fingered the open flaps over her breasts. A yank on the zipper broke the tab. The metal teeth parted, and the gap widened, revealing the round inner curves of her breasts. A hint of her nipples. Dusky pink. All the way down to the dent of her navel.

Her mouth pinched. He thought she might hiss. Possibly sharpen her claws on him. "What are you doing here?" came out softer than he'd expected.

"I came to see you."

"You're seeing a lot of me."

That he was. "Need help?" he offered. He wouldn't mind touching her.

She flattened one palm over the opening in the costume, and shook her head in defeat. Her color heightened. "I rented out the medium size an hour ago, and thought I could squeeze into the small. I can't, and it's all your fault," she blamed him. "I ate that burger and fries last night, and I'm still bloated. I'm one big gap."

He liked her gap. He had a solution. "If you can't get the zipper up, I can help you take it down."

Silence collected in the dressing room. The mirrors reflected her uncertainty. She breathed in. He breathed out. The air had that quiet-before-the-storm quality. Expectancy, awareness. The swell of the inevitable.

"I'm naked underneath."

"Commando here, too."

One corner of her mouth tipped up. "Something else we have in common."

He moved toward her, stepped around the chair. Closing in, he finger-traced her cleavage. She didn't flinch or cringe, which encouraged him to say, "I'll take off my shirt, so you don't feel alone when I peel down your top."

"Once our tops are off?"

"We work our way down."

"Down . . ."

"No surprises. You had my big reveal under the table at Amelia's during lunch. Thanks to Archie."

Grace had gotten an eyeful. She was ready for a second look. She needed to clear the air first. "I've been thinking, and have come to a decision. I won't push Halloween on you ever again. You have every right to avoid the night."

"Too late. I've changed my mind. I'll go to Amelia's party. I'll even wear a costume. Preferably a T-shirt."

"That's a one-eighty."

"Relationships require compromise."

"We're in a relationship?" she echoed his words.

"Let's see how the sex goes, then we'll decide."

"I haven't had a lot of partners." She felt he should know.

"You're not perfect in bed?"

"I'm sure you're good enough for both of us."

"Bet on it, babe." He laughed.

He hooked his fingers in the hem of his T-shirt, tugged it over his head. His hair fell over his brow. His lean cheekbones slashed to his jaw. His mouth was sexy. The three-way mirrors picked up his muscular physique, added depth and definition. Power. He was his own super-hero.

Off came her mask, the better to see him. Her skin was warm, and the catsuit stuck to her. He inched the leather over her shoulders and down her arms, exposing her breasts and belly. She flipped back her hair, baring her neck. Astonishment etched his features.

"You have a cat tat." He sounded incredulous.

"A henna tattoo for Halloween."

"Catwoman," he said. "I saw the tattoo in the crystal ball."

"I saw your hands."

"Was I touching you?"

"Not then, but feel free now."

He did. Hunger glittered in his eyes. Desire flared his nostrils. He went down on one knee, helped her out of her boots. Her socks. He stood again, heel-toed his tennis shoes. Kicked them aside.

Her catsuit came next. One minute the leather hung off her hips, the next, it wrapped her ankles. Cade's jeans disappeared as quickly. But not before he snagged a condom from his wallet, stripped the foil packet, and sheathed himself. They faced each other naked. Anticipation played between them, a sexual tease.

"Sit or stand?" he asked.

"I'll straddle you."

He positioned the chair, and sat. She slipped onto his lap, as if she was meant to sit there.

Breast to chest.

Thigh to thigh.

Sex to sex.

Every part of their bodies sought its counterpart.

Arousal brought his mouth down on hers, and he kissed her with a thoroughness and intensity that stole all breath and thought. His tongue thrust between her lips, tasted and seduced. She kissed him back, giving, taking, craving him.

He touched her, all over. Her shoulders and breasts. He circled her nipple, then her navel with his forefinger. Sensations overtook her. She squirmed, dug her nails into his shoulder. Her breath bathed his neck, his chest.

More kissing. More touching. More moans.

He embraced her and drank in her soft sighs.

She fanned out her fingers, ran them up and down his back, feeling the flex and flow of his muscles. The man was built. Her legs tightened around him. He felt good wedged between her thighs. Primal intimacy.

Hot, heavy, their breathing came together.

As did their bodies.

He cupped her bottom, angled her to accept him. She was wet, slick, when he entered her. They caught their reflection in the mirrors. His penetration, the roll of his hips, the rocking of their bodies, their building climax. Their raw need. Triple sexual.

Time went away and she began to unravel. Her orgasm stretched to the breaking point. She moaned. Stiffened. Shattered.

He came a second after her. His release of breath was rough, rushed. His expression going from pain to pleasure.

Spent and satisfied, he held her with the possessiveness of a forever lover. There was no doubt this was the beginning of a relationship like none they'd ever known. His chin rested on the top of her head. Her cheek pressed his chest. She listened as his heartbeat slowed. Steady and comforting.

"We're going to be late for the party," Cade finally commented, his voice low, not wanting to disturb their closeness.

"Very late."

"Our costumes?"

She tipped back her head, affectionately nipped his bottom lip before saying, "I rented out everything but a few T-shirts. You can choose between orange shirts designed with either *I Don't Do Costumes, Now Step Aside, You're Standing on My Invisible Dog,* or *If One Door Closes and Another One Opens, Start Worrying, 'Cause Your House Is Probably Haunted.*"

"That's it?"

She pursed her lips. "There is one more. . . ."

"I'll wear it."

"Only if you're absolutely sure."

"I'm sure."

Halloweener was the most remembered costume at the party.

Mesmerized by You

JENNIFER DAWSON

Chapter 1

"Oh dear. I'm afraid we have a problem." Aunt Iris's worried voice sounded over the cell, raising the hairs on the nape of Chloe Armstrong's neck.

"Problem?" Chloe asked, keeping her voice light and airy. Problems were the last thing she needed. She'd coerced her workaholic best friend into taking this trip. Chloe had promised a stress-free, chill Halloween weekend. If she didn't deliver she'd never get him out of the emergency room again. She crossed her fingers for extra luck and cautiously said, "I hope nothing is wrong."

Jack Swanson, best friend in question, gave her a sharp glance from his position in the driver's seat.

Chloe shrugged and hoped her expression was reassuring.

"Well, see, I had an unpleasant visit from the exterminator, and I'm afraid I have bees," Iris said, as though that explained everything.

"Bees?" Chloe prompted.

Jack rolled his melted-chocolate eyes and grinned,

shaking his head. He was used to her family's antics and no longer took them all that seriously.

Which was smart. After all, how could bees possibly impact their weekend trip to the small town of Moonbright, Maine?

Chloe relaxed into the seat and took in the brilliant fall foliage that lined I-95. The vibrant reds, oranges, and yellows of the leaves were gorgeous this time of year in this part of the country. They'd just passed a billboard advertising the world's largest pumpkin patch when Aunt Iris spoke again.

"Bees. In the walls." Her voice lowered several octaves, like she was a CIA agent relaying a precious secret code that would save the world. "I'm afraid the house has to be evacuated immediately."

Chloe straightened in her seat and rubbed her temple. Oh no.

They were supposed to stay at Aunt Iris's large, colonial house for the weekend. Chloe leaned her forehead against the window.

No good deed went unpunished.

Her mom, concerned about Aunt Iris, who'd been a widow for the past six months, had begged Chloe to go visit the older woman. Seeing as she'd always loved a good road trip, and not wanting to be alone with her aunt all weekend, she'd decided to turn it into an adventure.

And all adventures required Jack, no matter how reluctant he was.

He might not understand, but it was her duty to make sure he had fun and he'd been working way too hard lately. They were only thirty and Chloe worried he'd have a heart attack if he didn't relax.

She'd sold the trip as the perfect, stress-free break. Fall colors, pumpkins, and long walks down Main Street where nobody knew them. They could walk around and not have to stop and talk to anyone. People in the big city took for granted the luxury of anonymity. In a small town she couldn't even run to the grocery store without someone stopping her for a chat.

She'd created the perfect fall getaway, and Moon-bright had been deemed the only place in coastal Maine to celebrate Halloween. Now they'd been on the road for the past three hours, and it was the town's busiest weekend all year; where on earth were they going to stay?

Chloe took a deep breath. Okay, maybe she'd misunderstood. "Bees? In the walls?"

"Yes, dear," Aunt Iris said. "I understand this isn't ideal."

Chloe gritted her teeth. Oh yes, how perfect. A house filled with bees. Not a disaster. Just not ideal.

Jack's easy expression pinched back up and he glanced at her, the questions clear.

Chloe offered him a reassuring smile, that he didn't come close to buying, then turned to the issue at hand. "I'm sure it will be fine, could you maybe have the exterminator come Sunday when we're gone?"

There was a soft sigh over the line. "I'm afraid he's said the house isn't safe to stay in."

Great. "So should we turn around and go back home?"

Jack flashed her a horrified look and mouthed, "*Home?*"

She waved him off and he narrowed his eyes at her.

She pointed frantically at the road.

He pinched her and shifted his attention back to the highway.

"Oh no!" Aunt Iris's voice rose to normal levels. "I have it all arranged. We're going to be staying at my friend Amelia Rose's bed-and-breakfast. I have it all set up. You and Jack have a room, and I'll stay with Amelia Rose in her quarters. There's a big party that starts at five and goes until the witching hour. It will be great fun. The whole town shows up over the evening, and everyone is dressed in costumes. There are trick-or-treaters, candy, food, and punch. I'm positive you'll love it. Much more fun than my stuffy old house."

"Auntie, I didn't bring a costume." Chloe assumed they'd be spending the night on the couch watching old Cary Grant movies, walking around the small town, and sitting by the water. She'd brought jeans, sweatpants, T-shirts, and sweaters.

Jack gave her another *what-the-fuck* look.

Aunt Iris made reassuring noises. "All taken care of. I got the last costumes in town for you and Jack. They'll be adorable."

Oh God, this was going to be a disaster. Jack wasn't much of a costume guy. He'd hate this.

Okay, so Chloe would delay that little surprise. And really, once he got into the spirit of things, he'd have a good time, she'd make sure of it. She always did. She phrased her question carefully, so as to not tingle his spidey senses. "I see, and what might that be?"

She crossed her fingers and prayed for Batman and Catwoman.

"Well, since it's Halloween, there wasn't much left to choose from. The only costumes they had in your size were Dorothy and the Scarecrow, or Tarzan and Jane." Aunt Iris giggled, sounding like she was enjoying herself far too much. "I thought Jack's good looks would be wasted as a scarecrow."

Chloe had to choke down the laugh.

He was going to kill her.

Murder her in her sleep.

He'd find out he'd be walking around half-naked all night soon enough, but until then, she'd keep that bit of information to herself.

At least they had a place to sleep. And it would be fun.

They just needed to adjust their expectations.

Chloe put her hand on the GPS button. "What's the address?"

"Eight-sixteen Vine. It's the cottage on the corner of Pumpkin and Vine."

"Cute," Chloe said, already inputing the new coordinates. "We'll see you soon."

"Can't wait, dear," Iris said and the call disconnected.

Brow raised, Jack glanced at her. "And what was that about?"

Chloe beamed at him, giving him her most winning smile. "So, you know how I promised you a quiet weekend in the country?"

"Yes." His voice low, and slow. Filled with wary suspicion. Ah, alas, he knew her too well.

"There's been a change in plans."

"Why do I not want to hear this?" His voice that of the truly resigned.

She widened her smile even further and bounced around in her seat. They'd have fun. She was sure of it. "Come on, where's your sense of adventure?"

His too-handsome face winced. "I expended my sense of adventure when we were twelve and you dragged me into the woods and we got lost for twenty-four hours."

She crossed her arms over her chest. "Um, excuse me, but that was your fault."

"How was it my fault?" His voice rose, but he couldn't hide his amusement.

It was one of their oldest, most hotly contested arguments, all delivered in good fun, of course. "You didn't bring the compass."

"Chloe, how was I supposed to know I needed a compass?"

"I told you we were going into the woods."

"Not off the path."

She gave him a pout and fluttered her lashes "Where's my thanks for giving you a story you can tell eighteen years later?"

He shook his head, then turned his attention back to the road. "Don't distract me. What's going on?"

She took a deep breath. "Aunt Iris has bees in the walls and so—"

"Wait? How is that even a thing?"

She scrunched up her nose. "I don't know. You can Google it later. Anyway, her house is being bug-bombed, so we have to stay at her friend's bed-and-breakfast. See, no big deal."

"That doesn't sound too bad." He tilted his head and squinted against the sunlight. The cloud cover suddenly cleared to bright, glaring light. Reflexively, she took his sunglasses out of the glove compartment and handed them to him.

He put them on and smiled.

"You look hot in those aviators." She grinned at him. "Like a real badass."

"Chloe," he said, using the same tone Ricky Ricardo used on Lucy.

She shrugged. "Well, you do."

He did. Jack Swanson was a six-four, broad-shouldered, emergency room doctor. In their town he practically dropped panties whenever he walked down the street. There were rumors women showed up in the ER with fake illnesses just to feel his hands on their skin.

Of course, she was immune—they'd been best friends since the beginning of time—but that didn't mean she didn't appreciate his hotness as an abject observer. She hadn't entertained a sex thought about him in forever. Sex was for guys who didn't mean as much to her as Jack did.

But he was gorgeous. That was just fact.

"Anytime you tell me I'm hot, you are up to something." His voice was deep and smooth, too. Probably very reassuring to those panicked patients who filled his ER.

"You're paranoid." She kept her voice flippant and repressed the smile on her lips.

"I've known you twenty-nine of your thirty years. Now, spill."

Sorting through her selective disclosure, she held up her thumb and index finger. "There's kind of a small, tiny, town-wide Halloween party at the B&B tonight."

He groaned. "Woman, I've been working forty-eight hours straight, I don't want to go to some crazy party."

She waved. "Jack, it's a small town. The average age of bed-and-breakfast guests is probably eighty. How crazy could it be?"

Chapter 2

Jack knew *exactly* how crazy it could be.

Chloe was involved. Everything was crazy when Chloe was involved.

It was her best and worst trait.

He took his eyes off the road to scrutinize her. She gave him a wide, green-eyed, innocent stare.

Instincts borne from years of friendship kicked in. "What aren't you telling me?"

She bit her full bottom lip. "Isn't that enough?"

It was, but he knew her too well. The little vixen was hiding something. Not that she'd tell him until she was good and ready.

He reached over and squeezed her jeans-clad thigh. "Don't think I'm not on to you."

She flashed him another dazzling smile, one that displayed those perfect dimples that charmed everyone, him included. "Trust me, this is going to be fun."

She flipped her long hair and blew him a kiss.

Yep, she was trouble. No question about it.

Five minutes later, following the directions from the

electronic-voiced map, turning onto streets actually named Haystack Lane and All Saints Boulevard, he pulled into a long drive. The house was one of the prettiest he'd ever seen, straight out of a Norman Rockwell painting, decorated in whimsical Halloween decorations. Skeletons, witches, and cobwebs with big spiders lined the porch, and mountains of pumpkins lined a cobblestone walkway.

He eyed the big house, waiting for the other shoe to drop, but nothing seemed out of the ordinary. "This doesn't look so bad."

"Oh my God," Chloe said, squirming in her seat. "I love it. This is going to be fantastic."

He grinned at her. In that moment he decided to get into the spirit of the weekend. How bad could it be? He was with Chloe, who always kept his life interesting.

No matter what trouble she caused.

He shut off the car and they climbed out. Chloe ran ahead of him, her dark honey hair flying behind her as she jogged up the steps. She spun around, her long waves brushing her cheeks, as she beckoned to him with the crook of her finger. "Come on, let's take a selfie."

He'd been asked, by practically every man in their small Connecticut town where they grew up, how he could be just friends with Chloe. He got it—she was gorgeous, vivacious, and had a body that would not quit.

The truth, he didn't have a good answer for them.

He just was.

Yes, he'd had a few wayward thoughts about her during puberty, but once he'd started having regular sex with girls in the backseat of his Dad's Buick, he was able to keep her firmly in the friend category.

Chloe was a part of his life. As much family to him as his own, and he couldn't imagine his world without her.

As far as he was concerned, that was better than sex.

Sex, chemistry, those things faded, but Chloe was forever.

He laughed. "You and your selfies."

"I promised I'd text our moms when we got here. They'll love it."

She positioned them in front of one of the webs so it looked like the big blowup spider was about to crawl on top of their heads. Jack leaned down close to her face, pressing his rough, stubbled cheek against her soft one while she snapped their picture.

Just as Chloe shot off the text, the front door flew open, and Chloe's aunt Iris flew out. Jack stood aside as the two women hugged and kissed, generally talking over each other in greeting.

He didn't say a word as Iris talked a mile a minute as she ushered them inside.

The foyer of the house contained a makeshift front desk, adorned with pumpkin garland and what Chloe informed him were called twinkle lights. The house was open with a large piano in the living room and a big common table with large candles running down the center.

It was all quite charming and beautiful. Chloe was going to have a field day in this place. She lived for stuff like this, and Jack found he couldn't quite be mad about the bees entrenched in Aunt Iris's walls.

There was a woman standing at the desk, looking custom-designed to match the décor. Jack had no idea how old she was. She could have been forty; she could have been a hundred. She had that wise look about her he sometimes saw in the elderly patients he treated, but her face was virtually unlined. Expression serene, she had long gray hair and matching eyes.

There were also beads. Lots and lots of beads. She

looked like an exotic Christmas tree from a faraway land.

She smiled and clapped her bejeweled hands. The woman clearly had a thing for jewelry, but in fairness, she wore it well.

"Ah, I'm so glad you could join us this lovely weekend." Her unusual silver-gray eyes twinkled. "It's going to be a magical night, filled with wonderful surprises."

Yeah, that's exactly what Jack was afraid of.

Aunt Iris patted Jack's arm. "I'm so sorry about this, I hope you don't mind."

"Of course not"—he gave the older woman a squeeze—"we're just happy to be here."

"I promise you'll have fun." She held out her hands as though presenting the woman behind the counter. "This is Amelia Rose. She's the owner of this marvelous place. Now, I know you've been inconvenienced, but I promise you this is a special treat. People come from all over just for a chance to stay at Rose Cottage on Halloween night."

Chloe turned around, her expression fixed in that happy, excited look she got. She grinned. "This place is fantastic. I love it."

"Thank you, Chloe," Amelia Rose said, her voice light and lyrical. "After you and your Jack get settled, I'd like to invite you for tea and cookies."

Maybe Chloe was right about this being a quiet party.

Tea and cookies didn't exactly evoke the same images as the night they'd spent on Bourbon Street in New Orleans celebrating their twenty-first birthdays.

Half that night was still a black hole where his memory should be.

Not that he had anything against parties, because he liked having a good time as much as the next person.

Only he was burnt out, working far too much lately. Insane, grueling hours at the hospital, and he needed a break from crazy.

What he really needed was a nap.

Chloe jumped up and down with apparent glee. "We'd love that, wouldn't we, Jack?"

Iris and Amelia Rose looked at him, gazes questioning.

He patted his stomach. "I do love cookies."

Just then a woman juggling a huge pumpkin cake flew through the living room on her way to the dining room.

Jack grimaced. "Does she need help?"

"All's well," Amelia Rose said, in her calm voice. She had an accent but it was hard to distinguish the region "Let me show you to your room."

A single skeleton key dangled from a rose key chain off her slim fingers.

Jack stared at the key, then turned and raised a brow at Chloe.

A small frown formed at her lips, before her expression brightened. She grabbed the key from the woman's hand, then tilted her head pointedly at him. "Jack needs his key, too."

The woman glanced first at Chloe and then at Jack. "I'm afraid I only had one room available, and I only have that because of a last-minute cancelation, but Iris assured me that wouldn't be a problem."

Chloe swung in her aunt's direction. "Aunt Iris, you said you had rooms for us."

The older lady cleared her throat. "I said I had a room."

Chloe's brow creased, as though concentrating, before she sighed. "You did." She turned toward him. "Do you mind?"

He was exhausted and all he wanted was to kick his feet up and relax, maybe shut his eyes for five minutes.

He shrugged one shoulder. "Not a big deal."

So they had to share a room. Yes, being able to lie around in his boxer-briefs would have been nice, but such was life. Chloe was an easy person to be around and they'd probably be together every second anyway, unless they were sleeping.

Besides, they'd shared plenty of rooms in their long acquaintance. They'd grown up next-door neighbors. They'd camped out in backyard tents, snuck into each other's rooms as kids. Now she occasionally crashed at his house or he at hers. Sleeping in a double room wasn't the end of the world.

And all he really wanted was to lie down.

Chloe tucked her hair behind her ear. "Are you sure? I know you've had a tough couple of shifts and probably want to veg."

She was right, but she didn't infringe on that, except for the underwear part, and sweatpants were just as comfortable. He'd ditch the boxers and probably be even more comfortable. "I can veg with you there."

She smiled. "I'll be quiet as a mouse."

He loved her, but quiet she was not. "Chloe, if you stay quiet for five minutes I'll consider it a miracle."

She stuck her tongue out at him, then made a motion with her hand like she zipped her lips, before she tossed the imaginary key over her shoulder.

Amelia Rose pointed down the hallway. "You're in room number three, a lucky number, you know."

For reasons unknown to him, a bad feeling settled in Jack's chest, but he shook it off. There was nothing to worry about. This was not the first in a series of unpleasant events. Everything would be fine.

"No, I didn't know," Chloe said.

Amelia Rose nodded. "I modeled the room with the three of cups in mind. From the tarot. It's one of the best cards to get in a reading."

"How fascinating," Chloe said. "What does it mean?"

The woman gave Chloe a peaceful smile. "When you come to tea I'll tell you. In fact, I'll do even better and give you a reading, if you're interested."

Chloe's expression lit with excitement. "I'd love to. I've always wanted to get my cards done, but never found the opportunity."

"You've come to the right place," Amelia Rose said, her face shrouded in mystery. She gestured down the hall to their room. "Your fortune awaits."

Chloe hooked her arm in his. "This is going to be excellent."

Jack chuckled. "Let's go check out our room."

As they walked down the hall to door number three, a slither of unease slid down his spine. He had the sudden urge to look over his shoulder, but he didn't know why.

Chloe slid the key into the lock.

Jack's heart gave a hard *thump*.

The door opened.

"Oh," Chloe said. Her voice a bit breathless.

He peered over her head.

There was only one bed. One very small bed.

So far the number three was anything but lucky.

Chapter 3

Chloe turned to Jack and held up her hands. "Okay, don't freak out."

"I do not freak out." Jack narrowed his eyes on the bed, then glanced around the room. "I never freak out."

He didn't look at all happy, and Chloe couldn't blame him. It was one thing to accidentally fall asleep together while they watched a movie, but consciously sleeping together in the same bed seemed a little different.

Chloe glanced around the small room. It was pretty and quaint. A sitting area with two chairs and a reading table in between nestled against the windows, but there was no couch.

Chloe looked down. The floors were hardwood.

The bed was the only sleeping option. She'd offer to take the floor, but Jack would never go for that in a million years.

"Isn't it lovely?" Iris said, a sly smile on her lips.

Okay, she could handle this. So they'd have to share a bed; it wasn't a big deal. This was Jack. They'd slept together—platonically—plenty of times. Yes, by accident, but it wasn't a huge deal.

She thought of the last time they'd fallen asleep on the couch and bit her bottom lip.

Jack crossed his arms over his chest. "Where are we supposed to sleep?"

Iris looked at the bed, then back at Jack. "Why, on the bed, of course."

Jack took a deep breath, as though he worked to control his temper.

Chloe hurried in and held up her hands. She'd at least make the offer. What else could she do? "It's not a big deal, Jack. I'll sleep on the floor. You know I can sleep anywhere."

"You are *not* sleeping on the floor," Jack said, his voice strained. "I'll sleep on the floor."

"You will not!" Chloe would not allow that. The guy had probably slept less than eight hours in the past three days. He needed his sleep.

Jack pointed to the bed. "Then there's only one option."

"I'm totally fine," she said, her voice too rushed. She *was* fine with it. They just didn't normally crawl into bed with their pj's on.

Iris wrung her hands. "I know it's not ideal, but it was the best I could do on short notice. I didn't think you'd mind, because you're such good friends. I remember you used to have campouts all the time in the backyard when you were little."

Exactly. There was no difference between sleeping in a tent at eleven and being smashed together in what could barely be called a double bed at thirty. No difference at all.

Iris's expression twisted with worry, and Chloe rushed

over and gave her aunt a little hug. "Of course it's fine. Don't worry about it, we'll work it out."

Jack sat on the bed and pressed a finger to his temple.

It was time for Iris to go. Chloe ushered her aunt toward the door. Iris dragged her feet, looking back at Jack, before saying urgently to Chloe, "Tea's in thirty minutes. You can't miss it." She clasped Chloe's hand and squeezed. "You and Jack have to come. Everyone wants Amelia Rose to tell their fortune, but only a select few get the chance. She offered to read your cards, you have to promise me you'll be there."

Dramatic as always, but Aunt Iris didn't need to fret Chloe wouldn't miss the chance. She'd always wanted to have her fortune read.

"We'll be there." Chloe crossed her heart and kissed her fingertips. "I promise."

Iris gave Jack a smile. "Do you promise?"

"Sure," Jack said, but his voice already sounded sleepy.

Appeased, Iris nodded and slipped from the room, the door clicking closed behind her as she left.

Chloe took a deep breath and turned to Jack. "It's not a big deal, right? It's not like we haven't slept together before."

Jack's brow rose. "It's not that."

"Then what's wrong?"

He gestured over the ivory quilt. "I'm six-four, it's a double bed. There's barely enough room for me."

Chloe shrugged. "I won't take up much room. I'll scrunch over to the side and it will be fine."

Jack flopped down, stretching out his arms.

She sat next to him and poked his thigh. "It's only for one night."

He nodded, pressing his open palm on the curve of her back.

She pointed to the open door that led to a small bathroom. "And look, we have a bath, we should consider ourselves lucky. Wouldn't you rather have a private bathroom than your own bed?"

"True." He rubbed his hand over her spine in a slow circle. "As long as you're comfortable, I'm comfortable."

She craned her neck and looked down at him. "It's hardly like I have to worry about you taking advantage of me."

Dark lashes brushed his cheeks as his eyes drifted closed. "Never."

He'd always been the one man she could trust. The one she could depend on. He was her rock, her confidant, so engrained in her life she couldn't imagine it without him.

Nobody understood. Not even her best girlfriends, who kept insisting that they should do it already and get it over with. But it wasn't like that with Jack. Their friendship was far too important to ruin with relationship stuff. Every relationship she ever had ended in disaster.

Besides, she didn't think of Jack that way. He was her best friend. She certainly had no qualms or worries about sleeping in the same bed with him. Definitely not.

His fingers ran a slow path over her spine and, eyes still closed, he said, "I can feel you thinking."

"Do you need a nap?" She lay down next to him and he curled his arms around her shoulders and flung his other arm over his eyes.

"Just let me rest for a few minutes."

"I can let you sleep and go get my fortune read."

A smile played over his lips. "I don't want to miss that. Besides, I promised Aunt Iris. Wake me in twenty."

She slid her leg over his thighs. "Deal."

She curled in close to him and closed her eyes. "See, this isn't so bad."

His fingers stroked over her waist and when he spoke his voice was sleepy. "Not bad at all."

Twenty minutes later, Chloe woke from a catnap refreshed and full of energy. She got up from the bed, stretched, and looked down at a peaceful, sleeping Jack.

She'd said she'd wake him, but didn't have the heart. He worked so hard and he was so tired. Jack worked in the only trauma center in a fifty-mile radius; everything bad and horrible came his way. A job he loved but it wore on him. The stress. The pressure. The long hours. Life and death hanging in his capable hands.

Better to let him sleep; he didn't believe in fortune and fate anyway.

She scribbled a note and tiptoed out of the room. Ten minutes later she drank tea out of a delicate flowered cup in the innkeeper's quarters with her aunt and the enigmatic Amelia Rose.

Chloe took a sip of her spiced flavored tea and glanced around the spacious room, which matched the china cups. Antique and as lovely as the rest of the cottage. "I love this place, how long has it been open?"

The woman gave her a smile. "Rose Cottage has been in my family for generations."

Aunt Iris leaned close and said in a loud whisper, "They say it's magic."

Amelia Rose waved a hand. "An old wives' tale."

Iris glanced around the room before lowering her

voice. "They say anyone who sleeps here on Halloween night is destined to find true love."

"Don't be silly, Iris," Amelia Rose said.

Chloe grinned. "How fascinating." Aunt Iris was a die-hard romantic. According to her, Prince Charming came knocking on her door one day and it had been love at first sight. She'd believed in magic ever since.

Chloe didn't believe in love at first sight.

But she absolutely believed magic existed.

Aunt Iris took a sip of her tea. "Your mom told me you were dating someone. What was his name? How's that going?"

Chloe cleared her throat and said lightly, "His name was Greg and it's not going at all. We broke up."

Iris's expression twisted into sympathy and she *tsked*. "That's too bad, dear, your mom said he was a lovely boy."

"He was." Chloe didn't have a bad word to say about him. Greg had been pleasant enough and they'd had a good time. He was a perfect boyfriend if she was being honest. Good-looking and smart, he was the assistant principal at the school. He'd been passionate about literacy, something as a librarian she appreciated. He'd been nice, kissed like a dream, and was damn fine in bed. He'd always made sure she came twice to his once. He'd been absolutely perfect.

Chloe didn't understand why she didn't miss him.

"What happened?" Iris asked, still sipping delicately at her tea, pinkie raised.

Chloe shrugged and stared down into the dull brown liquid. "He broke up with me."

"You?" And the incredulity in Iris's voice could only belong to family. "But you're perfect."

"I guess he disagreed."

Before Aunt Iris could say anything else, there was a

male throat clearing. The older women looked over Chloe's shoulder and beamed.

"Jack, you made it." Iris's voice was as excited as a schoolgirl's. "Chloe said you were sleeping."

Chloe craned her neck to glance back at him.

Jack's eyes narrowed on her for a fraction of a second before he moved into the room and sat down on the chair next to her. "Chloe was supposed to wake me."

Other than a little sleep-rumpled he looked much fresher. Chloe smiled. "I thought you needed your sleep more than tea."

He gave her a searching look, expression intent, as though trying to read something on her face. "That's why I set my alarm. I know you too well."

Amelia Rose waved her hands, her thick gray hair flowing over one shoulder. "It all worked out the way it's supposed to."

Chloe straightened, excited to change the subject from her failed relationship to her fortune. Much better to focus on the future. She rubbed her hands together. "So, what's this about tarot cards?"

Amelia turned to the side table, opened the drawer, and pulled out a packet wrapped in a brilliantly colored scarf.

"Ooohhh," Chloe said, admiration in her voice. "That's a gorgeous scarf."

Amelia Rose smiled. "Thank you, dear. The cards are as old as my family, and this scarf was handcrafted by my great-great-great-grandmother and has always been used to wrap the cards."

With careful hands, Amelia unwrapped the package, revealing a stack of beautiful, intricate cards. They were old and ancient-looking, yellowed with age, but it was the artwork that captivated Chloe. The scrolled pattern in reds and yellows were almost hypnotic.

Fascinated, Chloe sat forward. "How does it work?"

"I'll show you." Amelia Rose peered at Jack. "You must have them read, too."

Jack grinned. "Thanks, but I'm not a believer. I'd much rather watch Chloe."

"Jack's a doctor," Aunt Iris added, helpfully. "A man of science."

Amelia Rose shook her head. "It doesn't matter if you believe or you don't, you both must have the cards read."

The hair on the back of Chloe's neck tingled, and a sudden rush of goose bumps raced across her skin.

Jack chuckled and shrugged. "All right, then."

Chloe shook off the odd sensation.

"Good." Amelia Rose handed the deck to Chloe. "Here, shuffle the cards. First you, then hand them to the doctor. He must shuffle them, too."

Surprise flickered through Chloe. "You're going to read them together?"

A nod.

"How interesting." Chloe turned the deck over in her hands, studying the card with the words *Wheel of Fortune* on top. The card appeared hand-drawn, with a large dial in the center, surrounded by angels. Chloe traced the picture with her thumb.

"You must shuffle facedown," Amelia Rose said.

With careful hands, Chloe turned them back over, and shuffled the large deck.

"Stop when you feel it's time," the older woman said, a serene smile on her face.

Chloe took the instruction very seriously, concentrating on the deck and shuffling, until she heard the word *stop* in her head.

Then she handed them to Jack. He grinned at her, clearly treating the reading as a game. He, too, shuffled the cards a few times, then held them out to Amelia Rose.

She shook her head. "Put them on the table. Chloe will cut the cards once, then Jack, you cut the cards again."

They both did as they were told, and then the woman piled them back up again into a single deck and laid out five cards on the table. There was a blindfolded woman holding two swords, two naked figures, their hands interwoven, men holding two gold cups, a woman on a throne, and a man sitting in front of a wall of cups. The pictures were beautiful, but Chloe wasn't able to decipher anything from them.

Amelia Rose nodded, the beads around her neck creating a musical tinkling. "Ah, just as I suspected."

Chloe leaned forward, searching the cards for what the woman saw, but they were a mystery to her.

Amelia Rose nodded again, straightened the cards as she continued to study them in silence. When she finally raised her head, Chloe was on the edge of her seat with anticipation. She looked first at Jack and then at her. "Your futures are intertwined."

Well, that didn't take magic to figure out. They were best friends; of course their futures were intertwined.

Jack gave a little eye roll.

"That makes sense. We're best friends," Chloe explained.

"Are you?" Amelia Rose's expression turned questioning.

"Yes, since we were one year old," Chloe said. "We grew up next door to each other, and our families are very close."

"I see," Amelia Rose said and pointed to the card with the blindfolded woman. "Your blindness is your greatest obstacle. To find happiness, your fate, you must be willing to strip the blinders away."

Chloe's brow furrowed. She had no idea what that meant. She glanced at Jack, but he just shrugged.

Amelia Rose continued, pointing at a card. "This is you, Chloe." She pointed to another. "And this is the good doctor. You need to learn to see each other without the veil of the past in order to ensure your future."

Okay, now Chloe was really confused. Who knew her better than Jack? Nobody. Her own mother didn't even know her as well as he did. "I don't know what that means."

Amelia Rose smiled, serene and peaceful, her gray eyes filled with mystery. "That's for you to figure out."

How cryptic. And frustrating.

Jack's expression turned sly. "What aren't you telling me, Chlo?"

"I have no idea." She laughed. "Jack knows all my secrets."

Amelia Rose pointed to another card. "Tonight, all will be revealed, by the light of the full moon."

Okay, then. This had been most unhelpful. Chloe offered a polite smile. "Thank you, what a lovely notion."

The woman was clearly off her rocker. Maybe she was a little disappointed not to learn anything profound, but it had still been fun.

Jack studied the cards. "Anything else we should know?"

Amelia Rose gave him a narrow-eyed stare. "Don't be afraid."

Jack chuckled. "I'll do my best." He shot a sideways glance at Chloe. "How about a walk down by the lake?"

What did the older woman mean by that? What could Jack possibly be afraid of? She peered at him, but he didn't appear the least bit distressed.

It was clearly nothing. Besides, the cards didn't hold any real answers, just a bunch of nonsensical messages that added up to a big fat nothing. Like opening a fortune cookie. Suddenly, the room felt a bit stifling. "I'd love a walk after the car ride."

Aunt Iris clapped her hands. "Isn't this exciting?"

"Indeed," Amelia Rose said.

Chloe couldn't see one exciting thing about what had been said, but Aunt Iris was happy so that was something.

"The lake is lovely this time of year," Amelia Rose said. "But before you go, I insist you have a cookie."

She rose, and walked out of the room, returning seconds later with two cookies.

Chloe blinked at them. "They're tarot cards."

They were gorgeous. The pictures appeared embedded into the cookie. A picture of a couple waving to a rainbow of cups. Delighted, Chloe pointed at the scene. "Cups seem to be a theme."

"Indeed." With a napkin, Amelia Rose took one cookie and handed it to Jack. "This is for you." Then she gave the remaining one to Chloe. "And this is for you."

They moved to stand, but she shook her head. "Please. You must eat them right now."

Chloe laughed. "Not that I'm going to turn down cookies, but why's that?"

"They are magic," Aunt Iris whispered.

Okay, maybe her mom was right to be concerned. Aunt Iris was clearly getting a bit loopy.

Amelia Rose smiled, shaking her head. "Nonsense. They are sugar cookies. One of my specialties, I like to see the pleasure on people's faces when they eat them."

Far be it from her to deny the woman who'd been so

gracious. Chloe looked at Jack and they gave each other "oh my God, they're crazy" smiles, but each took a bite.

And they both moaned.

Crazy or not, this might be the best cookie she'd ever had in her life. It almost melted in her mouth, crumbled and dissolved like something magical over her tongue. She took another bite. "Wow. I hope you sell these."

"Christ, that's good," Jack said, and shoved the whole thing in his mouth. "I could eat a truckload."

Chloe took the last bite and mourned its loss as she swallowed.

Amelia Rose smiled. "I'm afraid that's the last of them. They were meant for you."

Chloe had no idea what that meant, but she wanted more.

A feeling of well-being swept through her, stilling her for an instant, before it evaporated into the air.

"I'll have more later tonight for the party if you so desire," Amelia Rose said, her voice light and musical.

"Call us as soon as they're out of the oven," Jack said, the amusement clear in his tone.

Amelia Rose gave Jack a sly smile. "I'll make a believer out of you."

Jack laughed. "I believe in those cookies."

"Me too." Chloe placed a hand on her stomach. "They were divine."

"Thank you, Chloe. You two have fun," Amelia Rose said.

Aunt Iris waved them toward the door. "Now, go take your walk."

Jack and Chloe thanked them, and right before the door clicked shut, she heard her aunt say, "Do you think it worked?"

Chloe frowned. What on earth were they up to?

Chapter 4

Well, that was strange.

As he and Chloe walked down the path toward the lake, they were both silent, hands stuffed into their pockets.

Jack didn't want to admit it, but he was a bit unnerved over the reading they'd received from the strange Amelia Rose. He didn't know why, she hadn't really said anything significant, or even particularly revealing. Besides, he thought tarot cards were full of shit. He didn't believe in magic.

Although he did believe in the power of the full moon. Every doctor did. The ER was always packed. More women went into labor. There were more accidents. More drunks. More craziness.

It wasn't until Amelia Rose mentioned the full moon that Jack gave the reading any real thought. When she'd looked him dead in the eye and told him not to be afraid, he'd brushed it off, but his survival instincts still kicked in.

And then there was that cookie. Which might be the

best thing he'd ever put in his mouth, and he didn't even have a sweet tooth. He'd wanted to beg for more. They were that good. After he'd swallowed the last bite, a strange sense of . . . something washed over him. It had made him dizzy for a second, and he'd wondered if the proprietor had spiked the cookies. But just as soon as he felt it, it was gone, making him wonder if he'd imagined it.

Something else niggled at him. Something he needed to ask Chloe.

When they got to the water's edge, they stopped.

Jack stared into the water, rippling and glittering in the autumn sun. The trees surrounding the lake were in their full fall glory, deep reds, vivid yellows, and bright oranges. It could be a postcard it was that perfect.

Chloe took a deep breath. "It's beautiful here."

He looked at her, still watching the water, her honey-eyed hair blowing, her high cheekbones, and flawless skin. He visually traced the line of her jaw, the slope and curve of her neck.

She was beautiful. Too beautiful.

He blinked, startled by the thought. Where had that come from?

He shook his head and cleared his throat, returning his attention to the sparkling water. "Yeah, it is."

"What did you think of our reading?"

He opened his mouth to say it was complete crap, but those weren't the words that came out of his mouth. "Chloe, why did Greg break up with you?"

She'd told him they'd decided to stop seeing each other. That it had been mutual. But she'd told her aunt the idiot had broken up with her.

Which just proved the guy's stupidity.

Jack hadn't particularly liked Greg. Sure, he was a nice guy, respectable. Most of all he'd treated Chloe awesome, as she deserved. None of that mattered. Jack still hadn't thought the guy was good enough for her.

Chloe needed someone different. Someone special. Someone who would feed her sense of adventure and keep her from getting bored.

Jack just didn't believe Greg was that guy.

Chloe's head snapped to him, then snapped away before she shrugged. "He didn't think we were compatible."

It was a lie. She always hunched her shoulders when she lied. "What aren't you telling me?"

"Nothing," She smiled at him and waved her hand. "We weren't even going out that long, it's not a big deal. I wasn't attached to him or anything. I didn't even watch a romantic comedy after he left."

It sounded good. Jack believed she hadn't been attached. But there was something she wasn't telling him. He didn't want to ask, but did it anyway. "Was it because of that night?"

She looked away and didn't answer.

"Chloe?" he pressed, suddenly filled with a relentless desire to discover what happened. When she didn't answer him, he took her arm and spun her toward him. "Tell me."

She swallowed. "It's not a big deal."

The vague answer confirmed the suspicions he'd harbored for weeks. "It was because of me, wasn't it? I'm the reason he broke up with you."

She took a little breath before releasing it. "Let's just say you didn't help."

Jack ran a hand through his hair. He was such an asshole.

He'd had a rough night. A kid had died on his table. The six-year-old little boy had been in a terrible car accident and Jack had done everything in his power to save him, but it hadn't been enough. Jack had to tell the parents their lives had changed forever. As a doctor he was used to delivering bad news, and there was a certain level of detachedness he'd had to adopt to deal with it. But kids always got to him.

After his shift, instead of going home, he'd gone to Chloe's. She was the only person who could make him feel better. As soon as she'd opened the front door she'd known he was upset, and she'd done all the things that were special to Chloe.

That he loved about her.

They'd ordered pizza, drank beer, watched bad movies, and she made him laugh. After a while they'd grown tired. He'd stretched out on her couch, and she'd lain down next to him. Eventually, into the second bad movie they'd fallen asleep, his arm thrown over her waist, her hand on top of his.

This wasn't an uncommon occurrence. They'd done it hundreds of times before.

Only Greg had come over, unexpectedly, to surprise Chloe with breakfast. Jack had seen the look on his face when he'd spotted them on the couch together.

It hadn't been happiness. Not that Jack blamed him.

How many times had he ruined relationships for Chloe? How many times had Chloe ruined relationships for him? It was never intentional. Never deliberate. He wanted nothing but the best for her. Yet it had happened too many times to count.

He sighed and pulled her close. "I'm sorry."

She looked up at him, her green eyes enormous, a piercing vivid green that seemed to reach right into him. "It's not your fault."

He curled one hand around her neck and stroked his thumb over her jaw. "I'm not so sure about that."

She bit her lower lip, calling attention to her full, lush mouth. "The thing is, I would have chosen you over him. So that means it wasn't right."

Jack knew what she meant. He often judged women by Chloe's very long ruler. Asked himself if he'd rather spend time with the woman, or with Chloe, to gauge his interest.

Guess who was always the winner?

He continued to rub the line of her jaw. "This is a problem."

He had no idea why he'd said that. He hadn't meant to say it. Actually, he didn't want to talk about it. What he really wanted was to pretend that they could go on like this forever. Even though it was a lie.

She shook her head. "No, it's okay. When we meet the right people, we'll choose them. We just haven't met the right people."

It was a good, logical, sound reason he wanted to latch on to. But he couldn't, something stopped him, but he didn't know what or why. "The thing is, Chlo, do we ever really let it get that far?"

An array of emotions—worry, concern, and finally fear—flashed over her features. "What are you saying?"

He needed to stop this. Pull away from her. Change the subject and forget the strangeness that suddenly had sprung up around them. "Nothing. I don't know." He tightened his hold on the back of her neck and he thought he detected the slightest of tremors. "I don't want to be the cause of your unhappiness."

She rose to tiptoes and pressed a kiss on his cheek, twining herself around him like a cat, before whispering in his ear, "You're not. You are my happiness."

Out of nowhere, rushing through him like a speeding train, desire crashed into him, so strong and fierce it almost brought him to his knees.

What the fuck?

He did not think about Chloe this way.

That was off-limits. Had always been off-limits.

She slid back down his body and he gritted his teeth to keep his spontaneous lust in check. She leaned back and he looked down into her face. His attention settled on her mouth and stayed.

Her lips parted on a little gasp.

He had the overwhelming need to kiss her. To know what that goddamn mouth would feel like under his.

The moment caught. Held. Suspended.

A tension he'd never allowed to take root permeated the air between them.

Her fingers tightened on his arm, her chin tilted.

He grasped her waist. "Chloe."

Her breathing kicked up. She blinked. Then blinked again, confusion etching in the knit of her brow. "Jack."

Sanity rushed over him.

What in the hell did he think he was doing?

The tension cleared from the air, and with silent agreement they pulled away.

Both of them kind of laughed. A strained, uneasy sound.

She waved her hand. "Anyway, it's no big deal. I'm over him."

He nodded. "He wasn't good enough for you anyway."

She grinned. "We'll do better next time."

"That we will." He looked back over the water. "What time does the party start?"

"Five, but it's an open house–type deal, so we can go

whenever we want." She raised her hand against her forehead, shielding her eyes from the sun. "We should probably get back and relax before we get ready."

"Good idea."

He needed to get out of this fresh air so he could clear his fucking head.

Chapter 5

What was *that?*

Chloe had no idea what to make of the scene down by the lake. Or why she'd suddenly been struck with a serious case of the hots for her best friend. It was like one second they'd been going along fine, like normal, the silence comfortable. Then—*POW*—instant tension.

She was 99 percent positive he'd experienced the same thing.

His arms had tightened around her, his eyes had darkened, lingering a bit too long on her mouth. There'd been a fraction of a second when she'd thought they were going to go at it like a couple of crazed, wild animals.

But as quickly as the tension seized control, it evaporated. Leaving behind an unpleasant awkwardness.

Now they watched television, both as far away as humanly possible from each other without falling off opposite sides of the bed, staring too intently at the game show flickering across the television set.

They weren't relaxed.

His body appeared as rigid as hers.

She swallowed hard. What should she do? Ignore it?

She nibbled on her bottom lip. Ignoring it seemed the smart course of action. If they ignored it, by the time they got ready for the party they'd be back to normal, the strangeness forgotten.

She frowned. The words felt like they were bubbling in her throat, pressing against her lips to get out. It was the oddest sensation. She pressed her lips together. Counted to ten.

All she needed to do was wait until it passed.

The desire to confront the issue didn't abate. She started again, counting to twenty. The longer she repressed the urge to talk, the more insistent the desire became.

The pressure grew in her chest.

When she could finally stand it no more, the words burst forth, flying from her lips with a force that surprised her. "What was that? Out by the lake?"

He jerked, his head snapping toward her.

They looked at each other.

She gulped.

Suddenly the space on the bed between them became entirely too inviting. A flash of an image flooded her mind. Them, rolling across the bed, their legs entwined, him on top of her. Pressing into her.

She wanted to attack him. Devour him. The longing to turn that image into a reality was almost a compulsion.

It was the most disconcerting thought she'd ever had.

Not even as a teenager, in the throes of puberty, had she felt like this.

She flushed, and vaulted off the bed, moving to one of the sitting chairs that lined the bay window.

Jack's brows furrowed as she settled into the chair, crossed her leg, and her foot started to bounce. He picked up the remote that had rested against his flat stomach and pressed the OFF button, plunging the room into silence.

He blew out a long breath. "I honestly don't know."

Some of her tension eased; at least he wasn't going to deny it.

She laced her fingers and did her best not to fidget. "I'm not imagining things?"

He shook his head. "You're not."

She smiled. "One of the things I like best about you is that you don't ever play the 'you're a crazy girl' card."

"Never." He sat up, propping his back against the headboard. "Okay, let's approach this practically."

"Yes, let's." It was worth a try. Even though she wasn't feeling particularly practical right now.

"We had a moment."

"We did." She paused, thinking through the events of the afternoon before saying, "Here's my best guess. Amelia Rose put thoughts into our head. We went outside, talked relationship stuff, and well, you are a man and I am a woman."

"Makes sense." He nodded his head, his face easing in relief.

"It happens." Sure, never quite like that, but it *did* happen.

"And, let's face it—neither of us is hard on the eyes. There's bound to be an occasional slip."

They'd never had a slip before, but she wanted to build this story. Because it seemed like everything had changed since they'd walked out of that parlor. "Exactly. I've noticed you're good-looking before. And your body isn't bad, either." His body was spectacular.

"The same goes for you." He straightened. "I've noticed you that way before."

"When?" The word left her lips like a speeding bullet and she sounded way too eager.

He shrugged. "I don't have them written down on my calendar or anything, but I'm sure I've thought you looked hot every once in a while."

"Me too. I mean, you *are* hot. Okay, then, it happened. It was some strange thing, and now it's over. Right?"

Don't look at his mouth. Don't look at his mouth.

She looked anyway.

Once, drunk at her own bachelorette party, Cheryl Hanigan told Chloe that making out with Jack was better than any sex she'd ever had in her life. That she practically came just kissing him.

And Cheryl had made out with Jack at least ten years ago. Which meant he'd only have improved in time. With practice. She thought of his strong, steady hands as he worked on people in life-or-death situations.

What would it be like to have those capable hands roaming over her body? Playing with her breasts, stroking her—

"Chloe!" Jack's voice boomed through the room, shaking her from her erotic thoughts.

She blinked, straightening. "What did I miss?"

He raised a brow. "Really?"

"I . . . um . . ." The heat crawled up her neck. "Got distracted."

"Sure you did." He raked a hand through his hair. "Did you bring running clothes?"

She nodded.

"Maybe we should go for a run to help burn off this excess energy."

She jumped up. It might work. "Good option."

There was a knock on the door and she ran toward it like a lifeline. "I'll get it."

She flung it open and Aunt Iris stood there holding what looked like a dry cleaning bag. She held it out to Chloe. "Your costumes, dear. I forgot to give them to you."

"Great," Chloe snatched them. "Do you want to come in?"

Please come in. Please, please please.

Aunt Iris waved. "No, I have to help with the party. But you two have fun."

And then she was off, scurrying down the hallway, leaving Chloe alone with her best friend.

She closed the door and turned around, leaning against the wood.

"Costumes?" Jack asked, his tone wry.

"Yeah." She tried to smile and flutter her lashes like she normally did, but feared it kind of died a sudden death mid-charm. "Didn't I mention that?"

"You conveniently forgot." His voice was dry.

"Sorry." She held out the bag. "You're not going to be happy."

Jack shook his head. "Why don't I like the sound of this?"

"Experience?" she quipped.

He laughed. "What are we?"

What was so funny at the time, now seemed like a fate worse than death. She swallowed past her dry throat. "Tarzan and Jane."

"Absolutely not." He stood up in a huff she would have found hysterical an hour ago, but now she couldn't help thinking was kind of hot.

The way he prowled across the room.

Stalked.

His muscles flexing.

His jaw tight and hard.

He stopped in front of her, and she jerked her attention away from his body.

Oh God, what was wrong with her? She was so confused. She needed to get away from him.

He held out his hand.

She looked down at it blankly. "What?"

"The costume. Let me see it."

She handed it over. Trying to ignore the shiver of lust at his voice.

Help. She needed help.

He ripped off the plastic wrap and held up the scraps of material. "Absolutely. Fucking. Not. I did not go to four years of medical school to dress like a porn star."

The costumes were obscene. They might wear more clothes in porn.

Her costume was a skimpy loincloth that would barely cover her ass, and a bikini top. She'd look like Jane Fonda right out of *Barbarella*.

His was worse. A scrap of tan suede fabric and nothing else.

Normally she'd be on him, talking him into it, convincing him how much fun it would be. How he'd drive women wild. But she couldn't do any of that.

Because all she could think about was what he'd look like practically naked. How she'd have to stare at his bare chest all night. What if she licked him? What then?

What was Aunt Iris thinking?

She cleared her throat. "You don't have to wear it."

"I won't." He tossed the offending costume on the

chair. "Neither will you. I will not have you traipsing around half-naked for the whole town to see. And that's final."

Oh no, he did not! It didn't matter if she'd been struck with some weird case of hyperlust, there was no way he had the right to boss her around. She was her own woman. No man, especially Jack, told her what to wear.

Her brows rose practically up to her hairline. "What did you just say?"

His expression flashed as he waved an angry hand over the minuscule piece of fabric. "You cannot walk around like that."

"Why ever not?"

He let out a frustrated breath. "I don't know why, goddamn it, you just can't."

She opened her mouth to scream at him, and then stopped herself. They were about to fight. They never, ever fought. She held up her hands as though warding him off. "What are we doing?"

He dragged a hand through his hair, and his shoulders slumped. "I . . . shit. I'm sorry. I don't know what came over me. I can't explain it, it's like I don't want to say these words but they keep popping out anyway."

That was exactly what had happened to her. What in God's name was going on? She put her hand on the door. "Let's take a moment to ourselves, okay?"

"Maybe that's best." His voice was so soft it scared her.

She twisted the handle. "I'm going to take a walk alone. After we've had a chance to clear our heads, we'll be back to normal."

A shadow passed over his expression. "Chlo?"

"Yeah?"

"I . . ." He cleared his throat. "I think I should find another hotel room."

Her gaze flew to the bed, and her mind filled with them tumbling, sweaty and naked, on top of it.

The thought strangely defeated her. She nodded. "That's probably for the best."

Chapter 6

Jack sat on the edge of the bed in the now-empty room.

He was fucked. Screwed six ways till Sunday.

He'd called every hotel room in a fifty-mile radius and there wasn't one single room available. Not one. Apparently Halloween was the biggest weekend of the year in these parts and everything was booked.

He had two choices: Sleep in the car. Or sleep in the room.

With Chloe.

Two hours ago sleeping in a bed with Chloe had been no big deal. Earlier, she'd curled up next to him as though it was nothing. He'd run his hands down her back and it had been perfectly normal.

But now, out of nowhere, the thoughts that pummeled his brain were illegal in most states. Carnal, illicit, dirty images of her and him and that bed stormed through his mind and made him stupid.

Had he really ordered her not to wear that costume? Had he really been that dumb? Why had he even had the thought in the first place? He didn't get possessive over Chloe. He didn't tell her what to wear or how to look. Even if he was involved with a woman, he wasn't that kind of guy.

But it was the other thought lingering in the corner of his mind that really gave him pause. His actions had pretty much guaranteed she'd be strutting around that party dressed like a fantasy. And he didn't know if he could make it all night watching her.

So what in the hell had possessed him to say that?

The truth was, he had no idea. It was like he'd been taken over by a very stupid demon and the words had been flying out of his mouth before he could process them.

He blew out a hard breath. He needed to get this under control.

He picked up his phone and called Nick Jasper to talk some sense into him. Because Jack swore he was going out of his mind.

There'd been a moment, there at the end, when he'd almost pounced on her. He'd wanted to press her against the door, restrain her wrists, and devour her.

What a mess.

He pressed the CALL button and his friend answered on the second ring. "Hey."

"I've got a problem," Jack said as way of preamble.

"Having work withdrawal already? You've only been done five hours. Give it some time," Nick said, amused.

Nick worked with Jack in the ER. They'd started within two weeks of each other and had become fast friends. Nick also had the advantage of living in the own on the opposite side of the hospital, which meant Jack didn't have to worry about any leaks back home where gossip spread like wildfire. Nick had also met Chloe, so he didn't have to explain their complicated relationship.

"Not work. Chloe." Jack scrubbed a hand over his jaw.

"What could be wrong with Chloe?" Nick asked, his voice areful.

Did he really want to say this out loud? He'd already called, so he was committed. "She's fine. I am not."

"What's the problem?"

Jack cleared his throat. "I don't know what is wrong with me, but I can't stop thinking about doing terrible things to her."

Nick laughed. "What trouble has she caused now?"

"I don't mean that." Jack lowered his voice and glanced around the room. "I want her."

Silence.

The numbers on the alarm clock ticked over.

When Nick still didn't speak, Jack asked, "Did you hear me?"

"Yeah. What do you mean, you want her?"

"I mean we showed up here, everything was fine. Normal. We got our tarot cards read by some strange woman, we ate cookies, and since I left that room I can not stop thinking about getting Chloe naked."

"I see."

Jack blew out a frustrated breath. "That's it?"

"What do you want me to say?"

"Tell me it's stupid. Talk some sense into me." Jack shook his head. "I know it's crazy, but it's like a compul sion. I don't think I can resist her. And it's not just me. She's been struck, too. We talked about it, kind of, but then I ordered her not to wear a costume and she left. And I've called twenty hotels and there's not one room."

Muffled noises sounded from over the line.

Jack frowned. "Are you fucking laughing?"

The laughter boomed, and Jack held the phone awa

while Nick howled like a hyena. When he was finally under control he said, "Sorry. But, come on, you've got to see the humor in this."

"No, I don't see the humor. If I don't get away from her I'm going to do something stupid."

"So do something stupid," Nick said, as though it was no big deal. "There are worse things in life than taking our far-too-gorgeous friend to bed."

"Are you insane? This is Chloe. *My Chloe.* She's not some girl I can hook up with." Was he hysterical? Because he sounded hysterical.

"Calm down. I'm sorry, but I fail to see the problem."

Jack growled. "You're not helping."

"Look. You're practically married to the girl anyway, you should get the advantage of sex."

Jack held the phone away and looked at it like it might grow a second head, before holding it back up to his ear. "Forget it. You don't understand. I'll sleep in the car until this madness passes."

"Good luck with that."

Jack hung up, with Nick still laughing.

That was no help at all.

Jack stared at the bathroom door.

Time for a cold shower. Maybe that would cool him the fuck off.

"What do you mean, just do it already?" Chloe screeched into her cell phone.

Her friend, Nora Clyborn, was not taking this news the way Chloe expected. The way she needed her to.

"I mean," Nora said in a calm voice, "just do it already. You should have done it a million years ago."

Chloe leaned up against a tree and closed her eyes. This was a disaster. "Jack and I do not have sex."

"Well, you should," Nora shot back. "You really, reall should."

"Are you crazy? Did you have mimosas for breakfast?

"Nope." Nora was clearly amused. "Consider it you civic duty to all the single people in town."

Chloe's head started to pound, and she pressed he finger to her temple. Her friend had clearly gone craz right along with Chloe. "I don't even understand wha you're talking about."

Nora sighed. "If you and Jack finally got togethe you'd be putting every single person in town out c their misery. They could give up on you guys as an op tion."

Chloe gritted her teeth, vaulted off the tree, an paced through the leaves. She kicked them and watche them fly and flitter to the ground without the satisfyin force she needed. "Don't be ridiculous."

There was a pause on the line before Nora said, "D I need to remind you of Greg?"

Ugh! He was the last person she wanted to tal about.

"I don't see what the big deal was. He overreacted Chloe took another vicious swipe at the leaves, thinkin back to her conversation with Jack by the lake. *May(that's the problem, Chloe.*

No. She didn't have a problem. *They* didn't have problem. She liked her relationship with Jack exactly : it was.

"Chloe," Nora said, her voice soft. "Give the guy break, he went over to your house to surprise you wit your favorite breakfast and found you sleeping on th couch with Jack. Put yourself in his shoes."

"But that was nothing," Chloe insisted, her voi(stubborn even though something niggled away at he

"Jack had a bad night, we watched movies and fell asleep. It was totally innocent."

"So you're saying you'd be cool with your boyfriend curled up like that with another woman?"

"Jack is my friend, nothing more."

"How come when I have a bad day you don't snuggle up to me?"

Chloe just managed to keep herself from screaming, *"Because you're a girl!"* An argument that wouldn't help her case. She cleared her throat. "Look, I should go."

"Just think about it," Nora said. "Wait. Don't think about it. Just do it. Jump. He's your fate."

A sudden coldness washed over Chloe. Amelia Rose's words rang in her ears. Absently she said, "I'll talk to you later."

She hung up with Nora still talking.

Slowly, Chloe walked back to the room, her mind spinning. Okay, there had to be a way to get this under control.

They were adults.

In charge of their hormones and bodies.

They just needed to keep talking. Keep communicating.

Do what they did best. *As friends.*

She pulled the skeleton key out of her pocket.

Everything would be fine. Jack would get another room and tomorrow would be a new day. They'd forget all about this.

The lock clicked.

They'd get through this.

She twisted the doorknob.

They had thirty years of experience; they could make it through one more night.

Piece of cake.

She opened the door.

Jack came out of the bathroom wearing nothing but a towel.

Oh dear God, she was in trouble.

Chapter 7

Chloe's mouth went dry.

Her gaze swept over him, standing there, hair slicked back and wet. Water sliding over his tanned skin.

She gulped.

Unable to tear her gaze away from all his hard muscles.

They stood there, frozen, staring at each other as though they'd never seen each other before.

She took in his broad shoulders. The tat, a scrolling tribal shield of protection in black, on his left bicep. She'd been there when he'd gotten it. They were supposed to do it together but she'd backed out, not willing to commit to one thing gracing her skin for the rest of her life.

She wanted to trace the pattern with her tongue.

She flushed hot at the thought, the image so clear in her mind she could almost taste his skin.

A rivulet of water trailed a slow path, starting at his chest, down his ridiculous stomach, before disappearing under his towel.

He was a work of art.

Her lungs burned and she realized she held her breath. She exhaled and it sounded like a harsh gasp. Needy. Revealing.

"Chloe," Jack said, breaking the spell.

She ripped her gaze away from his body. "I'm sorry."

"Don't be." His gaze dipped to her mouth and lingered.

She pressed against the closed door.

"I'm having a hard time not coming over there." His voice was so low and gruff it sent a shiver through her.

Her breath kicked up. She meant to say he should go put some clothes on, but those weren't the words that came out of her mouth. "What would you do?"

He crossed his arms, propping one shoulder against the bathroom door as his gaze raked over her. "It wouldn't be pretty."

She licked her lips. "I don't like pretty."

His expression darkened. "And what do you like?"

She really needed to put a stop to this. Right now. Her attention flicked to the bed. "I wouldn't mind breaking the bed."

"That can be arranged."

"I certainly hope so."

He took two steps toward her and she took two steps toward him.

She was going to tear him apart.

They both jerked to a stop and blinked at each other.

Jack ran a hand through his hair. "Christ. I . . . I don't know what came over me."

"Me, either." She didn't know what was stronger, the relief or the disappointment.

"We need to talk about this."

She nodded. "We do." She bit her lip and glanced

behind him. "But do you think you could put some clothes on first?"

He looked down, as though surprised to find himself almost naked. "Good idea."

Then he went into the bathroom and slammed the door behind him.

Chloe sank onto the bed.

This was a total disaster.

Jack stared at himself in the bathroom mirror.

I don't like pretty. Chloe's words filled his head, making him stupid. Oh, so fucking stupid.

He had no idea what happened out there but it ended now. He quickly toweled off, put on jeans and a black knit shirt.

They just had to figure out a plan.

He took a deep breath and slowly exhaled before entering the bedroom.

She sat on the edge of the bed, and he quickly veered around her to sit on one of the chairs lining the bay window of the room.

He rested his elbows on his knees and laced his fingers. "How do you want to handle this?"

Her gaze darted toward him and quickly away. "Did you find another room?"

"There's not one hotel room available in a fifty-mile radius." He shook his head. "I'll sleep in the car."

Her brows knit. "No, you can't do that."

"Let's worry about it later." Right now, that seemed too far away and he needed to concentrate on the here and now. Getting through the next fifteen minutes without breaking the bed. "I don't get it, Chlo."

"Me, either. It's like as soon as we left that room with Aunt Iris and Amelia Rose, something came over me and now I can't stop thinking of you . . ." She cleared her throat. "That way."

He was a man of science. He did not believe in magic or fortunes or fate. So he could not believe he was going to say this, but he was. "Do you think there was something in those cookies?"

"Like what?" She tilted her head. "Is there some sort of powerful aphrodisiac the world doesn't know about?"

Yep, it sounded as crazy as he thought. "Not that I'm aware of."

She tapped her chin. "There must be another explanation. Is it possible we're undersexed and we're all that's available at the moment?"

Yes, that must be it. What other explanation could there be? He cocked a brow. "Should we test the theory?"

"How?"

"The party . . . it's starting soon, right?"

She nodded, and Jack tried not to get distracted by the spun honey gold in her hair hitting the sunlight.

He frowned. What the hell? He didn't have those kinds of thoughts about regular women, let alone Chloe. *Spun honey gold?* Pretty soon he'd have to start writing for fucking Hallmark. "I see no other choice but to hit on other people and see if that helps."

The words tasted like dirt. He forced his hands to relax instead of curling into fists at the thought of another man hitting on her.

She stared at him for a full thirty seconds before her chin tilted. "We have no other choice."

"No, we don't."

Her lips curled into a smile. "Let the games begin."

Chapter 8

She wore the costume.

Of course she wore the costume. It was Chloe, after all.

Jack had stuck to his jeans and a black pullover while she walked around half-naked. How was he supposed to hit on other women with her looking like that?

The party was in full swing, the house lit with jack-o'-lanterns and candles, strung with some sort of orange and black elaborate garland, and packed with about every conceivable Halloween decoration imaginable. There were plenty of available women making their way through the bed-and-breakfast.

And plenty available men, all making a beeline in Chloe's direction.

Jack gritted his teeth. What the hell? This was supposed to be a family town.

Unfortunately, Jack didn't blame them. Living in a small town, he understood; anyone new was like shark bait. Instantly attractive by their novelty alone.

When they looked like Chloe, it was even worse.

Tonight, in her barely there costume, she looked unbelievable. Her hair was a wild mess, making her look like she had indeed been living in the jungle. Her makeup was dark and smoky, giving her a mysterious flair.

He wanted to go over and claim her.

It was absolutely ridiculous.

Currently, she talked to some guy. He was tall and a little too slick-looking for Jack's comfort. In fact, he didn't like the look of the man one bit. Nor did he like the way he looked at Chloe. All hungry and conniving, like he was plotting to kidnap her.

By mutual agreement they'd agreed to stay away from each other, giving the sexual tension between them a chance to wear off.

It hadn't.

Over the guy's shoulder Chloe's eyes locked on his. Sucking him in. Making him want her.

He should look away, but couldn't.

He kept staring at her like he'd never seen her before. It was like a veil had been lifted from his eyes.

His heart gave a hard *thump* as he remembered the fortune from this afternoon and an eerie sense of foreboding raised the hair on the back of his neck.

Was he losing his mind?

"Is everything okay?" The soft, female voice ripped him from his thoughts.

Jack blinked down at the blond-haired woman staring up at him with huge, doe-like brown eyes. She was just his type. All soft and adorable. But he'd forgotten she was there.

He cleared his throat. "I'm sorry."

She gave him a sweet smile and tilted her head in Chloe's direction. "You should go get her. It's obvious she's the only woman in the room for you."

Jack shook his head. "It's not like that. She's my best friend."

"Well, you and your best friend are burning up the place." She laughed.

What was the woman's name? Jack searched his mind, drawing a complete blank, before he gave up. He shrugged. "Everyone thinks that, but I swear, we're just friends."

"Maybe everyone thinks that for a reason," she said, her voice low and soothing.

The statement stopped him cold.

Was that true? Even before today Chloe had always been a source of contention between him and other women. Women he always kept at a distance, never letting them get too close or slip too deep into his life. His reasons had always been clear in his mind. His life was full. He had a demanding job. He was young and not interested in being tied down. He liked to keep his relationships with women as uncomplicated as possible.

But was there another motive he didn't want to think about? That he didn't admit, even to himself?

Was Chloe that reason?

No, he wasn't that stupid. Until today he'd never allowed himself to think about Chloe sexually. He just liked her company more than anyone else's. That was why she was his best friend. It didn't mean more than that.

Did it?

"Go get her," the woman next to him said.

Once again he glanced in Chloe's direction to find her watching him. She looked at the woman and scowled. He looked at the man next to her and scowled.

They both looked away.

What was happening?

As crazy as it sounded, he was sure it had something

to do with those cookies. That fortune. And he intended to find out what was going on so he could put an end to it.

He smiled at the blonde. "I hope you have a good time."

She smiled back. "I will. The annual Halloween party at Rose Cottage is legendary."

Again the hair on the back of his neck rose and he cocked a brow. "How's that?"

A lilting laugh. "It's said that when people attend the party they find their true love."

A shiver raced down his spine. "Isn't that supposed to be Valentine's Day?"

"Not here. In Moonbright, it's Halloween that's magic."

Before he could process the information any further, Chloe came over with her new friend—whom Jack wanted to punch in the face.

She smiled at Jack, her lips a full and glossy pink. She put a hand on the man's forearm. "Jack, this is Anthony, he's the fire chief."

Great, a fucking fireman. Because women never went for the hero type. Jack clenched the bottle of beer he'd been drinking and nodded. "Jack Swanson."

Anthony gave Jack a good-natured grin. "Good to meet you, mate."

He had a goddamn Australian accent.

Chloe loved accents. She constantly raved about them, gushing over English, French, Irish, and Italian accents like they were panty-melting crack.

So, wait, did this mean she'd found someone to take her mind off Jack? Was this all going to be one-sided? Was he going to have to endure a hard case of lust that would not quit while she entertained herself with the fire chief?

Clearly Jack was trapped in one of Dante's nine circles of hell. There was no other reasonable explanation.

Chloe looked expectantly at the woman he'd been talking to.

Jack made no move to introduce her, because he had no idea what her name was. Something with an *M*? An *N*?

Chloe held out her hand. "I'm Chloe Armstrong, Iris is my aunt."

"Olivia Barnes." She shook Chloe's hand.

He was close on the name. *O* was the next letter in the alphabet.

Olivia was dressed as an angel, and she shifted her wings. "I know Iris, she's such a help at the school."

Chloe's brows furrowed and she tucked a lock of hair behind her ear. "Are you a teacher?"

Olivia nodded. "I teach second grade."

"How lovely," Chloe said, then turned to Fire Boy. "Do you know Olivia?"

Anthony's eyes locked on to Olivia. "I can't say I've had the pleasure."

Olivia bit her lip and a pretty blush stained her cheeks. "It's nice to meet you."

In the small space, their hands met.

They both went still, appearing not to breathe.

Jack raised a brow at Chloe, who shrugged, before she beamed. "Well, if you'll excuse us . . ."

The fire chief and the schoolteacher didn't even notice when they walked away.

They strolled out of the main room and into the open foyer. Jack grabbed Chloe's bare arm, swinging her around to face him. "Were you playing matchmaker?"

"I thought they might hit it off," Chloe said with a nonchalant shrug.

"Why? He looked like your type. Complete with the coveted accent." The jealousy still sang in his blood, not yet caught up to the fact that he had nothing to worry about. Or that he shouldn't be worrying in the first place.

"I . . ." She trailed off, expression pained.

Jack's attention fell to her mouth. "It's not working."

She smiled and it completely dazzled him. "I know. I wanted to claw her eyes out."

His mood lightened considerably. "I thought about punching the guy in his stupid five-o'clock-shadowed jaw."

Chloe shook her head. "We're a mess."

"We are." He spotted Amelia Rose, leaning down to a small child, handing out candy. "There's something strange going on here. And I'm going to find out what it is."

Chloe's attention settled in the proprietress's direction. "I say we start with her."

"Good plan. Let's go."

Chapter 9

As they started to walk toward Amelia Rose, Jack took Chloe's hand as he normally would, and something akin to an electric shock jolted up her arm. Jack looked back at her, scowled at their joined hands, and kept right on going.

By the time they reached the lovely hostess of the party, Chloe's arm tingled all the way up to her shoulder. Amelia Rose was busy marveling over a little blond girl's princess costume. Admiring her crown, and blue dress. The little girl curtsied. "I'm Cinderella."

"You certainly are." Amelia Rose pointed to the Cinderella pumpkin in the yard. "You left your slippers in my yard."

She giggled.

The older woman held out a big bowl of seemingly every type of candy ever created. "Take whatever you want."

The little girl studied the assortment, and then her eyes went wide when she found her favorite. She took it in her small hand. "Thank you."

"You're quite welcome." Amelia Rose straightened, then smoothed a hand over the girl's silky blond hair before turning to Jack and Chloe. "Enjoying your stay?"

"It's lovely," Chloe said.

Jack dropped Chloe's hand and stepped forward. "Do you have a moment? We have a few questions."

"Ah, yes, of course." Amelia Rose didn't appear surprised. They walked back into the room where the party was being held, and the older woman waved at several people before she turned back to Jack and Chloe. Her eyes twinkled. "Where's your costume, dear?"

Jack frowned. "It was a scrap of fabric."

Amelia Rose chuckled and patted him on the arm. "I wouldn't have thought you the shy type."

"I'm not shy." Jack's expression turned disgruntled. "But I'm also not looking for a career as a male stripper."

"Too bad." Amelia Rose's gaze ran over the length of him. "You'd be quite good. And you have that secret dancing talent. Such a shame to waste it."

Jack blushed to the tips of his ears, and Chloe stared at him wide-eyed and openmouthed.

What secret dancing talent?

Jack shook his head, started to speak, failed, cleared his throat, then started again. "I don't know what you're talking about."

"Of course, dear." Amelia Rose smiled, her expression peaceful.

Jack was lying. He knew exactly what the other woman was talking about. Chloe looked around the house, decorated to the gills with exquisite, upscale Halloween decorations.

Was Aunt Iris right? Was this place magical somehow? Was Amelia Rose herself magical?

"Back to the point," Jack said, ripping her attention

away from the room and back to the conversation at hand.

Amelia Rose smiled again. "Ah yes, the cookies. Have you discovered my secret ingredient yet?"

Jack's face filled with relief and he pointed at the older woman. "I knew it. You put something in those cookies."

Amelia Rose nodded. "I thought you two needed a little extra push. After all, you've been resisting each other so long, I knew seeing your fortune wouldn't be enough."

So . . . all this craziness, all this lust and consuming desire . . . was a drug interaction? That was it? Jack's shoulders relaxed, and all his muscles seemed to uncoil. Chloe waited for the same relief to take hold of her, to ease her body and wash over her.

But it didn't come.

She frowned. She felt . . . disappointed.

But *why* did she feel disappointed?

"You drugged us?" Jack said, his voice ripping her from her thoughts. "What did you put in those cookies? I'll need to check to make sure whatever you put in there is safe."

Amelia Rose laughed. "I didn't drug you, young man. That would be unethical."

Chloe's ears perked up. "Then what?"

"Because something was in those cookies," Jack repeated.

"Yes, there is. Intention," Amelia Rose said as though that explained everything.

"What?" Chloe shook her head.

Amelia Rose smiled. "It's quite simple. I set a very simple intention."

Jack crossed his arms over his chest. "And what was that?"

"That your true desires be revealed." Her voice took on a quiet, faraway tone. "And that those desires would be impossible to ignore."

Chloe's skin broke out in a rush of goose bumps, exploding over her arms. She hugged herself. "What does that mean?"

Before the woman could answer, Jack rushed in, his jaw set in a hard, stubborn line. "I think this is bullshit. I think you put something *real* in there."

Amelia Rose appeared completely calm. "You're a man of science, and I can appreciate that. But ask yourself, what type of known drug could I have put in there? And more important, why?"

Chloe nibbled her bottom lip while Jack's brow creased.

The woman raised a brow. "This establishment has been in this town since its creation. Do you really believe I would risk all that is sacred to me, to drug a couple of strangers? Now, does that seem logical?"

Jack's shoulders slumped and he lost the aggressive set of his features.

Amelia Rose waved a hand over to the table filled with food. "But if you don't believe me, the cookies are right over there. Go ahead and have them tested. You'll find there's nothing in them but flour, butter, sugar, and a little vanilla extract."

Chloe wasn't really paying attention any longer. She was still trying to process her emotions. She didn't understand one thing about what was going on here. But something about what Amelia Rose said resonated deep inside her.

Was there part of her that wanted Jack? She'd never thought so before, but had she been fooling herself?

Jack started to talk, but Chloe cut him off. "Thank

you, Amelia Rose. We've taken up enough of your time . . . enjoy the party."

"You, too." Amelia Rose patted her arm. "I see you're already starting to accept. Good. Life is always easier when you embrace your future."

The older woman wandered off, leaving Jack and Chloe alone.

"That didn't provide any answers at all," Jack said, staring over at the plate of cookies.

It might not have for him, but it had for her. It made her think.

She needed to be alone. To get away from him for a bit. She rubbed her arms. "I need to be alone."

"Chloe—" Jack started, but she cut him off.

"Seriously, Jack, just leave me alone." Then she turned and ran off, hoping he wouldn't follow her.

She wandered through the house, looking for a place that wasn't filled with people, and finally found what she was looking for. A sunroom in the back, deserted as the party was in the front of the house. Chloe sat on the wicker couch and stared out the back window.

What was going on with her?

The lust she could handle. It made sense: Jack was gorgeous, and it had been a while since she'd had sex. Lust she could pass off as some sort of anomaly, effecting them because of hormones, or something in the air, or the confines of the small room. That she could explain away.

It was the disappointment that stopped her cold. That made her really think.

Because, for that split second, when she'd thought they'd been drugged, she should have been relieved. Like Jack had been. There were a million things she should have felt, but disappointment wasn't one of them.

She thought of her last conversation with Greg, what he'd said that she'd never told anyone.

Chloe had dismissed his anger, saying everyone knew there was nothing going on with Jack. That he was her best friend and Greg needed to accept that.

He had shaken his head, and resignation had crossed his features. "You're the delusional one, Chloe, not me."

She'd sighed, slightly irritated he didn't understand, that nobody else seemed to understand. "I promise you're making too big of a deal about this."

He'd stared at her for a long time before saying, "I promise you, it is a big deal. I've never once curled up next to my best friend to watch a movie."

She hadn't known how to explain to him that that was just the way she and Jack were. That it didn't mean anything. "It was nothing."

He'd pinched the bridge of his nose. "You're in love with him, Chloe."

She'd actually laughed. "Don't be crazy, of course I'm not."

"You are. You're just too blind to see it." Greg shook his head. "Too scared to expand the box you've put him into to see the truth. But you're in love with him."

Chloe had dismissed the idea, telling herself that Greg just didn't understand. She wasn't going to give up Jack to appease him. He was the unreasonable one, not her.

But after today, sitting here, the doubts crept in.

Because Greg hadn't been the only one.

How many men had she dumped because they hadn't lived up to the expectations set by Jack? How many men had broken up with her because they hadn't wanted to deal with the Jack issue? She'd always laughed them off, telling herself the kind of man she wanted would be confident enough to handle her friendship with Jack.

But when was the last time she'd let a man like that get close to her?

And what about Jack? When was the last time he'd even brought a woman around?

She knew he saw women. Went on dates. Certainly he had sex, but he never brought them around her. Why? If they were best friends, why wouldn't she meet his girlfriends?

"There you are." Jack's voice had her head shooting up.

She looked at him, strolling toward her, his legs long, his shoulders broad. His handsome face, all carved and chiseled. How many times had she looked at a guy and thought, *Well, he's not as good-looking as Jack, but he'll do?*

Was she blind? Was she scared? Had she kept him in the friend box for so long that she didn't want to admit to anyone, least of all herself, that he'd outgrown it?

She remembered when they'd first checked in and he'd curled up next to him on the bed, pressing her body into his while he rubbed her back. Was that normal? Would she do that with Nora? Or what about Ted, one of her other long-standing guy friends?

She wouldn't. Not in a million years. She didn't even call Ted. They hung out in their standard Friday night group at the local bar, playing darts and pool. They laughed and shot the shit and drank together, but she didn't really talk to him. Didn't even think of him when he wasn't around.

She met Jack's eyes.

She called him every single day. Other than her mother, he was the only person she talked to daily without fail. Not her dad, her brother, or her sister, not Nora.

Jack.

He sat down next to her, and his gaze glanced down her body. "We need to talk."

She was past talking. She had to know.

Accept your future. That was what Amelia Rose had said.

Jack frowned. "Chlo—talk to me, we can figure this out."

The truth swept through her in a rush. She *was* afraid.

She went hot, then cold, as the blood drained from her face. The blinders ripped away, showing her the undeniable truth.

She was so, so stupid.

She wanted Jack. She loved him. Had probably loved him forever, but she'd refused to even think about it because she'd never sensed anything back from him, so she'd blocked it out and pretended it didn't exist. That it wasn't true for her.

No man ever lived up to him because none of them *were* him.

"Chloe, please." He put his hand on her neck.

She met his gaze. His expression was troubled. This whole thing was upsetting him because he didn't want to want her.

But he did. Tonight, on Halloween, surrounded by pumpkins and bats and skeletons and ghosts, he fought his desire for her.

Now faced with the truth, she was no longer able to let the fear stop her.

He could fight it if he wanted, but she was done. It was time she dealt with her feelings. There was no going back—regardless of what happened when they left this place, they'd be changed.

She had to know. There was no other option.

She took a deep breath, curled her hand around his neck, and kissed him.

Chapter 10

Jack was so surprised when Chloe's mouth met his, he froze. Shocked still as her hands pulled him close and her lips pressed against him.

He'd wanted her so bad, all day the urge to take her had been tugging at him, and now she was here. He gave one fleeting thought to stopping. To inject some sanity into the madness.

But the tip of her tongue touched his lips, seeking entrance. He groaned and gave up the fight. His mouth opened, their tongues tangled, and he was lost. Everything about her felt hot and eager, so damn right.

Better than anything he'd felt in . . . well, forever.

In an instant, the kiss transformed as he went from passive to active participant.

He wrapped his arms around her, his fingers sliding over the smooth skin of her stomach. Skin he'd touched a thousand times, but never like this.

She trembled under his touch.

The kiss turned hotter. Wetter.

He gripped her tight, pulling her close.

She didn't hesitate, climbing on top of him and strad-
dling his thighs.

He clasped her hips. Dug his fingers into her soft
flesh.

Christ.

She clutched his shoulders, her mouth growing more
insistent.

He wanted to consume her.

He slanted his head, increasing their connection.
Deepening the angle.

Getting lost in her.

Chloe. Fuck. He was kissing Chloe. His Chloe. His
best friend.

And it was incredible.

He couldn't get enough. He swept his palms up her
body, barely clothed in her tiny costume. He tangled his
fingers in her hair, fisting the length to drag her closer.
So much closer.

She gasped and moaned, sliding her hips forward.

When his cock slid between her thighs, he about lost
his goddamn mind.

She rocked. He surged.

The heat, the slide, the friction.

It was everything that had ever been missing in a kiss.
She was everything he'd been missing.

"Oh!" a soft voice exclaimed. "I'm sorry."

They jerked apart. Breathing hard, they stared at
each other, Chloe's green eyes as dazed as he felt. She
scrambled off him, and they looked at the woman
who'd interrupted them.

Chloe blushed, and cleared her throat, tucking her
hair behind her ears. "Aunt Iris."

The older woman gave them a huge smile. "I didn't
mean to interrupt. You surprised me."

Chloe shook her head. "You didn't. We were . . . um . . . we were . . ." She shot a glance at him.

Jack sat back on the sofa. "We were making out."

Chloe's expression went wide, and she slapped him across the arm. "Jack!"

Aunt Iris laughed. "I can see that."

"It was nothing." Chloe waved a hand. "We were . . . experimenting."

"Yes, dear," Aunt Iris said, her voice filled with amusement. "Your mother will be so pleased."

Really now? That was an interesting piece of information.

Chloe's brows creased. "Wait. No. It's not what you think."

He cocked a brow at her. "It isn't?"

She frowned at him. She turned back to Aunt Iris. "See, Jack's last girlfriend said he was a bad kisser and I was . . . Um . . . Helping him out."

"Hey!" Jack protested. He was confused, turned on, and screwed six ways till Sunday, but he refused to have her aunt Iris believe he was a terrible kisser. "You take that back."

Chloe patted his leg. "It's okay."

Aunt Iris's lips trembled with what Jack was pretty sure was suppressed mirth. "You two go on with your experiments. I was just passing through."

Then she turned around and left, leaving Jack and Chloe alone.

It was much easier to address the attack on his manhood than to think too much about what had just transpired between them. "Bad kisser, huh?"

Chloe's face flushed. "Yes, well, the last thing I want is our mothers finding out about this, and I had to come up with something."

"And you went with I'm a bad kisser and need lessons?"

Chloe's lips tilted. "Seemed logical."

He meant to take it further, to ignore the elephant sitting on the couch between them, but when he spoke, those weren't the words he said. "Why did you kiss me, Chloe?"

She swallowed hard and looked away. "Didn't you like it?"

"Five more minutes, and Aunt Iris would have walked in on something much more pornographic." Jack shifted in his seat, trying to adjust and find a comfortable spot with a raging erection. "But it doesn't answer my question."

She shrugged. "It seemed the thing to do."

"There's more."

"This is crazy." She ran her hand through her hair. "I don't know what's come over us this weekend."

"Me, either," Jack admitted. He only knew he couldn't seem to stop it. No matter the logic.

Chloe looked down at her lap and started nibbling at her bottom lip.

He slid his hand along the back of the sofa, before running a finger down her neck. "Tell me what's on your mind. That's one thing we've always been good at, and it shouldn't change now that we've shared the kiss to end all kisses."

Her head shot up. "It was good?"

"Are you serious?"

She shook her head. "It was so awesome I can't even think straight."

He leaned closer, meeting her eyes. "It was better than sex."

"It was." Her breath caught.

He tangled his hand in her hair. "All I can think about is taking you to bed."

"Me too." She clasped her hands. "We shouldn't."

"I know." It would change everything between them.

She batted his hand away. "Stop that. I can't think when you're doing that."

He rested his hand on the couch. "This is not good, Chloe. I can't resist you right now."

She pressed her lips together, remaining silent, her head tilting to the side. Jack knew her well enough to know she was thinking, contemplating their next move, and he let her.

After a minute, she cleared her throat. "Here's what I'm thinking. Let's get through this night, go home, and then, if we still feel this way in a week, we can revisit it." She glanced around. "Because this place has cast some kind of spell on us. We need to clear our heads so we can make rational decisions."

It wasn't a bad plan. It made sense. And their relationship was too important to ruin with impulsive sex. All he needed to do was get through this night without touching her. Once they got back home, they could retreat to their separate houses and gather their thoughts.

The problem was not touching her.

Something easy this morning that now seemed an impossible feat.

It was at least a direction, though, and he nodded. "Sounds like a plan."

Her shoulders straightened. "When we get home, we should take a break for a bit. Are you working on Friday?"

He shook his head.

"Good. We'll wait until next Friday, and if we still feel like we do now, we'll talk. Deal?"

Next Friday? That was a lifetime from now. But it was for the good of their friendship. "Deal."

Chapter 11

They rejoined the party. They ate. They drank. They marveled at the decorations. Talked to the townspeople. Laughed. On the surface, they'd put the scene in the sunroom out of their minds.

An hour had passed.

But Chloe couldn't stop thinking about the way Jack kissed her.

Couldn't stop looking at him.

And he couldn't stop looking at her.

By silent, mutual agreement they had made sure not to touch each other.

But every look brimmed with tension.

It was eleven thirty and neither one of them made any mention of going back to their room. Their room with the tiny bed and nowhere else to sleep.

Jack's gaze met hers. Lingered far too long. Her skin heated.

She couldn't look away.

The way he'd kissed her. His mouth, hard and demanding on hers.

The press of his cock between her legs, the thrust of his hips.

She sucked in a breath.

It was a kiss. Just a kiss.

His attention drifted to her lips, his gaze seemed to trace the bow of her mouth.

God, she needed some air.

Abruptly, she pulled away from the conversation and turned to the zombie bride and groom they'd been talking to. "If you'll excuse me, I'm going to get some air."

Jack watched her. "I'll go with you."

Ack! No. She couldn't be alone with him. She held up a hand. "That's not necessary."

As fast as she could, without appearing to run, she turned, weaved a path through the partygoers, and stepped outside.

The cold air hit her bare skin and she shivered. Even though it was still reasonably warm for October, she shouldn't be out here half-naked. But she didn't care. Maybe the cold would knock some sense into her.

She ran down the steps, turned, and headed down the path to the lake. When she got there, she stopped at the water's edge and stared up into the night sky, filled with a million stars. The moon was huge, bright and white, making the dark water sparkle like magic.

It was breathtaking and calming. She took a deep breath and exhaled.

She could handle this.

The cold air numbed her skin and she hugged herself, running her hands over her arms.

It was one week. If she still wanted to jump his bones next Friday, she could. But she had to be smart about this. It was Jack. His friendship was one of the most important things in her life.

She was a naturally impulsive person. She was not risk-averse. But this was Jack. She needed to take her time.

The sound of shoes hitting the ground sounded behind her, signaling someone coming down the path. She craned her neck and looked behind her to find Jack, carrying her coat in his hands.

Of course he'd come find her.

She frowned. If she needed to resist the temptation of him, why had she removed herself from the party and come to a place guaranteed to make him follow? Rose Cottage was making her stupid.

When he reached her, he put the jacket around her shoulders. "I thought you'd be cold."

She slipped her arms into the sleeves and shivered as the fleece slid against her skin. "Thank you."

She looked back over the lake and he stood behind her in silence.

She took a deep breath. "Have you ever seen anything so beautiful?"

"Yes," he said, his voice soft.

She could feel the heat of his body. The moon hung low and full, beckoning her. She swallowed hard. "Jack?"

"Yes, Chlo?"

Her name never sounded so good as when it came from his lips. From his gorgeous mouth that was now imprinted on her skin, that she could still feel against her lips. "Don't sleep in the car."

A beat of silence. "What are you saying?"

"I'm saying I don't want you to sleep in the car." She cleared her throat. "As soon as we fall asleep we'll be fine."

"We're still waiting until Friday?"

"Yes." Friday seemed an eternity away. "It's the smart move."

"It is." His arms wrapped around her, and he bent to whisper in her ear, "It would be easier to be smart if I didn't want to be inside you. Didn't want to feel you come."

She shuddered. Sex had always been a subject they'd never discussed. One of those taboo topics they avoided. It was strange to hear him utter those words, say things she'd never envisioned him saying to her, but they lit her on fire. "If we still feel this way on Friday, maybe you will."

His lips brushed her throat, raising the fine hairs there. "I can give you an orgasm and not fuck you."

She closed her eyes and fought against her base desires. "I don't think that's realistic."

He pressed an openmouthed kiss on the curve of her throat. "Probably not."

She melted against him, craning her neck and arching. "Maybe we should revise our plan to Thursday."

"Monday," he countered.

She licked her lips. "Wednesday."

His tongue licked across her pounding pulse. "Tuesday."

She moaned. "Don't you work?"

"I can come over at midnight on Monday—technically it will be Tuesday." His breath was hot against her inflamed skin.

"Isn't that cheating?"

"It will be Tuesday."

Two days, she could make that. It was enough time. "All right. Use your key. I'll be naked."

"Jesus, Chloe." He twined his fingers in her hair, and she turned her head, looking up at him.

His mouth was on hers in an instant.

His tongue moving against hers. His lips insistent.

His palm splayed over her stomach, warm against her cold skin.

Desire crashed through her, threatening to suck her under. She twisted, needing to get closer. His hands were everywhere. Leaving a blazing trail in his wake. His thumbs brushed the undercurve of her breasts. She moaned, rising to tiptoes to get closer.

What were they doing?

He pulled away and whispered against her mouth, "Now."

"Yes." She was past sanity.

His grip on her hair tightened. "We need to go inside."

She nodded.

He pulled away and took her hand.

In silence they walked back to the cottage. When they got to the steps, Amelia Rose was there, saying good-bye to some of the guests. She nodded. "You've given in to the magic."

Jack ignored her as they made a beeline to the hallway where their room was.

But Chloe's blood ran cold. Was that all this was? Some spell? Intention? The power of suggestion? Was it this house that was making them give in to a feeling that didn't really exist? She didn't know how that was possible, but then, why? Why after all this time was this happening? Why now, at thirty, couldn't they keep their hands off each other?

It was strange. And tonight, with her desire for him bordering on compulsion, she believed that it was this house, this place, the suggestion of their future affecting them. If they gave in now, they risked ruining a friendship for temporary insanity.

It wasn't worth it.

Jack pulled the key out of his pocket. She put her hand on his arm.

"Jack, we can't."

He turned back to look at her, his expression pained. "It's two days. What's two days?"

Nothing. Nothing at all. She swallowed. "It's not that." She gestured behind them, into the empty hallway. "It's this house. How do we know it's not this place casting a spell on us?"

He turned back around to face her. "Do you honestly believe that? That this is a spell?"

She frowned. "I don't know what to believe. But ask yourself, why now? Are you saying we just had better control over our bodies at sixteen than we do now?"

His brow furrowed. "Okay, I'll admit you have a point."

Her attention snagged on his mouth, and she bit her bottom lip, still remembering the taste of him. "Does this not feel out of control?"

"Yes." He stepped closer. "It's like I can't keep my hands off you."

"Exactly." She took a deep breath. "We've got years of friendship at stake, and I don't want to mess it up. Do you?"

Chapter 12

Christ. When she looked at him with those huge eyes, he couldn't think straight.

But he knew this was important to her. She was important to him. In fact, she was the most important thing in his life and he would do anything to keep her happy. And she had a point. He sighed and nodded. "You're right."

Something flashed across her features, a mixture of regret and relief. "If we still feel like this after we leave, we'll figure out what to do. Okay?"

"Okay." He could do this. He was a man of self-control. It was one night. He could keep his hands to himself for one night.

He twisted the door handle and flicked on the light, plunging the room into a soft glow. He looked at the bed. "How should we do this?"

She stood beside him, arms crossed, scowling at the bed. "First things first, lots of clothes."

Even as she said the words, she shrugged off her coat. He took in her bare skin, flat stomach, the curve of her waist and the swell of her hips. The long legs, firm and toned. The plunge of cleavage. He waved a hand at her. "That outfit has to go."

She looked down at herself. "Agreed."

"You have sweatpants, right?"

She nodded. "Do you?"

"I do."

"That's a start." He jutted his chin toward the bathroom. "Do you want the bathroom?"

"Sure." She gave him an overly bright smile. "We can do this."

"Piece of cake." He nodded toward the open doorway. "Now, go, and please, dress as matronly as possible."

She laughed and went into the bathroom.

He shrugged out of his jeans and tossed on a pair of sweats, leaving his pullover in place. He stared at the bed.

Fuck, it was small.

But if they were doing this, he needed to act as normal as possible. And normally he'd stretch out and make himself comfortable. Maybe that was the key. Being normal. Acting as he always had. Except, no touching.

It was a solid plan. He grabbed the remote and flicked on the TV, sat on the bed, and stretched out. He tossed his cell on the nightstand, and mindlessly flipped through channels while he kept an ear cocked for the bathroom door.

He settled on the History Channel. Watched some scientist talk about evolution without paying the slightest attention to what was being said. Finally, the bathroom door opened and Chloe stepped out.

He frowned at her.

She looked all . . . puffy.

She held out her hands. "This is about as unsexy as I can make myself."

He blinked at her. "What are you wearing?"

"About four layers of clothes." Hair in a slicked-back ponytail, her face free of makeup. She cocked a grin at him. "My own personal chastity belt."

He laughed. God, she was adorable.

He wanted to eat her up.

No. Wait. He wasn't supposed to be thinking of that.

She glanced nervously around the room. "Should I turn off the light?"

"Sure." He cleared his throat. "No problem."

She put her hands on her lumpy hips. "We're under control?"

"Completely." He was a liar. Even with her dressed like the Stay Puft Marshmallow Man, he wanted to devour her.

She glanced nervously at the bed, back at him, then back at the bed again.

Jack held his breath, waiting for what she might do, half-expecting her to run screaming from the room.

She padded over on bare feet, the only part of her body, besides her hands, not covered. She sat cautiously on the bed, and craned her neck to look back at him. "Tuesday."

He flexed his fingers. "Tuesday."

She nodded, then lay back against the headboard, precariously balancing herself on the very edge of the mattress.

And, suddenly, it irritated him. Not her, but the situation. That years of easy, comfortable friendship had all been ruined by some stupid, sudden burning attraction.

Eyes glued to the screen, she asked, "What are you watching?"

"The History Channel." His stomach tightened. His gaze skimmed down her overly padded body instead of staying on the television where it belonged.

There wasn't one thing sexy about her.

Not one.

Sure, she looked kind of cute, but she did not look sexy.

She was lumpy, and covered more effectively than a nun.

And he still wanted her.

Was still hard. Still fighting the urge to roll over toward her.

For as much temptation as she provided, she might as well have been wearing black lace lingerie.

He blew out a breath.

She blinked at him. "Is this okay?"

He shook his head. "Chlo, I hate you being so tentative. So far away."

"Me too." She rolled over, propping her head up on her open palm to look at him. "But I don't know what else to do."

His attention snagged on her lips, lingering far too long. "Can't we just act normal?"

Her teeth scraped along her bottom lip. "Yes, of course, that's what I want, too."

Gaze roaming over her, he said, "Normally you'd be lying next to me, your head on my shoulder."

Was he daring her? What exactly was wrong with him? If he was supposed to resist her until two days from now then her curled up next to him wasn't a smart idea.

But his brain had run off to parts unknown.

Besides, he did want them to be normal.

It had only been a couple of hours and he already missed her.

She took a stuttery little breath. "I can do that."

He rolled onto his back and patted the space next to him. "Good."

She stared at him for a good fifteen seconds, then slid next to him, before resting her head on his shoulder.

He tensed, his body tightening with desire he tried to ignore.

Her fingers slid across his stomach before coming to rest.

He had to bite back the groan.

He cleared his throat. "See, just like normal."

"Yep, totally normal." Her hand twitched on his stomach.

To his horror, his cock went from semi-erect, to full-on raging hard-on. Impossible to hide in sweatpants.

"Oh." She let out a gasp.

"Sorry." Christ. This was worse than being a sixteen-year-old kid.

She went to move away, but he tightened an arm around her. "Please, don't. Just give me a minute."

She settled against him, but she was no more relaxed. "This seems . . . like a bad idea."

"It's okay." He closed his eyes and willed his body to calm. "I miss you already."

"Me too."

"This is so awkward."

She laughed, and buried her head into the crook of his arm. "It is."

He ran a hand down her back. "At least I can't feel anything."

Her fingers moved a bit over his stomach. "I wish I could say the same."

He did groan now. "Don't say things like that."

"I'm sorry."

He rolled his neck, shifting to find a comfortable

spot. He could do this. He handed her the remote. "Put on what you want."

She flicked through stations at lightning speed before settling on a black-and-white movie with Cary Grant racing around on the screen. She dropped the controller to the bed. "*Arsenic and Old Lace.*"

"A classic."

Her fingers splayed over his stomach, the muscles tensing under her touch.

They lay there like that, for he didn't know how long, both of them breathing slow and deep, almost meditative.

He didn't pay the slightest bit of attention to the television.

He only focused on her hand. The taper of her fingers. The curve of her palm. The fine bones of her wrists.

He envisioned encircling her wrists with his hands. How his fingers would wrap around her, the squeeze of her bones in his grasp. Holding them over her head.

His body on top of hers.

Thrusting into her.

The image. It was so damn vivid.

His cock roared back to life. He moved a palm down her back.

She seemed to stop breathing.

He ran his thumb over the edge of her sweatpants.

Her fingers dipped lower on his stomach.

He pulled up one layer of fabric.

She inched lower.

He peeled away another piece of cotton.

Her leg slid up his thigh.

He bunched up a top.

Her hand dipped down to rest on his waistband.

He was so fucking hard.

Tension and sex practically vibrated the air between them.

He worked his way under the last layer of clothes, his palm settling on her bare back, her skin hot to his touch.

She gasped. Shifting closer.

Her fingers brushed his bare stomach.

Neither one of them spoke.

Neither one of them dared to breathe.

Chapter 13

Chloe was burning alive.

She was so hot. So turned on. She couldn't think of anything but touching Jack. It was as though her hand had a mind of its own, because she could not help herself.

His fingers played over the curve of her spine.

She shifted, her leg riding higher, closer to where his arousal was obvious. She worked her way under his shirt, stroking over his flat abdomen. Marveling at the way his muscles tensed under her.

They still hadn't spoken.

It was like they had some silent agreement between them not to say anything.

As wrong as it was, as much as she knew it was stupid, she didn't want anything to break this spell.

She hadn't felt like this in forever.

Hadn't lusted this hard in a million years. Maybe not ever. It was exciting and exhilarating. Too addictive to stop, despite the protests in her brain.

Her breath kicked up.

Jack's did the same.

He traced a path down the curve of her waist.

She raked her nails over his stomach.

He jerked, inhaling sharply.

It was too much.

It wasn't enough.

She didn't want to speak.

But she wanted more. Needed more. Closer.

She shifted; his big hand covered her ribs.

Her thigh journeyed higher.

Their breathing turned harsh.

Touch me. Touch me. Touch me. A chant in her head. Begging, really.

She tilted her hips, brushing her soft center against his leg.

He moved his thigh, pressing up and hard, creating a friction she was desperate for.

The tips of his fingers brushed the undercurve of her breast. Just the barest hint. Just enough to make her ache.

The temptation to touch warred with the temptation not to break the final barrier that would change their friendship forever.

She walked a path over his ribs.

The air grew hot. Humid. She thought she might suffocate with all these clothes on.

She nudged his balls with her knee. He moaned, the sound thrilling.

"Christ." His voice, low and guttural. He tightened his hold for one fraction of a second, then flipped her over onto her back.

His mouth covered hers.

And all that barely contained sexual energy exploded around them.

His tongue licked into her mouth. She groaned, tangling her hands in his hair.

The kiss turned hotter, wetter. Dirtier.

She shuddered. His leg pressed between her thighs, and she ground against his hard muscle, unable to help herself.

He ripped away from her. He shifted. "Too many clothes."

He yanked at her sweatshirt, and she arched, letting him whisk it over her head.

He growled and fisted the fabric of the next layer.

That went over her head, too.

She sat up, and, both of them kneeling, she grabbed his head, bringing him close.

Their lips tangled. Their hands searched. She slanted her head, deepening the angle of the kiss. It was everything a kiss should be, and it increased her frustration by about a thousand.

He pulled the next shirt over her head, looked down at her, and said in a voice that sounded like pure sex, "How many fucking tops do you have on?"

"One more." She pulled at his shirt, and over his head it went.

Then hers was gone, and their mouths met, their skin touched. It was like a bomb went off, detonating through the room with its force.

They went at it. Their mouths a frantic, searching quest. As though they were trying to make up for thirty years of longing in this one kiss. He bit her lower lip and she raked her nails down his back.

They tumbled to the bed, and his body was finally, deliciously covering hers.

She arched.

He surged.

They rocked.

She dug her nails into the base of his back.

His hand came up to cup her breast, his thumb stroking over the nipple.

She cried out, and he caught the sound with his lips.

He ripped away from her, slid down her body, and captured her nipple with his lips, while his free hand snaked down into her yoga pants.

He licked at the hard bud. Sucked.

Her hips arched off the bed as he tugged harder and harder.

When his teeth scraped over her oversensitive flesh, she keened and she couldn't stop the words from falling from her lips. "Jack. God. Jack. Yes. More."

He groaned, the sound vibrating over her skin. He pulled her deeper into his mouth. His fingers slid down her waistband and into her panties. Her legs parted. His fingers brushed her clit. She bowed off the bed.

He circled the bundle of nerves and lifted his head. "So damn wet."

She could feel how wet she was, how slippery. "More."

He pushed one long finger inside her, and kissed her, brushing his mouth over her lips. "You feel like heaven."

She arched into his touch as his thumb relentlessly circled her clit. Around and around. Over and over. Until she thought she'd go mad with sheer need. "Jack. Please."

He plunged two fingers inside her, hooking on a spot so good she lost focus.

"Please what, Chlo?"

His voice, oh God, his voice. Achingly familiar and yet strange all at once.

He swiped over her flesh and she keened again as her body tightened. "Stop." Her head rolled back. "I'm going to come."

He increased his pressure and whispered against the shell of her ear, "Then come."

She fought against the tide riding fast and desperate. Desire rolled through her. She gasped out, "No, please."

"Please what?"

She put her hand on his wrist, relentlessly driving her crazy. "Not without you."

He groaned and kissed her, hard and passionate, before rolling away from her to sit up on the edge of the mattress.

She rose on her elbows, breathing hard. "Where are you going?"

He looked back at her and in that moment, with the moonlight streaming in, his hair a mess, his jaw strong, his shoulders broad, he was the most gorgeous man she'd ever seen. She had no idea how she'd ever resisted him, or why she'd even want to.

"Condom." He grinned at her, and her heart squeezed before skipping a beat.

She flushed. "Oh."

He got up and went into the bathroom, and when he returned he dropped about five onto the bedside table.

Her brows rose. "Why did you bring condoms?"

"I always carry them in my bag."

"Just in case?" Somehow irritated at the notion.

With one foil packet still in his hand, he climbed onto the bed and settled on his haunches between her legs. He dropped the condom on her stomach, and gripped her ankles. "Are you saying you're not a tiny bit happy I'm prepared?" His hands moved up her legs to her hips.

She sucked in a breath at the look in his eye. "Maybe a tiny bit."

He tugged down her pants, taking her underwear along with them, and tossing them to the floor.

Then he stopped, and stared.

She was naked, except for the condom packet that rested in the dip of her ribs, and he took in every single inch of her.

He shook his head. "My whole life men have asked me how I could possibly be just friends with you."

She bit her lip, blinking up at him.

"And in this moment I have no fucking idea."

He leaned down and kissed her stomach, her hip bones, while his big hands held her in place. Then his mouth was on her, covering her, licking over her clit.

She arched up, crying out as his tongue slid over her folds, making her mindless and crazy. She clutched the pillow, burying her head into the softness as he sucked and licked, nipping over her skin.

She clamped her thighs around his head. Whimpered.

He was going to drive her right over the edge.

His tongue lapped over her clit.

"Jack, stop," she said, her voice harsh and panting. "I'm going to . . . God . . . No . . . I want . . ."

He didn't stop. Didn't ease up. He just pushed her harder.

His tongue. It was magic.

The condom packet slid off her stomach as she planted her feet and rocked into him. Giving up, surrendering to his will and determination. Everything that made Jack, Jack.

She coiled tight and then she exploded. She bit her lip, stifling her moans as she rode out wave after wave of delicious sensation.

She couldn't think, couldn't put together a sentence, but then he was on her, over her. His palm on her neck, his fingers on her jaw, twisting her face to meet his.

His mouth covered hers.

He tasted like sex.

And lust.

His grasp was tight on her jaw, and the way he kissed her, devoured her, sucked her right back under.

It was a raw, dirty kiss that consumed her. Her fingers came up to where he held her, and she dug her nails into his wrists.

He growled against her lips, biting her, sucking.

And the kiss went on and on and on.

He finally pulled away, grabbed the condom, and tore open the package. He tossed it onto her body again, ridding himself of his sweats, and then he was naked.

And she could only gape at him. Her gaze wide.

He had the best cock she'd ever seen in her life. Long and thick. A work of goddamn art.

She reached for him, but he grabbed her wrist, shaking his head. "I can't wait, Chlo."

He picked up the condom, threw the packet on the floor somewhere and rolled the condom down his hard shaft.

She breathed out his name. "Jack."

He leaned down, kissing her again, soft and sweet. His erection nudged between her legs. "Just let me inside."

She nodded, some distant part of her mind grasping the fact that she was about to have sex with Jack.

Her best friend.

The one person who knew her better than anyone. Knew all her secrets. Her likes. The things she hated. Her hopes and fears.

He'd seen her at her very best, and her absolute worst.

He'd held her hair when she was sick. Listened to her rant, supported her even when everyone else thought she was crazy.

Jack entered her, filling her. Stretching her tight and opening her eyes to what she'd refused to see all these years.

When he was seated to the hilt, their eyes met, gazes locked and held.

And she knew the truth.

He was her one true love.

Chapter 14

Nothing on this earth had ever felt as good as being inside Chloe.

He gritted his teeth, hanging on to the last remnants of sanity he possessed, as he tried to calm enough not to take her like some primal beast.

The grip of her.

The silky heat.

He braced his elbow next to her head and their eyes locked.

He was fucking Chloe.

This was going to change them forever.

He experienced a rush of panic that quickly dimmed as her thighs clasped his hips and she arched to meet him, gasping.

Her hands fell to his waist, nails digging into his skin.

He moved, gripped her wrists, and brought them up over her head. They were touching everywhere, the length of him sliding into her. Her breasts against his chest. Her inner muscles clamped around him and he cursed, thrusting inside her.

He'd think later. Much, much later.

He covered her mouth with his, his tongue sliding against hers. The air grew thick and humid. Tinged with a desperate, urgent lust. He ripped away and groaned.

Pumped harder inside her.

Her head pressed into the pillow and her neck arched.

He held her wrists tighter; he bit her exposed throat, before soothing the skin with his tongue.

She cried out. Her nails dug harder. Her thighs clenched.

Their movements deepened. Quickened.

He let her go, levered up, and rammed hard inside her, circling his hips. Grinding against her. Thrusting harder. Faster. Deeper.

The bed frame banged its frantic beat against the wall.

Over and over and over again.

Her body rippled down the length of his cock.

He jerked, losing what little control he had as he came in a loud shout, just as her orgasm rushed through her, milking him for everything he was worth, his vision dimming as intense pleasure tore through him in endless waves.

He had no idea how long they went on like that. Pushing and pulsing together mindlessly, lost in the aftershocks of bone-deep satisfaction. He collapsed on top of her, burying his face in the crook of her neck, inhaling that special scent, unique to Chloe. He licked her skin. Tasting salt and sex.

All her muscles relaxed under him, and he lifted his head to look at her.

Her eyes were closed. He brushed a lock of hair off her cheek, before rubbing a thumb over her swollen lips. "You okay?"

She nodded.

He brushed his mouth over hers. "Are you sorry?"

Her thick lashes fluttered open. "No. Are you?"

"Not even a little bit."

Her expression flashed. "Good."

He pulled out of her and rolled onto his back, looking at the ceiling. He'd just had his mind blown. He didn't even know what to say, where to begin, or how to process what they'd just done. He raked a hand through his hair. He smelled her everywhere, like she'd seeped into his skin and become a part of him. "Chlo?"

"Yeah?" Her voice as reflective as he felt.

He looked at her, that profile he knew as well as his own. Utterly beautiful. "That was the best sex I've ever had."

She turned to look at him. "Oh yeah?"

"By a mile."

"Me too."

Late that night, exhausted, Chloe stared out the window that overlooked the lake, wearing nothing but Jack's shirt. He lay asleep on the bed, taking up almost all the space, not that it mattered.

She couldn't sleep.

They'd taken catnaps, in between rounds of hot sweaty, mind-blowing sex. But after the last round she'd grown restless.

By some sort of mutual, silent agreement they hadn't talked about what was happening. Instead, they'd been insatiable. He'd taken her over and over again, in every conceivable position. Like they couldn't get enough. Like they were making up for years of lost time.

And she was shaken to her very core. Because she couldn't escape the truth. She loved him. Maybe she'd been in love with him her whole life and hadn't realized it. Could she have been that blind?

She thought of all the ways they were together. The way they never wanted to be far apart. The way she cuddled close to him. The way she needed to talk to him when she'd had a bad day.

She gulped. The way she picked Jack over every other man in her life.

She took a deep breath. She'd been blind, but she wasn't now.

But what if Jack didn't feel the same way?

What if it was this place, their fortune, and the moon that made him want her?

Their friendship would be ruined forever. Because she knew the truth now. She couldn't go back. She could no longer pretend that he was just her friend when he clearly wasn't.

"Chloe?" Jack's sleepy voice filled the room.

She turned and peered over her shoulder. Heart skipping a beat at the sight of him sprawled on the bed. The moonlight streamed in through the window, casting him in its white light, highlighting his magnificence.

"Come back to bed." He rolled to look at her, his chest bare and beautiful, his hair tousled. "I want you again."

If she was only going to have one night, she wasn't going to waste a second.

The morning was only a few hours away.

And then she'd learn what her fate really held.

Chapter 15

The bright sun blinding, they stared at each other.

Chloe sat on the chair in the bay window, all her muscles tense and coiled tight.

Awkward didn't begin to describe the situation. It was like as soon as the dawn had broken, sanity had reared its ugly head.

Jack sat on the edge of the bed in jeans and a long-sleeved navy T-shirt, watching her.

He was uncomfortable. Unsure.

The problem with sleeping with someone she knew like the back of her hand was that she didn't have to guess at his mood. Right now it was debatable if that was a blessing or a curse.

He glanced beyond her and cleared his throat. "So. Now what?"

She didn't want to have this conversation. Because now they had to decide and she didn't know what she'd do if he thought it was all a mistake.

She took a deep breath. She'd done the crime and now she had to pay the price. Even if that price was the loss of her best friend. "I don't know. Can we forget it happened?"

His expression clouded. "I can't forget it happened."

She looked out the window. "Can you go back to being just friends?"

Please say no.

He was silent for a long time and she couldn't bear to look at him.

He cleared his throat. "I can't lose you as a friend."

Her stomach sank. She closed her eyes, remembering the way he moved so desperately inside her last night. His whispered words. The way he chanted her name, low and sweet. Her lashes fluttered open. "Okay. You won't lose me."

"Do you promise?" His voice was soft.

He was breaking her heart. She would try her very best to pretend, because she loved him. "I promise."

There was silence. Tension filled the room.

"So . . ." he trailed off, shifted on the bed, before running a hand through his hair. "Do we go back to normal?"

"What choice do we have?" Besides the obvious one sitting right in front of them that neither of them wanted to speak out loud.

"I guess there isn't any."

If she didn't get out of here, she was going to cry. She glanced at the clock. "What time do we have to check out?"

"Eleven."

She nodded and stood. "I'm going to go for a walk."

She started toward the door, and he grabbed her wrist. She looked down at him and hope surged deep and strong.

Don't let me go. Please don't let me go.

He searched her face, his grasp tight on her. "It already feels different."

The hope died a swift, sudden death. "It's going to take a little time."

"I don't want that. I want it to be the way it was, the way it's always been." His expression clouded, his frown deepening on his lips.

Lips that had kissed her like she was his salvation, like he was starving for her not hours ago.

She wanted to scream at him. How could he want that after last night? How could he want to go back to the way they had been? To stuff her back in that box after everything they'd just shared?

And suddenly she was furious. Furious at him. Furious at herself for being so goddamn stupid. She ripped out of his grasp. "I'm sorry, Jack. It's going to take me more than an hour to be your best friend again."

Then she stormed out of the room and didn't look back.

Jack flinched as the door slammed shut behind Chloe.

He'd screwed up. The whole time he was talking he'd known it was going horribly, but he had been helpless to stop the descent.

He hadn't known what to say. How to put into words what he was feeling. He was terrified. Chloe was the most important thing in the world to him, more important than his parents or his brother and sister. More important than any of his other friends.

It had always been the two of them, thick as thieves.

She was everything. He couldn't lose her.

But last night . . . He cursed under his breath and dragged his hand through his hair.

Last night, Chloe had single-handedly blown away every sexual encounter he'd ever had in his entire life. She'd obliterated every other woman from his mind. Permanently. He had no idea how to go back to looking at her as a platonic friend.

Every time he looked at her, all he could think about was how she felt coming around his cock and the look in her eyes as she ran a finger over his jaw. The way she'd said his name in that pleading little whisper. Begging him to take her harder, faster.

He'd made her orgasm in every possible way. Addicted to the sight, the intake of her breath, the swell of her chest, the flush that spread over her breasts. The feel of her nipples in his mouth, rolling over his tongue.

But he couldn't lose her as his best friend. He just couldn't.

She was too important to him.

He had to find a way to make this right.

He shot off the bed, grabbing the key to the room, determined to find her.

She'd said she wanted to walk, so he'd have to search the grounds for her. He walked down the hall to the foyer and spotted Amelia Rose behind the desk. He stalked over to her.

She gave him that serene, peaceful smile. "Good morning, Jack, how was your evening?"

Terrible. Awesome. Terrifying. Mind-blowing.

He clenched his jaw. "Fine. Have you seen Chloe?"

She *tsked*. "She looked quite upset."

He tried his best not to let his annoyance show; after all, it wasn't Amelia Rose's fault his life had just been blown to hell because of her fortune-telling. "Yeah, I know, that's why I have to find her."

She patted his hand. "It's okay, you know."

He frowned. "What do you mean?"

Another reassuring pat. "I mean, it's okay to love her. It's your destiny. *She's* your destiny."

All the air whooshed from Jack's lungs and the room spun, twirling away as his mind grappled with the implications of what the older woman was saying. He felt a wave of nausea, a rush of panic, and then, just as suddenly as the turmoil began, it stilled. Settled.

His entire perception of the world changed and everything made sense. He blinked at Amelia Rose. "I'm in love with Chloe."

She smiled. "Yes, I know, dear. It's written all over you. I knew the second I saw you."

All he could do was stare at the woman and repeat, "I'm in love with Chloe."

Amelia Rose nodded. "Maybe you should tell her that."

"I'm afraid." He had no idea why he was telling the woman this, but he couldn't seem to help himself.

"It's okay, men often are." She laughed, and it was a light, lyrical sound. "You'll survive."

Jack could only stand there, trying to come to terms with this life-changing turn of events.

He loved Chloe.

He'd *always* been in love with Chloe. She meant everything to him because that's what she actually was. Everything.

Amelia Rose pointed toward the front door. "She went outside. I believe I saw her wander off in the direction of the woods."

He sucked air into his lungs. "Thank you."

"You're welcome."

Jack took off, practically running. He needed to find her. He prayed to God she somehow felt the same way.

Because he couldn't live without her for one more second.

Chapter 16

Chloe stood in the center of a deep wooded area, staring up at the brilliant red, gold, and orange leaves of the tallest tree, crying.

What had she done?

How could they ever recover from this?

Heart heavy, she could only let the tears flow.

Somehow she had to learn to be friends with him. To accept that he didn't feel the same way about her as she did about him. She'd have to find a way, because she'd promised him and she couldn't break her promise.

"Chloe!" Jack yelled from off in the distance.

She pressed her lips together, frantically brushing the tears from her cheeks.

He couldn't see her cry. She had to pull it together.

He yelled her name again, this time his voice louder, closer. She scrubbed at her face with the hem of her shirt.

He crashed through the leaves, leaping over a fallen tree, before coming to a sudden halt. A deep frown marred his perfect features. "You're crying."

Of course she couldn't fool him. She shrugged. "I'm sorry I'm not taking this as coolly as you are."

He took three steps toward her, stopped, and then shoved his hands into the pockets of his jeans. "I'm not taking this coolly, Chloe."

Anger bubbled up inside her and she let it take over her sadness, using it as fuel, as a shield to protect her breaking heart. "You certainly seem like you are."

He shook his head. "I'm a fucking mess."

Because he didn't want to ruin their friendship.

She just needed to find a way to deal with it. She was not an avoider. She straightened her shoulders. All her life she'd been honest with Jack, and she wasn't going to change now just because they'd slept together. Not about something this important. She had to tell him the truth, and since they were best friends he'd have to understand. That was the way they did things.

She took a deep breath. "I have to tell you something."

"I have to tell you something, too." He moved closer and she held up a hand to stop him.

"Me first."

He opened his mouth as though he was going to say something but stopped. "Okay."

"Last night, when we thought for a moment we'd been drugged, I didn't feel the way I should." The tightness in her chest increased, but she trudged on, despite her fear.

"How did you feel?"

She steeled her spine. Confession was good for the soul, or so she'd been told. It would be hard to recover from, but eventually she'd get over the humiliation of secretly falling for her best friend. "I felt disappointed. I should have been relieved, as it would have given us a completely logical explanation for our sudden . . . um . . .

impulse-control problems. But I was disappointed instead."

His features widened. "You were?"

"Yes." She bit her bottom lip, still swollen from all the hours they'd kissed. Hard, soul-deep kisses that had taken her breath away. That she'd gotten lost in.

Her throat closed over. Here came the hard part. The truth she barely wanted to admit to herself, let alone him, but it had to be done. She clasped her hands tight in front of her, and tears welled in her eyes. "I'm sorry, Jack. I know this is unfair. I know I promised. But I can't do it. I can't be your friend." She let out a strangled sob. "Maybe, at some point, but I'm going to need time." Wetness spilled onto her cheeks. "I don't know how much. I'm sorry."

She started to cry in earnest, and she looked down at the leaf-strewn ground and waited for him to leave.

There was nothing but silence. A cold, eerie silence that stilled her heart and numbed her all over.

She heard the rustle of leaves. She choked back her hiccupy mess.

She didn't want to do this, but she had no other choice.

The truth was the only way.

Then his arms were around her, strong and warm. She wanted so badly to push him away, but she didn't have the strength. This one last time she'd let him comfort her. Soak in the feel of him as he held her tight.

He stroked her hair and she cried, pressing her face to his strong, capable chest. He ran a thumb over her cheek, down her jaw, before tilting her face up to his. He frowned as he took in her tear-streaked face.

She whispered, "I'm sorry, Jack."

He wiped away the wetness. "I love you, Chloe."

Everything inside her stilled. What did he say? "W-wh-hat?"

He ran the pad of his thumb over her lip. "I love you. I've always loved you. I think you've been in my life for so long, that you're so engrained into the very fabric of it, somewhere along the way I fell so in love with you I couldn't even comprehend it."

"You love me?" *Please, let it be true.*

"I don't want to be friends with you." He leaned down and brushed her lips with his. "Well, no, that's not right. I want you to be my best friend. I want to tell you about my bad days and my good days. I want to have dinner with you. I want to lie on the couch and watch movies with you. I want you to be the last person I talk to before I go to bed at night and the first person I talk to when I wake up in the morning."

A huge, trembling smile spread over her mouth. "We already do all that."

He grinned back. "Yeah, we do. But now I want the mind-blowing sex part, too."

She sucked in a breath. She wanted it, too. "You do?"

His attention dipped to her mouth. "I don't think I can live without screwing your brains out every night."

Laughter spurted from her lips, and she slapped him on the arm. "That's not romantic."

His arms tightened around her. "Chloe Armstrong, you have ruined me for all other women. I have loved you and worshiped you and compared everyone else I've ever met to you. And they *always* come up short. I have hated every guy you've ever been with, and now I know why, because I'm the only one who can have you. You have always been mine, and you will always be mine. I think it's time to make it official."

"Okay." All her stress and turmoil melted away. It was

right, they were right. They'd just been too blinded by their friendship to see it.

He pinched her. "Is that all you have to say? Don't you have *anything* else to tell me?"

She rose to her tiptoes and kissed him. "I love you, too." She grabbed the waistband of his jeans and tugged. "Now, take me."

He looked around. "Here?"

"Here." She was already unbuttoning his jeans.

He pulled her questing fingers away. "Are you kidding? There are probably ticks all over the place. I can't have you ending up with Lyme disease."

See, this was why they were so perfect for each other. She huffed, planting her hands on her hips. "Lyme disease? *Really?* I offer you my body, and you're thinking about ticks?"

He shrugged. "I'm a doctor. Best-case scenario you're out of commission for months. I don't like those odds. I've managed to last thirty years, I can make it back to the room."

"Well, fine, but as a concession I expect you to make it up to me."

He hooked his finger in her belt loop and yanked her close. "Name your price."

"I expect roadside car sex on the way home."

He pretended to think it over before he nodded. "Deal."

She laughed, her heart light and free. She got to have it all. Her best friend, exactly the way they'd always been, but now they'd be complete with nonstop sex and multiple orgasms.

No way life could get any better than this.

Chapter 17

Ready to take off back home, Jack grinned in amusement as Chloe's aunt took one look at them and clapped her hands, jumping up and down like a teenager. She beamed. "It worked!"

Jack raised a brow at Chloe, who furrowed her brow, then shrugged.

She turned to her aunt. "What worked?"

She gave them a sly little grin. "I have a confession to make."

Jack groaned.

"What did you do?" Chloe asked.

The older woman looked at Amelia Rose, who smiled. Iris giggled. "I might have fibbed a bit about my house. But your moms and I talked and decided you two needed a little push."

Chloe's cheeks flushed a pretty pink. "A push?"

Iris waved her hand back and forth at Jack and Chloe. "Are you saying you didn't get together? Because I saw Jack kissing you in the hallway not five minutes ago."

MESMERIZED BY YOU   191

That kiss had been nothing compared to what he'd been doing to Chloe twenty minutes ago. They'd barely made it inside the room. Jack laughed, shaking his head. "It worked."

"Are you saying *our mothers* planned this?!" Chloe's voice raised an octave.

Iris shrugged. "You two are made for each other, and everyone was getting tired of waiting for you to figure it out."

On principle, Jack should work up a little indignation, but it was hard to be upset when the results had so clearly worked in his favor. And Jack had to agree with her. He couldn't figure out what had taken them so long, either. It seemed so obvious now. They were complete idiots. Of course they were in love with each other.

"Even your fortune confirmed it, didn't it, Amelia Rose?" Iris said, as though that was the nail in the coffin.

Amelia nodded. "The cards never lie."

Chloe's expression was that of stern amusement. "Yes, well, I'll forgive you all this once, but we're going to have to have a talk about your interference."

Aunt Iris walked over and kissed Chloe on the cheek, giving her a long, tight hug. "Be happy, dear girl."

"I will be," Chloe said, squeezing back, grinning at Jack from over the older woman's shoulder.

Jack's heart gave a hard *thump*. Jesus, he loved her. He couldn't wait to get back home and start planning their life together. He had to hold himself in check from the millions of things he wanted to start right this second.

Aunt Iris let Chloe go and came over to hug Jack. He folded her small frame in his arms and she swayed a little. "I'm still disappointed you didn't wear your costume." She pulled away and gave him a little pout, and Jack got a sudden flash of Chloe as a little old lady, all fierce and meddling. "I told all my friends we were going to get to see some serious skin."

Chloe laughed. "Aunt Iris! Don't objectify him."

"Why ever not, dear?" She patted him on the cheek. "Abs like his shouldn't go to waste."

Jack rolled his eyes.

Chloe went to hug Amelia Rose. "Thank you."

Amelia Rose patted her on the back. "You're welcome. Everything worked out as it should."

"It did."

Jack sighed and folded Amelia Rose into a quick hug before giving her a kiss on the cheek. "I suppose I owe you a debt of gratitude."

The woman smiled, grasping his hands. "You can come back every year, that's gratitude enough."

"Deal." Jack winked at her. "Thank you."

"You're most welcome, dear boy."

He turned to the woman who was his past, present, and future. "Ready, Chlo?"

"Ready." She hefted her purse onto her shoulder and grinned at him.

And he fell into her eyes, her smile, and that face he knew as well as his own. She was his now, and he wasn't ever letting her go.

He picked up the bags, and Aunt Iris and Amelia Rose waved.

He walked out the door ready to start his future. With Chloe.

When they got to the last step, Amelia Rose called out to him, "Oh, and Jack."

He looked back at her. "Yeah?"

She gave her serene smile. "It's going to be a girl."

His mind flashed to the middle of last night, slipping nto Chloe's silken heat, half-asleep. Jack's heart tripped, ooped, and he fell all over again.

He was a believer.

Enchanted by You

SHARLA LOVELACE

To Jamie, Selena, and Shauna,
my fellow Diva Mamas at Divas, Ink.
I don't know how I did this thing
before you ladies had my back.
I love y'all forever!

Chapter 1

Sidney closed her eyes so the worst ass-chewing of her life wouldn't come with a visual.

"Don't you tune me out, Sidney Jensen," her boss spat. "I want you hearing every word. I want you feeling every penny *you—just—lost—me.*"

"I'm feeling it," Sidney said, her stomach clenching with *every overemphasized word.* "I promise."

"Oh, I don't think you really do," the woman said, rising to every bit of her five-foot-four inches and managing to strike fear in spite of her petite size. "Not yet, anyway. Not until it comes out of your paycheck."

"Orchid, please," Sidney breathed, ignoring the usual need to smirk over the ridiculous name. She didn't have the luxury of smirking. She didn't have the leeway of any of the smart-ass comebacks she usually had. For once, she had to toe the hated line.

"Don't *Orchid* me," she said. "I trusted you with this. You swore you were ready. I *believed* in you."

Oh, there it was. The cursed *belief* in her. The trust. Fuck all that, actually. It was the paycheck threat that

made Sidney's scalp sweat and added to the fine sheen
of perspiration that was making her fake silk blouse
stick to her back under her jacket.

Sidney had been an associate at the Boston law of-
fices of Finley and Blossom for longer than any of the
others. Every other associate in the building had fewer
years in the company, and they looked up to her and
her kick-ass work ethic. Everyone *she'd* started with,
however, was now a junior partner. It was beginning to
be a *thing*.

Not because she didn't do good work. She did great
work. She did phenomenal work. Sidney Jensen was a
workaholic who put everything she had into every case.
Lawyers wanted her on their cases. She was a research
savant and a machine who didn't believe in stopping
until the job was done. Every case she worked on, however, had a partner being the one to sell/lead/hold
hands with the client. Which worked out fabulously,
since Sidney was not blessed with those particular skills.
She didn't go to college to learn how to babysit adults,
she went to learn the law.

That being said, the partner she'd been paired with
from the day she landed there, Orchid Blossom, now senior and name partner although only five years older
than her, had decided it was time for Sidney to put on
her big-girl babysitting panties and learn how to lead a
case. If she ever wanted to move up and not be a career
associate. Translation: if she wanted to keep her job.

So when Orchid handed her one of her long-term
clients to set up a simple merger—on her own, from
start to finish, Sidney took a deep breath and swallowed
her pride at being handed such an entry-level case.
That was okay. But she'd show her boss. Sidney worked
double-time to prove that she was more than the re-
searcher with an eye for detail and an unstoppable

work ethic. And also to show that she didn't have to be the awkward sometimes-too-abrupt-or-too-harsh rambling-at-the-mouth attorney who turned polished and refined Bostonians away. She had to step out of her comfort zone.

And she had. Straight into the crosshairs between two CEOs with control issues and the need to dominate the other side. They didn't need pristine documents and extraordinary organization as negotiations fell apart; they needed body blocks and a referee. And before the meeting was done, they needed a new lawyer, because the firm of Finley and Blossom was no longer retained. And Sidney was left hyperventilating into her cold coffee.

"I know," Sidney said, licking her lips as she tried to placate her boss. "And I know I let you down, but—"

"Let me down?" Orchid said. "Carson Foods was my biggest client. One of the first of my career—I've had them forever. I gave them to you *because* they were so well established you couldn't screw it up!"

Sidney blanched at the words, feeling the air physically push her back. "You gave me a bullshit case?"

"I gave you something to cut your teeth on," Orchid said, curling her tiny fists at her sides. "And you chewed it up and vomited it all over my goodwill."

Sidney couldn't breathe. She'd been given a no-brainer, and she'd lost it. No matter how hard she had worked on the case, she'd lost it. Over—people skills. She *should* be a career associate. Hell, she should just be a paralegal and work in the research library with a table and a bottle of water.

She would not cry. She wouldn't show weakness. Not in front of the woman she most wanted to be like. A woman who was a force in the courtroom and a calculating businesswoman. A woman who had lived her life named after a flower and was badass enough not to change it when she became a lawyer. Not even when she had to put it on the letterhead.

"Am I—" Sidney stopped to clear her throat. "Am I fired?" she asked, sitting up straighter and willing the clamps around her heart to ease up.

"By God, you should be," Orchid said.

Should. She said *should*, not yes. "So—"

"I don't have the manpower to let you go right now," Orchid said, and Sidney felt her chest relax the tiniest bit. "Especially now that I have to try to mend fences with Carson Foods." She sat back down in a huff and smoothed hair that hadn't dared to move from the severe bun. "I'll have Monica cancel my trip to Maine this weekend."

"Your vacation?" Sidney said.

"It was a work vacation," Orchid said. "Heading upstate for a spa weekend with some old Harvard friends after stopping to help out my uncle with a legal issue."

"What legal issue?"

Orchid shook her head as if the topic were a buzzing fly. "A lease agreement he wants out of," she said.

"Let me do it," Sidney blurted. "The lease agreement, not the spa thing," she amended. "I can leave now. Since you have to stay and fix my crap, let me go deal with—"

"'My crap'?" Orchid finished. She laughed sarcastically. "You expect me to unleash you on my family now?"

"Come on, it's a lease agreement," Sidney said. "That's first-year finance, and I've done dozens of them." She paused and averted her eyes. "And I doubt your uncle will stop being your uncle if I fail."

"He already doesn't like me, so I doubt it'll matter much," Orchid said, blowing out a breath. "Fine." Then her eyes landed hard on Sidney's. "Still. You screw this one up, you don't deserve to even work in the mail room."

Sidney swallowed hard as she nodded. "Got it."

"Sidney," Orchid said. "You're good. You know the details, you know everything on paper, but you've got to get out of your own way and learn how to work with people."

She could wipe the floor with this woman's skinny ass, and she knew it. Orchid wouldn't have half the successes she had without Sidney's all-nighters digging up information for her cases—force or not. And here she was talking down to her like she was an errant child.

"I'll get you the file. Talk to Monica about the reservations," Orchid said. "It's a little over an hour's drive, so leave early in the morning."

"On Saturday?" Sidney asked. "Wait, wouldn't you be handling the business part today? Or Monday? Who's doing business on the weekend?"

"The kind of people who have pumpkin festivals and bake sales today," Orchid said. "It's Halloween. And my uncle lives in Mayberry. They live for that shit. And if you want to catch them all happy with their pants down, you don't wait till Monday." She picked up a pen to write something, then looked back up and pointed it at her. "Didn't you grow up in a small town?"

Sidney felt the jab to her gut, accompanied by the oh-so-familiar dread.

"Yes."

"Then you know how it is," Orchid said. "It's not about formal appointments or faxing paperwork to some office building. You go ring their doorbell over front porch coffee. Use that ridiculous Carolina accent of yours to charm them."

"Maine is farther north than we are now."

"Doesn't matter," Orchid said, dismissing the comment with a flip of her hand. "You reek of small town. Smile. Pet the dog. Adore the baby."

Sidney felt ill. *You reek of small town.*

"Then again, this might not be the best idea," Orchid said.

"Yes, it is," Sidney said before her tongue could rebel and agree with her boss. "I can do this. There's actually a town named Mayberry?"

"Moonbright," Orchid said, already flipping through a stack of papers, Sidney's plight losing her interest. "Moonbright, Maine. Same thing if you ask me."

Chapter 2

Sawyer stepped out of his truck and shut the door behind him, ignoring the squeak and grind that was getting louder every day. Some WD-40 would take care of that. Miss Amelia Rose would tell him a new truck would take care of it better, but he didn't need a new truck. Old Betsy had gotten him around just fine for the last decade. She helped him make a living and never nagged, complained, or got jealous of other women. Well, she wasn't particularly fond of that two-wheeled thing under the tarp in his garage—the thing he'd arrived in town on twelve years earlier. Betsy would probably be jealous if he still rode that, but that had gone by the wayside. Another lifetime ago. Another him.

He glanced back at the two white packages sitting neatly on the seat. Two beautiful steaks wrapped in butcher paper and just waiting to be lovingly caressed on the grill. Sawyer blew out a breath and pulled off his dirty cap, scrubbing fingers through his hair. After the grind he'd had today, getting everything ready at the cottage, he couldn't wait to just collapse into his recliner with a good hunk of meat.

He walked into the post office with his orange slip. The bullshit one that said they'd tried to deliver something but he wasn't there. Bullshit, because it was addressed to the Rose Cottage as it should be, and someone was always there.

Scrubbing a hand over the scruff that had covered his jaw since morning, he pasted on a smile. It was important to appear gracious as he approached the counter if he wanted his supplies to keep coming in. Even though it usually meant trying not to fall into the cleavage.

"Hey, Sawyer," said the pretty blonde with the medieval bar-wench dress.

Okay. So, more cleavage than usual.

"Hey, Tina," he said, his slower South Carolina drawl making her big blue eyes darken like he'd drooled honey. Shit, he needed to learn how to talk like a Northerner one day. "Interesting costume choice."

"Like it?" she asked, striking a pose, as if her boobs needed help with that. "I'm wearing this to the Renaissance Festival in Bangor next week, so I thought it'd make a great Halloween costume, too."

"And Chuck is okay with it?" Sawyer asked. The postmaster struck him as a bit more conservative, having gone through a major religious phase a few years back.

"He likes when we dress up for holidays," she said, propping up her—bustier. "Says it's more customer-oriented."

Sawyer chuckled and raised an eyebrow. "There's one perspective."

She leaned forward on her elbows with an innocent look he didn't buy, since her nipples were damn close to winking at him. "So, did you come in here to see what I'd be wearing?"

"Got one of these again," he said, waving the slip before the conversation went in a direction he wouldn't be able to angle out of.

Tina at least had the decency to shake her head and look amazed, even though he knew damn good and well she had orchestrated it.

"I don't know what's been going on with that route lately," she said, standing back up. "I'm so sorry, Sawyer. Let me go look for your package."

"Appreciate that," he said.

Tina lifted her hair and fanned her neck with it as she sauntered slowly to the back.

"Whew, they are cranking the heat a little too high today," she said. "Don't you think?"

Sawyer shook his head and headed to the post office boxes, pulling out a key for box number 262.

Twelve years he'd lived in Moonbright, and most of those had been decent and upright. The first few—well, he'd arrived at eighteen years of age, on a motorcycle, with a chip on his shoulder and an attitude. Back then, he was servicing cars by day and any woman he could get his hands on by night.

Tina was one of them. Three years older and a hell of a lot more experienced, she taught him plenty, but he did his part, too. Enough that she'd been shoving her tits in his face ever since.

It was a hot time in his life for sure, but then he grew up. Met Amelia Rose, who put him on the straight and narrow. Got a permanent job as a groundskeeper at her B&B, bought a house, made a life. Maybe a boring one. Maybe kind of a secluded one, but that was okay. He was good with that. Relationships—they weren't real. He learned early in life that forever was a lie. And Sawyer didn't have time for lies.

He also didn't have time for women like Tina anymore. Women who still dangled themselves before him but with an agenda and a timetable. At this time in their lives, they were either still single and desperate, or divorced and looking for Mister Number Two, and Sawyer wanted no part of either.

The little door of the box swung open, revealing the normal contents. Junk mail. Flyers. A couple of bills. Nothing personal. There wouldn't be. Outside of Moonbright, Sawyer Finn didn't exist. And no one in this town was going to send him mail unless it was a bill.

"You got a big one here," Tina cooed as she came back in, caressing a long box in a way that would probably mortify any other woman. Tina wasn't any other woman. She also wasn't known for boundaries. "Heavy, too."

Sawyer really needed to start using UPS.

She shoved the box onto the counter with a dramatic flair. "Here you go," she said, letting her chest rest against the box as she blinked up at him through long eyelashes.

"Thanks," he said, smiling. "Have fun."

"What are you doing for Halloween?" she asked as he started his turn. "Going to the Rose Cottage party?"

"Me?" Sawyer shrugged and threw out another endearing grin. "Oh, you know me, Tina, I don't get into all that. But I'll say, it looks pretty good. Been working all day to get the place looking perfect for that."

"I think you'd make an amazing Hercules. All that lugging things around making your muscles all—"

"Hercules?" Sawyer laughed.

"Or Tarzan," she added, fingering the little threads holding her boobs in.

"I'm really more of a Batman kind of guy," Sawyer said.

"Too many clothes," she whispered dramatically.

"Exactly," he said, chuckling as he made for the door.

"Maybe I'll see you there, anyway?" she called after him as the door swung closed.

"Not in this lifetime," he said under his breath as he set the box in the truck bed.

Halloween antics weren't his thing. Any holiday antics, really, but this one always got under his skin more than the others. The dressing up. The pretending. It was all bullshit. How he landed in a town named *Moonbright* that celebrated all that business—with street names like Pumpkin Boulevard, Haystack Lane, and All Souls Avenue—was beyond him.

But it was just a day. Well—a month, really, with residents getting giddy early and his employer needing all the yard decorations out as soon as the calendar said October. This year, especially, since Amelia Rose had hired a party planner to do up the place even crazier.

"Sawyer," said a gruff voice behind him.

He turned to see the jovial, lined face of old Mr. Madigan as he ambled down the sidewalk with his cane.

"Hey, Mr. Madigan," Sawyer said, pulling his dirty cap off to scrub fingers through his hair. "How's it going?"

The old man just smiled and nodded, focusing on his steps. Two other people smiled and nodded his way before he got in the truck, and it was a good feeling. He'd made a life here. Something real. Something much more real than the one he'd been born into.

"Mr. Finn!" said a little girl, running up to his door as he lowered the window.

"Madeline!" yelled a female voice from the sidewalk down the way. A voice that maybe *wasn't* quite as happy to see him.

"Hey, Miss Madeline," Sawyer said, grasping the little girl's hand as she stepped up on the running board. "How many feet did you grow this week?"

"Five!" she exclaimed. "And a half!"

"Well, of course the half," he responded, glancing toward her mom as she approached.

"Look!" Madeline said excitedly, pointing at a gap in her smile, front and center. "They finally came out! Both of them!"

"Good for you!" Sawyer said.

"Madeline," said her mom, advancing on her daughter like he might give her poisoned candy. "Get in the salon, they're waiting on you."

"I'm gonna be Medusa," Madeline said, her gappy grin going huge to match the sparkle in her big brown eyes. She was so damn adorable. As other people's kids went.

"Medusa?"

"Yeah, they're gonna make my hair look like snakes!" she said, stepping down.

"Cool!" Sawyer laughed as she ran into the salon.

Her mom hesitated on the curb, looking at the door her daughter just entered as if it had eaten her alive.

"I remember when princesses and ninja turtles were all the rage," he said, making her turn.

She smiled, her eyes casting away quickly. "Yeah," she said. "Well, good to see you, Sawyer." She turned to follow her daughter's path.

"Carol," he said. "We're okay, right? We're still friends?"

The pretty brunette managed about four shades of embarrassed before nodding, and that made Sawyer wish he hadn't said a word.

Carol Sims had been another one of his early conquests. She had been a wild-child college girl breaking out of a rich family legacy, wanting to break some rules. He'd been happy to help.

She grew up, too, got married, had a kid, had another one, and then found out her husband preferred different body parts. Carol got the house, a sprawling ranch-style creation on ten acres that required upkeep, and looked up Sawyer to do a little work on the side. Problem was, she was angling for another kind of side work, as well. And his stupid ass didn't see it coming. After a month and a half of twice-a-week yard duty and Madeline following him around like a constantly chattering puppy, he arrived one afternoon to find that the kid had been sent to her dad's for the day and Carol— Carol was dressed and ready. Posed in her bed. Crotchless panties, leather everything.

His fucking dream come true. But Carol was a friend. And she seemed—a little too breakable. He just couldn't do it. And she had kicked him out in sick mortification, avoiding him ever since.

"Of course," Carol said, her hands fluttering to her waist, her throat, and then crossing over her chest. "Good to see you again," she repeated before retreating into the salon.

"Shit," Sawyer said, rubbing his tired, gritty eyes. He had to be the only man alive thinking that women chasing him down for sex was a problem.

The sex wasn't the problem. Everything that came afterward was.

Putting his truck in Reverse, he started the trek home. Let all the crazies lose their senses tonight. Let Amelia Rose do her thing at the cottage. Sawyer had no need to hobnob with the Maine-iacs on Halloween. Or hand out copious amounts of candy to kids with snake hair. He and Duke, the old stray mutt that adopted him five years earlier, would be just fine lounging around fat and happy with their steaks.

Chapter 3

"What do you mean, you have no reservation?" Sidney asked, her hand stopping halfway into her bag. "You just mean it's early, right? I know it's way early for check-in, I was just hoping maybe you might *by chance* have the room ready so I could freshen up before—"

"Miss Jensen," the clerk interrupted, pasting on a polite if not slightly nervous smile. "I'm sorry, but I'm afraid there's actually no record of a reservation in your name."

Sidney blinked. "What?"

"I looked twice," the clerk said, pointing at her monitor as if that would prove it.

"That's impossible," Sidney said. "Monica made—wait, maybe it's still in my boss's name. Orchid Blossom?"

The clerk's eyes darted to meet hers, and Sidney nodded at the question in them.

"I know. Yes, that's a real name."

Fingers paused a second on the keyboard, second-guessing, and probably third-guessing because of Sidney's accent. Somehow, in the North, a Southern drawl sometimes equaled a lower IQ. Finally, she typed in the name. "Sorry," the clerk said. "Not in here, either."

Sidney huffed out a breath as she set her bag on the counter. "Hang on, let me call—or can you just book me into one now?"

"We are *completely* full," the clerk said.

"Full?" Sidney said, blinking fast. "What about after checkout?" She glanced at the sign. "At noon?"

"We are totally booked for the next three days," she said. "A convention in town."

"Jesus," Sidney breathed. "One second." She pulled her bag off the counter and walked over to an over-stuffed chair in the lobby, digging for her phone as she went.

She didn't have to get a hotel, theoretically. It was an hour and a half's drive, meaning she could technically drive home and back again in the morning. Assuming she'd need to. Assuming she didn't knock the deal out of the park today. But she couldn't plan on that, and her car was essentially held together with string and duct tape and the gallon of water she kept in the back-seat in case the radiator overheated again. She'd ex-hausted all of her prayers on the drive there.

"Monica!" she whispered urgently when the voice an-wered after four rings.

"Sidney?" she said. "It's Saturday."

Really? "I'm aware of that," Sidney said. "I'm standing in the lobby of the Crescent Hotel, wondering why they don't—"

"Oh shit," Monica said.

Sidney's shoulders slumped. She rubbed her fore-head. "Well, I guess that answers that."

"I'm so sorry, Sidney," Monica said. "I got so busy with Orchid yesterday and forgot."

"Well, it probably wouldn't have mattered," Sidney said. "They're booked solid. Where was Orchid staying?"

"She wasn't," Monica said. "She was hitting up her uncle's issue in Moonbright on her way upstate. She wasn't staying there."

Of course she wasn't. Because she was friggin' Superwoman.

"Hold on," Monica said, the sound of shuffling reaching Sidney's ear. "Let me look up what else is around there. Maybe there's something in Moonbright proper."

"It's supposed to be tiny," Sidney said, already shaking her head. "Outside of town would be bett—"

"They have a B&B!" Monica exclaimed.

Sidney closed her eyes. "Great."

"Well, I mean, I can look in Portland, but that's farther north," Monica said. "Do you want me to call this place? It's called the Rose Cottage."

Just shoot me.

"Then, if it takes you some time, you're right there," she said.

Because I'm not Orchid.

"Fine," Sidney said wearily, watching a couple get room keys and pull their happy little luggage to the elevators. "Give it a shot. I'll sit here till I hear back."

"I'll call you right back," Monica said, clicking off.

"Okay then," Sidney said to no one.

She leaned over, elbows on her knees. It could be worse. She could be fired. She could be spending the weekend poring the Internet looking for openings for law associates. Or Walmart greeters. So spending it in Podunk Hell was candy in comparison. And it probably wasn't that bad, anyway. Not like Derby, South Carolina, the hick town she'd left behind after high school. After her nana died and the bake shop closed. After everything that made that place bearable was gone.

Including him.

Her phone ringing startled her so badly, she nearly dropped it. Lord, where had *that* come from?

"Hello?"

"They have an opening," Monica gushed. "They had a big Halloween party last night, but everyone is leaving today," she said.

"Oh God, it really is Podunk," Sidney moaned.

"It'll be fine," Monica said. "Okay, so the Rose Cottage. Put it in your GPS. I'll text you the address, too, but it's on the corner of Pumpkin and Vine."

Sidney's eyebrows shot up. She felt them. "I'm sorry, what?"

"I know," Monica said. "I did the same thing. But I double-checked and Googled it twice. It's at 816 Vine, Moonbright, Maine."

Walmart wasn't sounding half-bad.

"I—I—"

"Owner's name to ask for is Amelia Rose. And get this—she's a fortune-teller." The sound of a baby's cry echoed in the background. "Crap, my son's up. I gotta go, Sidney. Good luck!"

"Uh-huh," Sidney managed, but the line was already dead.

Turning off I-95 toward the coast was an adventure in itself. Lots of winding, lots of nothing but trees, and more than one prominent billboard advertising the world's largest pumpkin patch. In Moonbright. Because the rest of it wasn't unbelievable enough.

It was like going home to Derby. On holiday steroids. Except that she'd never done that. Gone home. There was nothing for her there. No friends, no family—her nana long gone and her parents gone even longer be-

fore that, taken in a car crash when she was eight. And
the only person she could ever somewhat call a friend—
even as weird as it was—had disappeared.

Caleb James. God, he'd been so beautiful, so hot, so
every girl's secret fantasy. The rebel son of the high
school principal who skipped more classes than he at
tended and wore jeans and a leather jacket better than
anyone she'd ever seen. And stole her breath, her
words, and her heart every time he was near. Which was
a lot.

James and *Jensen* had put them together since grade
school, and lockered her under him all through high
school. Her kneeling down, looking up at him every
day as he grinned and walked away. Till senior year.
When a hand appeared in her face, and she followed
the arm all the way up to Caleb James. Holding out a
hand to help her up.

"I have a question for you," he'd said.

Nothing had come out of her mouth but air, so he contin
ued.

"I need tutoring if I'm gonna graduate," he said, that hon
eyed voice drawling the words. "My dad told me to find some
one or he will." His eyes faded a bit. "You're smart. Will you
help me?"

"I'm—I'm—I don't think—I mean, I'm not that smart,
she stuttered out like a five-year-old.

"Please," he said, one side of his mouth crooking up in
grin that nearly buckled her back to her knees. "You're smar
Sidney. You're squeaky clean, you should be class president o
something."

"That requires actually talking to people," Sidney sai
amazed that the words found their way out. And that he kne
her name.

*He laughed. And not at her, but like she'd said something
funny. Huh.*

"So, will you help me, Squeak?" he said, his eyes sparkling.

"Jesus," Sidney exclaimed, squeezing the steering
wheel as she shook her head. "What the hell?"

She hadn't thought about Caleb in years.

He'd used her for her help, but she hadn't cared at
the time. It put her in his world. Every other day. Actually talking. Laughing. Learning about the guy no one
really knew. Finding out that he wasn't so different
from her after all. She'd look into those impossibly dark
eyes and get lost. Watch his lips as he talked and dream
of kissing them. And every now and then, as she waxed
on about government or literature, she'd look up and
stop breathing as she caught him watching *her*.

And she hadn't thought about any of it, about her
old life, about much of anything outside of memories of
her nana, in so long. Now, because she was headed to
some small town, she was stumbling down memory lane?
No thanks. It wasn't that great the first time around. Except for—well, except for *that*. *That* had been pretty
great. *That* had been monumental. Until it wasn't.

She did not need to go there. She didn't need to
think about men, period, past, present, or future. Not
that there was a present . . . or much potential for the
future. But none of that mattered. She needed to think
about her case. The lease agreement. Finding Orchid's
uncle. Finding the dick who was giving him grief. Focus,
focus, focus. Yet, every curve, every turn, brought her
memory after memory of that night.

There it was, finally. A giant sign advertising Moonbright, Maine. Proud home of the world's largest pumpkin patch.

And not even that hideous monstrosity could keep her mind from straying. From tumbling backward ridiculously to graduation night. Twelve years ago.

". . . these, our last precious moments of our high school careers . . ."

"God, if she says 'precious' or 'behoove' one more time," Caleb said under his breath. "I swear I'm standing up on my chair and playing air guitar."

Sidney giggled. "I dare you."

Caleb turned and gave her one of those piercing looks that always made her breath catch.

"You should know better than to dare me, Squeak," he said, his voice going low and curling her toes in spite of the nickname she hated.

". . . if only we could look into a crystal ball and see what extraordinary futures we have yet to behold . . ."

"If only she'd wrap up this shit so we could get out of here," he groaned, letting his head fall back.

Sidney didn't care that the valedictorian's speech was ludicrous and long and flowery and full of dumb metaphors. Let her ramble on incessantly forever. Stretch out this night. This year. This moment of sitting next to Caleb James, his knee touching hers. His laugh warming her on an already steamy night. Before it was all over and he didn't need her anymore. And before there were no scheduled reasons to see each other every day.

That ended tonight.

She was all too aware of that.

". . . take the hand of the person next to you . . ."

Say what? Hold his hand? Did she hear that right? Her deodorant was failing by the second.

". . . in some way, that person has shaped your life. They have been present in your world every day for twelve years . .

Thomas King was on Sidney's right, and he'd brought her a candy bar in the sixth grade. So, that was something, right? His hand was sweaty and sticky as he grabbed hers, but Caleb's was warm and dry and impossibly perfect as he took hers. And laced his fingers through her fingers.

Laced. His. Fingers.

Jesus. God.

The world could end right there because it wasn't getting better than that. And then again maybe it was because there was that look again. Draining all the blood from her head.

"Couldn't have done this year without you, Squeak," he said.

She wanted to say something. Something profound. Something perfect. So she blinked.

"I mean, I literally wouldn't even be on this field if it weren't for you," he said.

"Your dad would have found someone else to tutor you if it wasn't me," she said finally, staring at their hands. Trying to memorize it.

"I wouldn't have listened to anyone else," he said, his voice going distant. "I probably would have skipped town like my mom."

His thumb started moving along hers, and things shot off to places she didn't dare talk about.

"No, you wouldn't have," she whispered, watching his thumb move back and forth. She wanted to do what she always did when he got angry talking about his mother leaving him, and tell him he was better than that. That it was her weakness, not his. But Sidney couldn't think in full sentences at the moment.

"Ever wish you could just disappear?" he asked, pulling her out of her stupor. "Just vanish, be invisible, start over somewhere new where no one knows you?"

Sidney turned to look at his profile. He was staring, unseeing, at the back of Kristin Callihan's head.

"I'm always invisible," she said. *"But yeah, starting over would be good."*

"What would your starting-over name be?" he asked, his voice soft.

"Jane Eyre?" Sidney said. Caleb gave her a look. *"I don't know,"* she said, chuckling. *"You asked! Cinderella?"*

"Cinderella?"

"What would yours be, then?" Sidney asked, daring to move her own thumb along his finger. She held her breath to see if he'd notice, and watched his eyes drop.

"If you're Cinderella, then I'd be Tom Sawyer," he said, his words slower.

Breathe. *"Well, of course,"* she said.

"Or Huckleberry Finn."

"Be creative," Sidney said. *"Mix it up and be Sawyer Finn."*

Chapter 4

"Smells good in here," Sawyer said, coming in the back door to grab a bottle of water from the stash that Amelia Rose kept in the fridge.

"Wipe your feet."

"On it," he said, scrubbing the bottoms of his work boots on the wiry doormat. "Cooking lunch so soon?"

"We have a guest coming this morning," Amelia Rose said, her small frame looking dwarfed by the large, old-fashioned stove she stood in front of, stirring a large pot of something. Her long, flowing clothes made her look even smaller.

"Already?" Sawyer asked. "Damn, we barely got rid of last night's heathens."

"Sawyer Finn," she said, turning with a hand on her hip. "Those *heathens* fund your paycheck."

"I know," he said, rubbing at his eyes. "I'm just cranky. All these damn pumpkins."

"They're adorable!" Amelia Rose said, her smile taking over her face as she turned back to her pot. "I've never seen such amazing carvings. And the Cinderella carriage!"

Cinderella. Something about that just pissed him off.

"You see amazing carvings all over the lawn," he said. "I see rotting pumpkin carnage that I have to haul off at a hundred pounds per load."

"Bah humbug," she said.

"Don't even get me started," he said. "So, how soon is this guest coming? How soon do I have to get all this mess cleaned up?"

"Don't sweat it," she said. "It's a lawyer from Boston. She's coming early, so I'm sure she'll understand that we have a little cleanup to do from last night. I just want to have some lunch ready."

"From Boston," Sawyer said, snatching a piece of corn bread from a plate. "Fancy."

"I don't know about that," she said. "But I know we were not her first choice." She threw a smirk over her shoulder. "I want to change her mind."

"Fancy and snooty," he said around a mouthful of corn bread. "How was the party?"

"Wonderful as always," she said.

"Anyone find out they're going to die?"

She turned with a frown. "What?"

"Your fortune-telling," he said. "Everyone always gets good news. I have a hard time believing that." She cut him a glance that always gave him a little bit of the willies. "I love you," he said. "I just, you know . . ."

"I tell the truth," she said. "I always tell the truth, but if I see something particularly bad—I'm not going to tell someone that. No one should know certain things about their own future." She shook her head. "It changes how you live if you know too much."

"So you lie?"

"So I refund their money and tell them I couldn't see

anything," she responded quietly. She sighed then and blinked quickly as if clearing her mind of the subject. "You should clean up a little."

Sawyer chuckled. "For what? I'm in the yard all day today with sour pumpkin guts and a giant muddy spider."

"For our guest."

"Since when?"

Amelia Rose sighed. "Because I feel like you should," she said. "Can't that be reason enough?"

"No," he said, laughing. "I promise, I'll stay out of the way."

"You know, you could do with making an impression or two," she said. "Maybe a bit of polishing."

Sawyer chuckled. "For what?"

"For the female population," she said.

"Please," he said. "I do just fine with the female population." He reached in the fridge for the water he'd forgotten about.

"Is that so?"

"That is so."

"When's the last time you had a date?" she asked.

"Who said anything about dating?" Sawyer said, washing down half the bottle. "Dating is a headache."

"It's getting to know someone."

"It's a waste of time," he countered, coming up behind her and squeezing her shoulders. "There isn't a woman out there worth all that."

"You don't get lonely?"

"I have Duke," he said, laughing when she rolled her eyes. "Besides, I'd never find the right mix of someone who'd put up with me. Next time you're brewing up potions, maybe you can craft me the perfect woman."

"Well, sure," Amelia Rose said, lifting a spoonful to smell the broth. "I'll get right on that."

Sawyer leaned over to sniff the pot. "Now works, too."

She chuckled. "Sorry, it's just soup."

"I said next time," he said, winking. "No rush."

"Well, since you're preordering," she said. "I assume forty-four, twenty-four, forty—"

"Surprise me," Sawyer said, snatching another piece of corn bread from the platter.

"Blue-eyed blonde who bats her eyes?" she asked, turning to flutter her eyelashes.

Sawyer laughed. "Blue eyes are good. But make it a brunette. Batting optional."

It was a joke he perpetuated—teasing her about her fabled "mystical" abilities. Amelia Rose was more than his employer. She'd been kind of a mother figure to him ever since he landed in town all those years ago. She looked out for him in a way, so he returned the favor. She never appeared to care one way or the other what people thought of her, and that was part of why he loved her, but he leaned toward the more realistic side of things. Fortune-telling and other magical hooey might be popular around this area, especially at Halloween, but he believed in setting his own fate. And changing it. No one person could look out there into the cosmos and point at an end result.

That being said, if anyone had a fifty-fifty shot at it, it was Amelia Rose. He'd seen enough in his twelve years in Moonbright to at least give him pause.

And if asked, he'd deny that a hundred different ways.

"So, have you ever been in love, Sawyer?" Amelia Rose asked, her tone dancing in that zone he recognized. The one that said none of this was random and she'd just been building up. "The real kind, I mean?"

"Love," Sawyer scoffed, leaning against the counter. "Now, *that's* smoke and mirrors."

Amelia Rose glanced over her shoulder. "So that's a *no,* I'm guessing?"

"Well, you've known me since I was eighteen," he responded.

"And I don't stalk you," she said, laughing. "*And* I've never read you."

"As it should be," Sawyer said. Whether he believed or not, he didn't take the chance of someone poking around his thoughts.

"Totally respect that," Amelia Rose said, waving a wooden spoon around. "But you didn't answer me."

Sawyer blew out a breath, feeling his grin fade a little with the memory. "Nah," he lied. "I never had time for that."

"Not even when you were young?" she asked.

His eyes landed on her, and the corn bread he'd just swallowed felt like it had hardened halfway down. "Why would you ask that?"

Amelia Rose shrugged. "Because I didn't know you then." She tapped the spoon on the rim of the pot and laid it on a plate. "And because you had a girl's class ring tied to the console of your motorcycle when you first got here."

A *zing* ran through his body at the mention of that ring. At the memory of the girl it belonged to, and the last time he'd seen her. *She'd been crying.*

"I don't know too many females who give up their jewelry," Amelia Rose said. "So I figured you either killed someone or had a bad breakup."

"Well, aren't you and your long-term memory the observant little pair," he said, shaking his head free of the images. That was a long time ago, and not a place he was up for revisiting.

"Part of my charm," she said, winking.

"Well, part of mine is getting back to work," he said, brushing his hands off on his jeans. "Thanks for the snacks."

"Like I had a choice?"

"I'm putting the gnomes back out, leaving a few of the bigger pumpkins, and tomorrow I'll deal with the cornucopia," he said.

"Sounds good, but get some help with that," she said. "I don't want you throwing your spine into a knot."

"Yes, ma'am," he said.

"You still didn't answer me," she added as he pushed open the back door.

He winked in her direction. "No, ma'am."

Sidney had to stop and take a breath when she pulled up in front of the B&B. Work her shoulders free of the stress and her neck free of the tension she'd worked up on the way. Not to mention the unwelcome memories flooding her brain. She could live with the worry over this case. That was expected. That, she could talk herself through. Old high school memories of the one who got away—the one she never even really had—that was something else. Something she had no business filling her busy head with right now.

Getting out of her car, she took in the scene before her. The Rose Cottage reminded her of something out of a fairy tale. Or an old and more comfortable time. Quaint and cozy and warm, with Halloween decorations still up and mountains of pumpkins and fall foliage tucked around. A giant spider on one side of the porch. Zombies crawling out of the ground. Okay, maybe that part wasn't so cozy, but someone definitely got into Halloween.

A man in a worn blue jean jacket, even more worn jeans, and aviator sunglasses was lugging large garden gnomes off of a low-boy trailer, so she could only imagine how much cheesier it was about to get.

"Good Lord," Sidney muttered as she slung her overnight bag over her shoulder and eyed her car. It was spitting and hissing and doing everything just short of a body shiver. It didn't look good. Stepping forward, she had to throw both arms out to steady herself. "Shit!"

Thin high heels and cobblestone. Great. Thank God she'd thought to throw in some flats.

She noticed the man working stopped to watch her, and she righted herself immediately, holding her chin up and tucking her hair behind her ear. He probably thought she looked ridiculous here in a pencil skirt and heels, and she wasn't about to give him more to amuse himself with.

He turned anyway, after his initial pause, striding back to the trailer. Something struck her as familiar, watching him. Something about his strong, purposeful gait.

"Quit ogling the gardener, Sidney," she whispered to herself. It had evidently been too long since she'd been with a man. Way too long. "Seriously. Find some normal."

The woman who opened the door before she reached it, however, beaming at Sidney with kind eyes, beads hanging down to her knees, and rings on every finger, probably wasn't going to fit that bill.

Sawyer grunted his way from the low-boy to the edge of the flower garden with his third gnome. Big ugly shit. He never could see the appeal. And Amelia Rose's gnomes weren't of the puny variety, either. Each one came up to his chest and weighed probably seventy-five pounds. So dragging them on and off the trailer was no small task. The giant cornucopia—now that, he'd need some help with, but these ugly trolls he could handle. Gnomes, trolls, it was all the same.

He just about dropped the fattest one while watching the fancy lady lawyer from Boston get out of her not-so-fancy car. Legs that went on for fucking days, followed by a tight little skirt, and she perched on impossible heels. All of it was concealed somewhat by a long, tailored coat once she stood, but that first glimpse was sweet. Then she hobbled over the cobblestone and nearly busted it, so it was all he could do to look away and give her some dignity.

Still, there was a familiarity about her. Something in the vulnerable way she tucked her hair behind her ear and held her chin. Something that struck a nerve. A protective one.

"Sleep deprivation is making you soft, old man," he said under his breath.

The early-morning cleanup from last night's party and departing guests on top of a couple of restless nights had Sawyer feeling a bit fuzzy.

He'd make it an early night tonight. Hit the bed early and not let his mind wander where it had been the last thirty minutes. Speeding back to a place he didn't need to go. To the last time he'd felt something. Another lifetime ago. Another version of him.

"Your room is all ready for you," Amelia Rose was saying. That's what she had said to call her. At first, Sidney thought it was her first and last name, but then she corrected her when she called her Amelia, so she assumed she was just mysterious like that. Like Madonna, or

Cher. To be honest, Sidney had a hard time concentrating on the woman's words, she was so distracted by the visuals and the warmth she felt surrounding her like a big embrace. Well, after she got past the shock of the big skeleton guard dog just inside the door.

A beautiful old antique upright piano adorned the front living room, old sheet music perched atop it, just waiting to be played. Black-and-white and sepia-toned photos were everywhere, capturing people there in the house, playing the piano, and some of what Sidney assumed to be the town of Moonbright. It was a warm and welcoming, homey place, marrying the past and the present perfectly. Wing-backed chairs lined the walls, inviting conversation or sitting with a book and a cup of coffee. The adjoining dining room had a beautiful long table with a buffet, the table adorned with three-wick candles placed every few feet.

"How long have you been here?" Sidney asked as they'd circled back to almost where they started, a quaint old skeleton key dangling from her fingers.

Amelia Rose just laughed, the long beads she wore tinkling against each other. Her long gray hair was beautiful, pulled over in front of one shoulder and woven with more beads. Sidney was at once captivated and amused by this woman. She didn't know whether to take her seriously or just sit back and enjoy the show.

"Oh, long enough," Amelia Rose said with a wink. "Let's have a sit in the kitchen, shall we? There's no one else here, we can kick back and visit a minute."

"Well, I really need to go start—" Sidney began.

"Just relax, take a breath," Amelia Rose said. "You can't start a business day with so much tension."

"You can tell I have tension?"

"I could build a house with the rocks your skin is

stretched over, dear," Amelia Rose replied. "Come unwind for a second."

They walked back into the large, old-fashioned kitchen, and Sidney's mouth watered at the aromas of soup bubbling on the stove and what smelled like cookies baking. Oh, she missed home cooking. And she missed cookies. She didn't indulge much since Nana died, and only when she made them herself. Store-bought was a joke.

"Dark chocolate chips and walnuts," Sidney said on a sigh as she sat down at a massive old oak table, doing everything she could not to drool.

"You have a good nose," Amelia Rose said.

"It's my favorite," Sidney said.

Amelia Rose checked the oven just long enough for the aroma to waft out in full force, then closed the door and picked up a large spoon to stir the soup.

"My nana had a bakery when I was growing up," Sidney said. "I worked with her there, and my favorite thing was to make the cookies."

"She taught you the old ways," Amelia Rose said, sitting down with two steaming mugs she'd never seen her make.

"Only from scratch," Sidney said. "Nothing else compares."

"Agreed."

"What's this?" Sidney asked, already sipping. "Mmm. Oh, wow."

"Spiced tea," she said. "My special recipe."

"It's amazing," Sidney said.

"Your accent," Amelia Rose said. "It's not Boston. There's a hint of it, but something else. Something—"

"Southern," Sidney finished for her, smiling. "South Carolina. But I've been in Boston for most of a decade, so I guess it's all blended up."

"Ah, I should have recognized that one," Amelia

Rose said. "My groundskeeper is from there, too. So, you left after your nana died?"

Sidney's brows moved together. "How'd you know that?"

"Because I get the feeling you would've stayed in that bakery otherwise," she answered.

Huh. "Yes, ma'am, probably so." Sidney said. "But she wanted me to get out of town, do something else. Something smarter. And I just couldn't stomach the small-town crap anymore, so—" *Jesus, Sidney, dial back trashing her world, will you?* "So—I left."

"Law school?" she asked. Sidney gave her another surprised look, and the older woman laughed, eyes twinkling. "No mystery. Your assistant told me when she called."

"Oh." Sidney chuckled.

"Although you do have that look about you," Amelia Rose added.

"Dressed up and desperate?"

Who *was* she? Laughing and talking like one of those people capable of that? Where was the awkward saying-everything-at-the-wrong-time, too-abrupt woman she lived with every day?

Amelia Rose laid her hand on Sidney's as she smiled with her, and a feeling like a warm blanket soaked in honey flowed over her. The older woman's eyes, sharp in spite of the soft lines that fanned from them with her smile, met Sidney's.

"Can I try something?" she asked, an odd lilt to her speech, as well. Like an accent that didn't really belong to anything or anyone but her.

"Um," Sidney said. "Like what?"

Reaching into a basket that Sidney would swear wasn't there before, she pulled out a tiny bottle of a golden liquid.

"It's just an essential oil," Amelia Rose said, popping

the tiny cork off and pouring two drops onto a nearby burning candle. "Give me your palm."

"Oh no," Sidney said on a laugh, pulling her hand back. "No thanks. I'm not interested in that stuff."

"There's no 'stuff,'" Amelia Rose said.

"You're a fortune-teller," Sidney said. "I already heard."

"I'm a truth teller," Amelia Rose replied. "Fortune or not." She winked at her. "And if you want that, I can provide, but that's not all I do." Her hands had been soft against Sidney's. Soothing. "I also know a bit about natural healing."

"I'm not sick," Sidney said.

"Not that kind of healing," she said. "It's just a natural way to put you at ease. Before you have to go do—whatever it is you have to do."

Sidney met her eyes, which looked almost the same gray as her hair.

"Which you already know?"

Amelia Rose shrugged. "Only if you want me to."

Sidney fidgeted on the bench. "What will this cost me?"

Amelia Rose shook her head. "You're my guest. It's on the house."

Hesitantly, Sidney pushed a hand forward, watching it as if it belonged to someone else. What was she doing? She didn't have time for this hooey. She needed to be finding Orchid's uncle, find the owner, and wrap up everything today. It was just a lease dispute. Surely she could manage something that minor without screwing it up.

Yeah, not even she could buy that. Not in person. Face-to-face.

And as soon as Amelia Rose took her hand in both of hers, she didn't care.

Chapter 5

Sidney never felt more relaxed, or at ease. Hell, she hadn't felt this good after a full day's treatment at the massage and spa place everyone at work always went on about. The one she splurged on for one day, and ended up weirded out by an overly enthusiastic masseuse.

One drop of whatever the hell that was in her palm, and she knew she wanted to buy it by the barrel. Amelia Rose's hands rubbing her hand and fingers—kind of like a hand massage times infinity—because Amelia Rose's voice was like soft butter dripping over the whole thing. Calming her nerves. Giving her confidence.

Butter.

That was the smell.

Between the cookies and the smell of butter, and whatever was in that soup, Sidney was floating on a comfy high of no stress. Damn, who knew all she had to do was sniff food to chill out?

"So you aren't actually reading my palm," Sidney said, her eyes fluttering closed as Amelia Rose worked her fingers.

"No," Amelia Rose said. "I don't need to."

"What do you mean?"

"When you let it all go like you just did," she said, "I can see what I need. Most people don't relax that fast."

"You're saying I'm easy?" Sidney asked.

Amelia Rose chuckled. "I'm saying I wish everyone was."

"So—theoretically," Sidney said, tilting her head. "What did you see? Since I'm so easy."

"Well," Amelia Rose began. "It's not like watching a movie, doing it this way."

Ah, here comes the bullshit disclaimer.

"It's more like a sense."

"Uh-huh," Sidney said. "And what sense is that?"

"First of all, something very familiar," Amelia Rose said, her brows coming together like she was puzzled. "Like we both know the same thing. That's new."

"Hmm," Sidney said, wondering if she could pay for her to do the other hand. She didn't buy the hokey "seeing" part, but the relaxation with the touch and the aromatherapy was worth just about anything.

"Your past will become your future."

Sidney's eyes shot open. "Pardon?"

"Is that disturbing to you?" Amelia Rose asked.

"Um," Sidney said, gently pulling her hand away. "Well, I've already been there, so driving in circles really isn't my thing."

"I can get a lot more detailed with other methods," Amelia Rose said.

"That's okay," Sidney said on a short laugh, taking a long sip of her tea and letting the heat go all the way to her toes. "I think I'm good."

"All right," Amelia Rose said, her eyes sparkling with humor. "Well, get settled in, you find Mr. Teasdale, and lunch will be ready at noon."

Sidney blinked. "How'd you know I was seeing Mr. Teasdale?" She shook her head. "I thought it wasn't like watching a movie." She held up a hand. "On second thought, I don't want to know."

Amelia Rose smiled and pushed to her feet as the back door swung open. The man who'd been working outside strode in, pulling his sunglasses off, his mouth open to pose a question. A question that died on his lips as soon as his eyes landed on Sidney.

"Sidney, this is my groundskeeper and overseer, Sawyer Finn," Amelia Rose said.

She kept talking. There were words about South Carolina and having things in common floating somewhere in the room, but Sidney was pretty sure he didn't hear any more than she did.

Sawyer Finn.

"Caleb," she breathed, the word not cracking a sound.

Caleb. Looking at her. Those dark eyes making her feet sprout roots into the rug. The blond hair was a little darker, the face was a little scruffier, the lips—they were the same.

He blinked, something—almost painful crossing his face.

"Squeak," he whispered.

And yet she started as if he'd yelled it through a megaphone. It was still a joke. He remembered what he did, even down to the nickname he had for her.

"Who?" Amelia Rose said. "You two know each other?"

Sidney shook her head, propelling her feet into motion. "No," she managed, her voice sounding odd to her ears. "Don't know him at all." Getting to her feet, she prayed her knees would hold her. "Excuse me, I need to go. I have—"

She couldn't finish the sentence. She couldn't finish

the thought. All the newly drunk and happy muscles proceeded to braid themselves tightly back together as she clickety-clacked her way out of the house, her heels moving faster than her brain.

"Sidney!" she heard him call behind her, but she kept going.

She yanked her shoes off and carried them, covering the cobblestone inches quickly in her bare feet. Got in her car and begged it to start. To hell with staying there. She'd sleep in her car in a parking lot somewhere before she—*shit*. Her overnight bag. And her coat. They were still sitting happily inside that house, probably drunk on cookie fumes, too.

Looking in the rearview mirror through hot tears she despised, she saw him standing in the front yard as she pulled away, watching her leave.

How ironic that was.

"Shit," Sawyer said through his teeth, turning as the car veered out of sight. He raked his fingers through his hair and wished he was wearing his cap so he could throw it.

"Well, that explains a few things," Amelia Rose began behind him. "Want to tell me—"

"No," he said. "I don't."

What were the odds? What were the damn odds that Sidney Jensen would show up here, hundreds of miles away from Derby, South Carolina, at this particular cottage? Looking at him with those eyes—those damn eyes that stripped him down every day of high school, that gazed up at him from her knees and made him think of all kinds of naughty things. That made him want to be better, be more, be *hers*. That gave him the courage to ask her to tutor him, to get to know more than just the body he already fantasized about. The eyes that ripped his heart out on that football field.

He couldn't care less what that chick had to say up on that podium. Or what his father had to say to them after that. He didn't hear any of it. All that was important in his world was how Sidney's fingers felt intertwined with his. The feel of her skin, the metal of her class ring under his fingers, the pulse at her wrist racing against his. How her thumb started moving, too. And how hard his dick was getting.

Everything about Sidney Jensen turned him on, and the kicker was that she had no idea. She actually believed that shit about being invisible. Good God, she had no clue just how wrecked she made him on a daily basis. How just watching her walk down the hall did him in. Watching her organize her locker like it was life and death. Watching those fucking sexy, full lips as she talked and the little crease above her nose when she concentrated. All the little things that got him through each day, and now it was about to be over. All his chances were about to go up in smoke. She was the only reason he'd stayed in school, that he'd stayed in town as long as he did, and now he was going. Somewhere. Anywhere. It didn't matter where. She'd be going off to college, and there was nothing to hang around for anymore.

Sawyer Finn.

That was a pretty cool idea.

"We have to stand," Sidney whispered, leaning over closer.

"So let's stand," he said with a grin, pulling her up with him.

He didn't let go, and she didn't, either. God, that was amazing.

". . . presenting the senior class of . . ."

And then everyone was moving their tassels over. Shit, it was over. It was over. The night, the year, he'd wasted it. He could have asked her out a hundred times, kissed her a thousand. Touched her. Wound his fingers up in that hair and— shit, he needed to quit before the baggy graduation gown didn't hide it.

But he hadn't. Hadn't wanted to bring her into his world. His world that his own mother didn't want. That she ditched. His world that consisted of frozen dinners and barbs and insults and notes to do his homework, because his father wasn't going to be home.

And now the time was running out, and she was standing next to him, her hand warm in his, and people were throwing their caps and yelling and hollering, and she wasn't. She was looking up at him. With those eyes that said this was it. This was his chance.

And he took it.

Letting go of Sidney's hand, he took her face in both of his, and the gasp that escaped her lips just about sent him over the edge as he covered that incredible mouth with his own.

Everyone else disappeared as he tasted her. Lips that tasted like strawberries and excitement. Lips that he'd fantasized about forever, that were just as hungry for him, as they parted for him and took him in. Her hands landing on his chest. Fingers curling into his gown. Fuck, he was toast. Pulling her to him, he took. Took all she was giving. Gave all he had. Ignored the hell out of the noise and snickers and comments of the others next to them, he didn't care.

"Sidney," he finally breathed against her mouth.

"Caleb," she said on a shuddering breath. God, she was beautiful.

"Come with me."

Those damn blue eyes shot open in shock. "Wh-what?"

"Come with me tonight," he said. Knowing it was crazy. Knowing she'd say no. Praying she'd say yes.

"What?" she repeated, her lips swollen and puffy from his kiss. Damn, he liked that. "Tonight—where? What are you—"

"I'm out of here," he said.

Her eyes filled with tears, socking him in the gut. She cared. Damn it. "Where are you going?" she asked.

"I don't know."

"For how long?" she asked, the words falling off at the end. Even in all the chaos, he could still hear her every word.

"I don't know," he repeated. "But you could come. Right now."

"Now?" Her eyes went huge.

He took two breaths and decided to throw it out there.

"Now," he said. "Right now. While everything's crazy."

"But—"

"For tonight or for forever, Sidney," he said, hearing his own words and feeling the excitement and terror they charged him with. "Your choice."

The adrenaline rushed through his veins. It was insane. It was terrifying. But it was the time to do it. Before things like logic and reality settled in. Before he had to endure another insult or jab or disappointed look. Or just absolute invisibility. Sidney had no idea what being invisible really was.

"Caleb, I can't," she breathed. "My nana's here, she's— she'll be down here on the field any second now. And your dad—"

"My dad won't even know I'm gone," he said, hearing the sourness in his tone and choking it back. "I'm good. You have family, so give her fifteen minutes of picture taking, and then meet me behind the field house," he said, his mind whirling. His hands twitching with the need to touch her again.

She laughed. Not at him, but just like he was crazy. Like they couldn't do that. Be that irresponsible. She was never irresponsible. She'd never even ridden on his bike, because her nana told her not to. It was against the rules. But shit, she was thinking about it. He could see it in her eyes.

"Fifteen minutes," she repeated, like she was calculating the time.

"Here," he said, pulling off his class ring. He grabbed her hand and pressed it into her palm, folding her fingers over it. "To show you I'm serious. That I'll be waiting for you."

Her breaths were choppy as she opened her hand and then closed it, holding her fist to her chest after she pulled hers off, too.

"You don't have to do that," he said.

She pressed it into his hand. "Kiss me again," she whispered.

How he heard the words, he had no idea, but he had her in his arms before she could change her mind. Lifting her off her feet. Making her laugh just before he held the back of her head and kissed her for all he was worth.

Sawyer stood with his hands on the scratched metal of his truck's side rails, feeling the tightening in his chest. In the breaths he took in. That was the memory he'd chosen to carry with him all these years. Sidney laughing. Sidney with her arms wrapped around his head, kissing him back with all she had, breathing fast, wanting him, carefree for once in her life. Not the one of her crying, arms wrapped around herself, fist held tight around his ring, thinking he'd left her behind. Not the gut-wrenching guilty one of watching the only person he ever loved finally give up after an hour in the dark alone and walk away.

And now—now, he'd watched her leave again. Upset again. Because of him. Again.

"Fuck," he muttered under his breath, gripping the metal tighter. Pushing that look from his mind.

He never thought he'd see her again. Certainly not

sitting in Amelia Rose's kitchen, his place of business, looking up at him with the same beautiful eyes and over a decade's worth of accusation.

He could go after her. Find her. Explain.

Apologize.

Or he could keep moving these stupid-ass gnomes.

Chapter 6

Sidney drove blindly through town, not bothering with the GPS, breathing hard as she looked determinedly for a street named All Souls Avenue.

"How hard can it be?" she yelled at the windshield. "It's a town of fifteen damn people!"

She swiped angrily at two more hot tears as they left her eyes, hating every second of the weakness she felt coursing through her veins. She was a strong woman now. No more of that insecure twit she used to be. The one who fawned over Caleb James like a starved puppy. Falling into his arms and his mouth on graduation night, buying the body language and the sexy words. Believing his lies that he wanted her with him, that he was serious.

Caleb James. Sawyer Finn. Whatever the hell he was calling himself. It was all a farce. And the fact that it had chased her out of the Rose Cottage like her ass was on fire just set her belly to boiling. Nothing was supposed to undo her like that. Ever again. That was why she was still single. No one got under her skin. No one could hurt her like that again.

"And why the hell am I crying about it now?" she yelled. Again. "Ugh!"

It was one damn night on the heels of an intense year. *Twelve* years ago. To look at her now, one would think she was engaged to the guy. Last week. Good grief, this was ridiculous.

"Get it together," she breathed, wiping another stray tear away. "Get it fucking together." She had a job to do. She didn't need to think about how he looked or the expression on his face or any of the other 459 little details she could obsess over if she let herself.

"What the hell street am I on?" she muttered, thinking maybe she did need to pull over and consult her GPS. But her car was making that weird clacking noise it had made on the way in, and she was a little afraid to stop. She might not get going again. "Seedling Street," she noted, passing a sign. "All Souls!"

It was straight ahead in front of her, and Sidney almost did a happy dance right there in the car. Thank God. Something else to focus on.

Turning onto All Souls Avenue, which was lined with a variety of pumpkins in front of each door, she glanced left and right, looking for the soda shop. She hadn't thought to ask if it still had a sign. Or what the sign might say. And she didn't remember what the name of the shop was, only that the address was 163. Okay. Maybe she could have studied the file a little closer before hitting the road, or had the professionalism to bring it with her, but she'd kind of planned on doing that while freshening up in her room before leaving. Which didn't happen. Because—*ugh*. The way she bolted out of there, she was lucky she'd had her damn wallet with her.

So she'd be winging it. With hopefully at least— please tell her she had a pad of paper somewhere in the car. God, she wasn't starting this off very well.

A picture of an ice cream soda in a tall glass caught her eye to the right, and she tapped the brakes in relief and pulled into a parking spot. A tiny 163 showed above the glass door, but it certainly wouldn't have been enough to wave and get her attention. Blowing out a breath, she rooted around in the console, found the small spiral she'd once used to track her mileage, a pen she tested quickly for ink, and set them next to her wallet. And the little skeleton key on the rose key chain.

Oh, this day.

Makeup—that would have been a grand plan. She took a quick look in the rearview mirror and did a swipe-and-repair job on her eyes. Did she look like a lawyer people could count on to take care of business?

"I look like a war orphan," she said to her reflection.

One more deep breath, and she cut the engine and palmed the keys, praying it would start again. She got out and patted the hood on her way to the door, trying not to smell the aroma of burning something-or-other. Surely her car wouldn't do that to her. It had gotten her this far.

Grasping the old door handle, she pulled it open.

"Mr. Teasdale?" she called, remembering the old woman's words. Had she checked up on her? How on earth did she know whom Sidney was there to see? Then again, small towns did tend to know everything. About everyone. She certainly knew that.

"Yes?" came an answering elderly voice.

"Mr. Teasdale, I'm Sidney Jensen?" Sidney called

again, stepping inside to way too much heat. "From Finley and Blossom—er—Orchid's firm?" And why was she posing everything as a question like a first-year associate? *Woman up, Sidney.*

"I know who you are," said the old man, coming around a corner, a cane taking on the brunt of the weight on his right side. His tone was gruff, but his eyes gave away a softer side. They were light blue and surrounded by wrinkles that proved a lifetime of laughter. A full head of white hair, meticulously groomed, and starched and ironed jeans proved he was related to Orchid. "You're the one my niece sent so that she didn't have to come trudging over here."

"No, actually, I offered," Sidney said, feeling the odd urge to defend her boss. "I needed the brownie points," she lied with a wink. "Still working my way up, you know."

She discreetly fanned herself with her blouse. He must have had the heat cranked up to ninety in there. A bit overkill for the low damp fifties that was outdoors.

Besides that, it was charming. An olden-days feel to the ambience, antique fixtures and an oversized soda fountain bar, round tables and wooden chairs, a chalkboard menu. It was adorable. And closed.

"So," Sidney began, looking around. "This place is amazing. Did it just not make it, or you closed on purpose?"

"I'm Arthur Teasdale," he said slowly, holding out a hand.

Shit. People skills.

"Sorry," Sidney said, shaking his hand and eternally grateful he didn't grasp hers as if it was a wet fish. "Very nice to meet you. Orchid had all nice things to say."

"No, she didn't," he said, propping his cane against a

chair, and pulling out another to sit in. He gestured for Sidney to do the same. "I'm surprised she even said we're related."

"Well," Sidney said, putting on what she hoped was a believable smile. "She's a busy lady. I hope to be as good as her one day."

"Don't hope for that," he said. "Don't turn into her."

Sidney started, surprised. This was his niece he was talking about. "Why?"

"Because she lost her soul along the way," he said, settling in with a long sigh. "Once upon a time, she was a sweet, funny little girl. Then my sister and her husband got some money and got snobby, and passed that crap on to Orchid." He scoffed. "Smith, by the way."

"What?"

"Her last name," he said. "It's not *Blossom*. It's Smith."

Sidney's eyebrows raised, and she laughed, the feeling relaxing her muscles again. "Seriously?"

"She changed it to that ridiculous name before she went to law school," he said, waving his hand. "Guess she thought it made her stand out more. Look all feminist or some such crap."

"Oh, wow," Sidney said, covering her mouth.

"Yeah," he said. "The things you learn, huh?" He pushed back his chair a little to spread his legs. "So, to answer your question, my wife died. That's why I closed this place."

"Oh, shit," Sidney said, clamping her lips closed on the word. *Thinking before speaking. Professionalism. Not cursing in front of clients.* "I'm so sorry."

"Don't be," he said. "Wasn't your fault, and I'm sure Orchid left that out, too. If she even remembered. No, God wanted my Layla back, unfortunately before me, and so she had to go." He rubbed at his face, not a whisker to be seen. "But this was her baby, not mine. Her passion. She had a way with it. With people." He narrowed his eyes. "I don't have that skill."

Sidney chuckled. "I know the feeling."

"I just didn't have it in me after she was gone," he said. "I tried, but—" He shook his head, and Sidney could see the sadness in spite of what he attempted to cover up. "So I just want to be done with it. I'm selling everything in here for whatever I can get, and moving on. Or if I can't move on—to pay the damn rent."

"So you're stuck in the contract?" she asked.

"Crane," he said, the sharp focus coming back to his eyes with the name. "Asshole has no compassion, no soul, no anything. All he cares about is his monthly rent."

"Crane," Sidney repeated, wishing like hell she'd brought the file so she could look remotely in the know. "I don't have your file in front of me, remind me of his name and—"

Out of the corner of her eye, an old green pickup truck slow-rolled past. One she'd seen—damn it, it had to be his. It had been hooked to that low-boy. Sidney felt her heart speed up like a jet readying for takeoff.

"Edmund Crane," Mr. Teasdale said, loud enough to be heard over the blood rushing through her ears. "He's kind of a business mogul around here. Owns a bunch of land and buildings. Doesn't give a rat's butt about the people who pay him to use them. My wife had patience with him. I don't."

Sidney rubbed the goose bumps down on her arms that had nothing to do with being cold. Not in this building.

"Known him since grade school," he said. "He was an ass then, too. Always stealing people's milk."

"And where can I find him?" she asked.

"You don't have that information?" he asked. "I e-mailed it all to Orchid."

Yes. Yes she did. Back at the cottage on her bed, where she left it when she bailed like a hormonal teenager. A place she didn't want to go back to right now—although it would be the time to do it while *he* was out driving around.

Why was he driving around?

Looking for her?

Stop it.

"Yes, but not with me," she said. "It's back at the cottage, where I'm staying. If you can tell me, it'll save me a little time. I can drive there straight from here."

"I can save you more than that," he said. "It's right across the street there." He pointed a slightly gnarled finger. "Catty-corner over to the left. Says 'EC Consolidated' on the window."

"He's across the—" The green truck came back the other way, turned around, and pulled in next to her. *Fuck. Is he—fuck.* She swallowed hard, and wiped her hand over her damp forehead. It was the heat. That was all it was. She fanned her blouse again. "Across the street, and he won't meet with you?"

"Always conveniently gone," Mr. Teasdale said. "Or busy. Or just plain tells me a deal's a deal. He's done that twice."

"That's ridiculous," Sidney said. "Any contract can be gotten out of. Especially something as simple as a lease. I mean, he can impose a penalty for early departure, but he can't legally force you to stay."

"Well, good luck finding him," he said.

The door pulled open, and Sidney felt her throat close up. Seriously? She was working. He was tracking her down while she was—

"Hey, Sawyer," Mr. Teasdale said, pushing to his feet.

"Hey, Mr. T," he said, holding out a palm as his eyes darted to Sidney. "Don't get up, I'll go get it."

Sidney's head spun. He wasn't there for her. "It?"

"Sawyer's picking up an antique desk for me—son, you can't manhandle that thing on your own," Mr. Teasdale said. "Why didn't you bring help?"

"My help isn't available till tomorrow," he said, his voice muffled from wherever he'd disappeared to. "And I need them to help me with Amelia Rose's cornucopia." He stuck his head back around a door frame. "I'm already bribing them with a six-pack," he said on a grin. "Didn't think I should throw in an extra job."

The grin made her fingertips go numb.

"You know Sawyer?" Mr. Teasdale asked, looking back at Sidney. "He works out at the cottage—didn't you say that's where you're staying? You kind of have that same accent, even. Where are you from?"

Know Sawyer? Hell no, she didn't know *Sawyer*.

"No, never met," she said, hearing the nasty dripping from her tone. *People skills.* "But he looks a lot like a guy I used to know. A long time ago."

"Well, they say we all have a double out there," Mr. Teasdale said.

Sawyer walked back around and leveled a gaze at her, as she felt the sweat trickle down her spine.

"I'll say," she said.

"Sawyer's indispensable around this town," Mr. Teasdale said. "Seems like he's got a hand in helping everybody do everything. So, how do you like the Rose Cottage?" Mr. Teasdale asked.

She couldn't look away from him. From Sawyer. From the boy she knew who now stood maybe six feet from her, a man. Now there was no obsessing over the little details, now she was looking right at them. The dark eyes that still could root her to the floor. The tiny lines showing next to them. The hair that was a darker blond than it used to be. Her gaze dropped to his hands where he crossed them over his chest. The hands were the same. She didn't let her gaze fall any further. She was having a hard enough time sucking in the hot air as it was.

"Um, it's—I really just got here, so I can't say," she managed. "In fact, if I can track down Mr. Crane today I probably won't have a reason to stay at all."

"Oh, well, that's a shame," Mr. Teasdale said. "Nice place. They say it's magic, you know."

Sidney did a double take. "I'm sorry, what?"

"The house?" Mr. Teasdale said, nodding. "Yes ma'am. Interesting things happen there."

Sidney laughed. "You mean because of Amelia Rose's fortune-telling business?"

"She's a lot more than that," he said. "She's—" He narrowed his eyes with a small smile. "She's whatever you need her to be."

"Oh, whatever," Sidney scoffed, trying not to think too hard on the oil and the butter smell and the way she'd felt. It was probably laced with something.

"Think what you want," Mr. Teasdale said. "But they also say that spending the night in that house will make you fall in love." He chuckled. "Of course, I guess you'd have to be spending the night there with another person."

Her mouth went dry as her eyes flew automatically to Sawyer's. "I guess." She fanned her blouse out again, feeling like the temperature got impossibly hotter. "Did you ever stay there?"

"Sure did," Mr. Teasdale said.

"And?"

He grinned, all his wrinkles standing out. "Married

fifty-two years." He tilted his head. "You ever been married, Miss Jensen?"

"No sir," she said, her eyes darting to Sawyer again. "Never found the right person."

Sawyer's expression faltered with the tightening of his jaw, and a quick blink before he turned back to Mr. Teasdale.

"I'll have to get my friends to help me with that desk later, after all," he said. "I was thinking it was more light-weight, that I could drag it out with a dolly, but that thing will take two people for sure. I can look at your sink while I'm here, though."

"No problem, Sawyer—"

"Let's see," Sidney said, pushing to her feet and kicking off the high-heeled Manolo knockoffs. "Maybe I can help."

Wait, what the hell did she just say? It was as if her feet were being controlled by aliens. Was she helping in order to get him to leave? Helping in order to be around him? She didn't really want the answer to that. No, it was just about helping sweet old Mr. Teasdale. That was it.

One eyebrow moved slowly higher on Sawyer's face. "Come again?"

She had to keep going. "I'm stronger than I look," Sidney said, breezing past him, refusing to look up into his face as she walked past, for fear of falling. Flailing. Puking. Any and all of those things were inherently possible.

Sidney inhaled slowly once she got around the corner into what was clearly a small office. She held her hair up off her neck and fanned herself with it as the bane of that day's existence walked in behind her.

Too close.

As she turned around, he was only a foot away, and

the look on his face made her entire body break out in goose bumps. That didn't mean anything. He didn't mean anything. She just needed to get laid and knock the edge off. She'd get right on that as soon as she got back home. Because—right.

"Sidney," he began, his voice no more than a whisper. "Just listen to me."

"I'll take this end," she managed to force her tongue to say. "It's lighter."

He paused, nodded, and blew out a breath through his nose, clearly figuring out that she wasn't going to talk or go tromping down explanation lane. That was good. Dear God, that was good.

"Fine," he said, moving to the other end. "Do you know how to lift correctly?"

"Just worry about your end," Sidney said.

He shook his head. Inside, she was shaking everything. The one man she'd ever let herself feel anything for—peaking out at eighteen, letting her heart and soul be crushed—whom she never thought she'd see again, was now moving furniture with her.

"On three," he said, his gaze burning a hole through her heart.

Chapter 7

It was like something from a twisted-up movie. The kind that made people think too much and leave exhausted. Sawyer was already there.

As he and Sidney walked past Mr. Teasdale with his antique desk, and maneuvered it through the door while she glared at him, Sawyer wanted to shake his own brain loose. He was surprised the thing didn't end up on the floor.

"Where is it going?" she asked, finally looking away, her voice sounding almost defeated by the fact that she'd spoken first.

"My truck," he said.

That brought those blue eyes back. "I realize that," she said wryly. "I meant, where are you taking it?"

"Why?" he said, turning so the desk was aimed correctly. "You in the market for one?"

"Won't quite fit in my backseat, so no," she said. "But it's nice, so I'm curious why he's getting rid of it."

"It was his wife's," Sawyer said. "He doesn't use it, and he doesn't want it going with the big sale chaos, so he's giving it to Mrs. Duggar's dress shop a few blocks over. She and his wife were friends."

"And you just so happened to be doing all this right this—*ooph*—moment?" She grunted as he shifted the desk against her so he could lower the tailgate. "Coming here at the same time I'm here?"

No, but Little Miss Haughty-Ass didn't need to know that.

He shoved the piece all the way to the end and slammed the tailgate closed.

"Here's a little tidbit of news for you," he said, turning around to face her, blocking her way. "I live here. I work here. I have a life and things I have to get done." He pointed a finger and then made a swirling motion with it. "You showed up in *my* world today, Squeak."

"Don't call me that," she said, brushing her hands off on her skirt, then scoffing at the dirt she left there. "I never liked that nickname, but I put up with it because it was some back-assward term of affection from someone I ca—" She stopped, and Sawyer saw the emotion in her eyes that matched what caught in her throat. *From someone she cared about?* Shit. "That person is gone—in fact, he probably never existed at all, so you can lose the joke."

"What joke?" he asked, close enough to smell her. To touch her if he wanted to. That thought made the words she was saying float around on tilt.

"The joke that was on me," she said, her words hard and suddenly icy. "That night. Probably all year, for that matter."

He felt his eyebrows pull together as he stared at her. "What?"

She blinked away the anger, the hurt, the resentment he saw there, and shook her head, her expression suddenly free of all of it, like it was never brought up. "Ancient history," she said, looking across the street. "Doesn't matter anymore. Excuse me," she added, pointing. "I have some business to do."

He watched her walk away, ass perfectly hugged in that little skirt of hers, head held high, hair swinging in the breeze that she was probably feeling big-time since her coat was still back at the cottage and she was barefoot. As if she heard his thoughts, she stopped and wheeled around. Passing him without so much as a darted glance, she disappeared into the old soda shop and reappeared ten seconds later, heels making her three inches taller.

"Good idea," he said, knowing he shouldn't provoke her, but unable to help himself. She wouldn't speak to him on a normal level, so if he had to irritate her to get interaction, then what the hell. She'd made a point, and he remembered her being stubborn enough to stick to it. Whatever the hell that point was.

He deserved her anger and resentment. She had every right to tell him to go to hell. But a *joke?* He didn't get that. He'd been an A-number-one prick twelve years ago, letting her believe he'd left her. Listening to—

No.

He wasn't going down that road. That path only led him to negative thoughts and rage, and he'd buried all that a long time ago.

Tearing his eyes from watching her cross the street, he turned and went back in the soda shop. He had a sink to check out. This was his life now.

Keep walking. Keep walking. Don't think about Huckleberry back there watching you walk away. Or the fact that he might not be. Because that would be somehow twistedly, infinitely worse.

"Shit, shit, shit," Sidney muttered, thankful at least that the tears were gone.

At least now she could act like a grown-up, she thought as she reached the frosted-glass door with EC CONSOLIDATED emblazoned over it. At least she wouldn't look like a sniveling, pining teenager—

"Shit!" she repeated, pushing the door that didn't budge.

Damn it, Crane wasn't there. Was he watching? Sidney turned partially, as if to look down the sidewalk, and checked her peripherals.

No. He was gone. Not *gone* gone, because his truck was still there, sporting the five-hundred-ton desk she probably threw her back out for, but she wasn't about to wuss out of carrying once she'd thrown down that gauntlet. But gone from the street, from the sidewalk, from the image that kept burning into her retinas. Him standing just inches away telling her she was in *his* world. He was right. But why? Why was Moonbright, Maine, his world? Not because people couldn't leave home, because she had, as well, but because of how he'd done it.

He'd just disappeared. She remembered the buzz around town. Principal James's son bolting after graduation, with no plan, no clothes, no note. Leaving his dad in very much the same way his mother had left them. With no warning.

With Sidney, he'd just twisted a little extra cruelty into the mix by telling her about it first. Asking her to meet him. Then being long gone when she got there.

And her, standing there on the curb like a stupid, sappy idiot, with her heart exposed and his senior ring clutched in her hand. Ready to jump off in an after-school special and have a bad-idea adventure and break the rules for once. *For tonight or forever.* That's what he'd said. Pretty words from a beautiful boy-man, used to trick the nerd girl. With kisses that had addled her brain enough to fall for it.

Until she'd finally given up and left. Heartbroken, angry, hurt, mortified at her own naïveté, and so tempted to throw his ring in the nearest trash bin. She thought she knew him. He knew *her* like no one ever had and ever would again, because how could she ever trust her own judgment again, much less anyone else?

Sidney remembered driving around for hours that night, unable to go home and tell her nana that her night with friends had been cancelled. It had been hard enough to pull off the lie when it was for something exciting; she couldn't do it for that. And part of her—she wouldn't let herself think it out loud—but part of her was looking for a blond-haired wild boy on a motorcycle.

She'd parked across the street from his house for a while just in case he showed up. Fuming and planning twenty different confrontations, waiting for the sound of his bike. By the time his dad got home and glanced over to where the old bike usually was parked, she knew what he didn't know then. That the bike wouldn't be back.

She checked a local pawnshop in the coming days for her ring, but it never came back, either. Caleb James was gone. A memory.

Off becoming Sawyer Finn.

Sidney felt the old burn in her belly as she walked back to her car. That was okay. That kind of burn was what she needed. To remember the anger and not let him get under her skin.

She paused as she opened her door. Any other place on earth that didn't have Ca—Sawyer hovering in the middle of it, being its pulse or whatever crap he did now, she would be hightailing it back inside to confer with her client. Let him know that Crane wasn't there and see where she might need to go to find him. Now there was no way in hell. She'd have to do it the hard way. Go get her laptop and do what she was best at. Research. Followed by probably knocking on some of the other businesses' doors and asking questions—not what she was best at.

Sidney smiled at two teenage boys walking down the sidewalk dressed in goth attire, and hoped it was a costume. Throwing one last glance at the old truck next to her, she bade it a silent farewell and closed her door. And cranked her engine—to nothing.

"Oh no," she said.

She tried again, closing her eyes, and again a third time adding a prayer. It wasn't a dead-battery kind of nothing. It was a sickly sounding wet kind of choking sound.

And then there were the white wisps of smoke curling up in tendrils from the general vicinity of her radiator.

"Great," Sidney breathed, opening her door and slamming a palm on the wheel.

"Dude, is your car going to blow up?" one of the boys asked as they slowed.

"*Dude,* I don't know," she said, stepping out. "Want to come sit inside so you can get a feel for it?"

"Man, a crazy bitch," the other one said, pushing his friend along. "Don't stop."

"Black lipstick isn't your friend!" she hollered.

Just as the soda shop door opened.

And it wasn't Mr. Teasdale.

"Problem?" Sawyer asked.

Why did he have to look like that? All manly and rugged and—ugh. *Remember the burn.*

"No," she lied, as his gaze fell on the smoking front of her car. *Traitorous piece of shit.* The car. Sort of.

"I can see that," he said.

"It just needs—"

"A new radiator," he said. "Possibly more, but I'd have to get under your hood to know for sure."

Their eyes met at the double entendre, and he at least had the decency to blink away as the indecent smirk tugged at the corners of his lips.

"Your car's hood," he corrected.

Sidney's neck went hot, and it had nothing to do with her car.

"Let me guess," she said, crossing her arms over her chest. "You work on cars now, too?"

"I did," he said, taking off his blue jean jacket and rolling up the sleeves of a flannel shirt. Oh, good God. All her female parts did a shimmy. "It was my first job."

"Never knew you as the working type before," Sidney said, cursing her own tongue. *Don't make small talk. Call a tow truck!*

He gave her a quick glance with a nod she took to mean to pop her hood.

"Well, things change when you're on your own," he said, leaning away from the steam when he raised the hood. "And you're fond of eating."

"I'd say that decision was on you," she said, wondering who was driving her mouth.

His head was hidden from view, but she saw one hand land on the side heavily. A second later, he leaned over, looking at her dead-on.

"I got the impression you didn't want to have this conversation," he said quietly, his eyes not blinking. "Has that changed?"

Sidney heard the seriousness in his tone, and she rearranged her weight on her feet.

"No," she said.

He nodded and went back to work.

"Yeah, your radiator's shot," he said after a few minutes. "You need a new timing belt and transmission, too, but those aren't dead, yet."

She closed her eyes and leaned against her car. Nothing was going according to plan. What now? How would she continue? How would she get home? She jumped as the hood slammed down.

"The owner of the auto care place and I are still— well, he owes me a favor," Sawyer said.

"Of course he does," she said wearily, running her hands over her face and back through her hair.

"And I can call that in," he added, his tone more acidic. "Unless you're hell-bent on hating me more than you want your car fixed."

Sidney looked at him. This would likely fall under those people skills, too. Graciousness.

"No, that would be good," she mumbled. "Thank you."

"Fine," he said. "Now, this car isn't going anywhere. I'll go let Mr. Teasdale know it's gonna be parked till they come pick it up, and then we'll go."

"We?"

Sawyer gave her a tired look. A look that said he was over the big surprise and he just wanted to get on with his day.

"You have a magic flying carpet under that skirt?" he asked.

She gave him a disgusted sneer. "Really?"

He just shrugged. "What's your plan, Squeak?"

Ugh. To pick up the nearest damn pumpkin and throw it at his smug face.

"I don't know, *Caleb*," she said, drawing out the name loudly. "I was thinking I'd wait for the tow truck like most people do. Get a rental car."

He chuckled and walked up close. Inches kind of close. The kind of close that becomes heady when you're backed against a car and can't move.

"This isn't Boston, Sid," he said softly, his voice trickling over her skin. The last time she was that close to him, he—She swallowed hard and concentrated on looking unaffected. However unaffected looked.

"I'm aware," she said.

"Then you should realize that this is Saturday and my guy isn't at the shop," Sawyer said. "He's most likely on his back porch working on his putt or at his grandson's soccer game. And while there'll be a tow truck coming," he continued. "There's no rental car."

"So I'm at your mercy?" she asked, tilting her head at him "You driving me home on Sunday, too?"

He blinked.

"I thought you weren't staying," he said

"Well, I have to find Edmund Crane," she said, pointing behind her. "I have some research to do, and evidently now some searching on foot. Unless you have Uber in this town?"

His expression was blank. "Have what?"

Sidney shook her head. "Cabs?

"Not likely," he said, backing up a step. "What do you need Crane for?"

"To talk to him about my client's lease," she said. "That's why I'm here."

Sawyer's eyebrows moved together in confusion, and he backed up another step and crossed his arms over his chest. Really good arms.

Stop.

"What?" he asked. "Your client?"

"Yes."

"Teasdale is your client?"

"Yes," Sidney repeated.

"Crane is working him over for the lease?" he asked. "That's why he's—" His jaw tightened. "Damn it."

Before Sidney could ask what he was suddenly so mad about, he was yanking open the door and swallowed back into the sauna.

Chapter 8

If it wasn't so damn hot in that place, Sawyer would've thought it was his own ire smoking out of his ears.

"Mr. T!" he yelled, vaguely aware of the door opening again behind him.

It didn't matter. If Sidney was now tied up with Edmund Crane, she needed to know whom she was dealing with. She just needed to stay back there. About six feet back there. Because her scent was making him crazy. Making him think more like the lovesick boy he used to be instead of the independent man he'd become.

"Who's yelling at me?" came Teasdale's voice, closely followed by the man himself, leaning heavily on his cane.

"Why didn't you tell me about Crane?" Sawyer said.

The old man's look of irritation crumpled into weariness and then annoyance.

"Who put that idiot's name in your head?" Teasdale said, his gaze looking past him to Sidney.

"I might have mentioned—" Sidney began.

"You're my lawyer!" Teasdale said, accentuating the last word with a hard pound of his cane. "Two seconds outside my door and you're blabbing my case to a stranger?"

"Hang on," Sawyer said, instinctively standing in front of her. And kicking himself in the ass for feeling protective. "It's not like that. Sidney and I have—" What did they have? "We grew up together. We—were friends once. And her car is broke down outside, so—"

"So you said you'd bring her to Crane, and she said that's where she was going anyway," Teasdale said, waving him off like a gnat. "I see the picture."

"Other way around, actually, but yeah," Sawyer said.

"Wait, what?" Sidney asked.

"Doesn't involve you," Sawyer said. *Please stay out of it.*

"The hell it doesn't," she said, looking like she gained a full inch. "Bring me to Crane? *He's* the car guy who owes you a favor?"

Sawyer blew out a breath. "Yeah."

"Oh, Jesus," Sidney said, lifting her hair off her neck and walking in a circle.

He wished she would quit that. He was having a hard enough time with her mouth. Exposing her neck like that made him want to back her up to a wall.

"I'm never getting out of here," she said.

"Quit being dramatic," Sawyer said, focusing back on Teasdale. "You. Why didn't you tell me that's why you're selling everything?"

"Because you'd go off half-cocked, boy," Teasdale said, lowering into a chair. "Get yourself in another pickle over *favors.*"

"Listen to me—"

"No, you listen to *me,*" Teasdale said. "I'm a pretty big boy. I don't need you getting involved with him again over me."

"Or me," Sidney piped in, grabbing his arm and then stopping dead, staring at her hand as if it had betrayed her. Clearing her throat, she let her fingers slide down his arm and pull away before they reached his hand. And the punch to his midsection was only intensified when those huge blue eyes gazed up at him. "Whatever the hell getting involved with him means. It's not worth it."

"Look, I just got his niece a job at the post office, and he was appreciative," Sawyer said. "I know someone there, and it was no big deal. Small change. So is pushing your car to the front of a line. It's all good."

"Well, I have a lawyer now," Teasdale said. "So you don't need to do squat for me." He raised an eyebrow at Sidney. "Right?"

"That's right," she said, tucking her hair behind one ear.

Her nervous tell. That was what had been familiar earlier. How the hell was he going to make it through this weekend, with Sidney Jensen in his wake?

Sidney being in his truck with him was brutal. Watching her slide across the vinyl, her skirt riding up on her thighs before she pulled it down. Being in the same enclosed space with her, only talking when they had to get out again to unload the desk, her scent surrounding him.

It was a longer drive to Edmund Crane's house on the outskirts of town, and the silence stretched. A particularly rough bump liberated the top button of her blouse from its fastener, and Sawyer was treated to the perfect inside cleavage of her right breast.

Fuck.

Screw this. He had to talk or lose his mind.

"So, what made you want to become a lawyer?" he asked.

"What made you become a mechanic-turned-gardener with a penchant for hanging out with bad guys?" she countered.

Sawyer huffed out a breath. "You first."

Sidney inhaled deeply and let it go as she crossed her arms. Pushing up and unknowingly putting more of that boob on display. Sawyer shook his head and tried to just focus on the road. He wasn't usually one to go stupid over a pair of tits, but once upon a time, this particular pair was on his daily fantasizing list. Now between that visual and the skirt inching up her legs again, his dick was starting to join the party.

"Wanted to make my nana proud, I guess," she said, gazing out the passenger window. "She left me a chunk of money when she died, and I felt like I needed to do something worthy of her with it." She let go of another breath. "I'm still working on that."

"Meaning?"

"Meaning I'm a very small fish swimming against high tide in a very lucrative corporate ocean," she said. "Not exactly where I saw myself landing."

"So then do something else," he said. The look she gave him could have melted steel. "What? I'm serious. You're smart, Sidney. You were always smart. If you don't like the direction you're walking in, turn around."

Her eyes narrowed, and her jaw tightened. "Your turn."

He held a palm up. "What do you want to know?"

"For starters," she said. "What's up with this Crane guy, and what did he do to you?"

Sawyer sighed. "Crane owned the shop I got a job at when I first hit town. He—I don't know, saw something in me, I guess, and took me under his wing. Taught me everything he knew. I told him my real name and he helped me create someone else. Made me Sawyer Finn on paper." He shrugged. "I should have seen the signs then, but I was blinded. He was kind of a dad figure, and—well, I was short on that."

"You left that."

He met her eyes as he rolled up to a red light. "No. I didn't. I may have a father. But I never had a dad."

The look that passed between them was full of every conversation they'd ever had, before she blinked and faced forward.

"You have to remember, I was eighteen and scared and pissed off and not knowing what I was going to do," he said, watching the little crease above her nose crinkle. He knew what question was coming. "Someone offering me a little attention and safety—I soaked that shit up. And eventually that led to him calling in favors. Errands. Some shady deals that I had to deliver paperwork on or keep people occupied while he had meetings off the book. Just a bunch of shit that I finally had enough of, and when I met Amelia Rose she gave me another job so that I could get away."

"Jesus, it sounds like the mob," Sidney said.

Sawyer laughed. "No. Just an ass. Sad thing is he was still more of a dad to me than mine ever was."

"So—what were *you* pissed off about?" Sidney asked, zeroing in on what he knew she would.

He nodded, making a turn next to a train car graveyard, and pulling over. He'd thought about this conversation, this apology, a million times over the years. Not once had it ever been staged as a hostile takeover in his truck.

"Someone saw us," he said finally.

"Some—what?" she stuttered, looking lost.

"That night," he said. "On the field. You and me."

She gasped, and then blinked away, frowning and swallowing hard like the sound gave her away. And maybe it did. And maybe he liked that a little too much.

"Wow, a stadium full of people saw teenagers kissing," Sidney said, chuckling. A sound that came out as nervous and fake. "I doubt that was life-altering for anyone."

"Depends on the eyes. They saw me leave. Probably assumed you would follow." Sawyer closed his eyes briefly.

"Imagine that," she said, deadpan.

"Okay, Sidney," he said. "I'm sorry. I—"

"Don't," she said, staring forward again. "Just—let's get to Crane's."

To hell with this. "'Don't,' my ass," he said. "You keep throwing little barbs at me, and that's fine. I deserve it. But we're not kids anymore. We're in my damn truck, and if I have something to say, I'm gonna say it."

He glanced sideways to see her jaw set. "Fine," she said, recrossing her arms. "Your truck. Babble away."

He blew out a breath.

"I'm sorry," he said.

"For what?" she said. "Lying to me? Making a fool out of me? Having to face me now? Owning up to the joke?"

Sawyer opened his mouth, but he was reeling at the rapid-fire acid that shot out of her mouth. To her credit, she was, too. She took a deep, kind of shaky breath afterward and held two fingers over her lips, as if it all fell out of its own accord.

"There was no joke," he said finally. "No lie. No—fool-making. Did I miss anything?"

"Don't insult me, Ca—*Sawyer,*" she said, rolling her eyes. "Whoever the hell you are now."

"You know where that came from," he said.

"I know about two kids having a silly conversation at graduation," she said. "You don't see me going by '*Cinderella*,' do you?"

"Could be an interesting lawyer name," he said.

"Please," she said, chuckling over the anger he still saw simmering. "One fake name per company is enough."

"What?"

She shook her head. "Nothing." Making a little hand flourish, she said. "Proceed."

"I'm sorry I left you there, Squeak," he said as the frown returned to her face. "I didn't plan it that way."

She scoffed. That was expected. He probably wouldn't believe him, either.

"What makes you think I even showed up?" she said, averting her gaze.

"Well, for starters, the raging hatred," Sawyer said. "And—" He faced forward, looking for the right words.

"You son of a bitch," she said, the words slow and full of awe. Her eyes narrowed and glimmered with the hint of hurt. Hurt he'd put there. "You were there."

How could he explain it? That he'd waited for her with more excitement and anticipation than he'd ever felt in his life. Until—

He spun in place, the familiar dread spreading over him. "Dad."

"I asked you what you're doing out here," his dad said. "The celebration's on the field, not behind it."

"I'm—going out with some friends," he said. "Meeting them."

"You don't have friends," his dad said.

There it was. The hatred, boiling in his belly. The kind that made his eyes go hot and fight crying when he was alone. He wouldn't cry tonight. He wouldn't give that man the satisfac-

tion. He'd graduated. Made it through this hellhole, thanks to Sidney, and his father's slung insults couldn't hurt him tonight. Nothing could hurt him tonight. He'd kissed her. She'd kissed him back. She was coming. His father could kiss his damn ass.

"You don't know what I have," he said.

"I know you were making out with Sidney Jensen on the field out there," he said, pointing behind him. "Looking like an idiot, and then heading off here." He held both hands out to his sides. "Not leaving. Not hanging out with anyone. Just standing here by yourself. It doesn't take a genius to figure out you're waiting for her."

"Don't even say her name," Caleb said through his teeth.

"Ooh, protective," his dad said. "How sweet. What's the plan? Go get a hotel? Ruin her future so she's as useless as you are? Run off together so she blows all the potential she has going for her?"

"You're just jealous," Caleb seethed.

His dad laughed. "Jealous? Astound me, son. What do you have that I would be jealous of?"

"A woman," Caleb said, his voice low. Knowing he was going somewhere he shouldn't as his dad's eyes changed. Knowing as the words were falling from his mouth that he was crossing a line he never crossed. "A woman who wants to be with me. Who cares enough to stick around."

"Watch your mouth."

"No, I mean, I get why she left me," he said, walking closer, feeling every button he was pushing and unable to stop. It was like a floodgate had opened and he was finally free. "I'm an ass, after all. That's what you're always telling me. She gave up on me, but you?" Caleb stepped close enough to hear him breathing fast through his nose. "Why did the great Principal James's wife ditch him?"

"Because she's a whore," his dad seethed, grabbing him by the collar. "They all are." Caleb shoved at him, pushing his *hands away.* "*You'll see. Shouldn't take too long for your own little whore to find someone a hell of a lot better than you.*"

Caleb's fist was up and smacking into his dad's jawbone before he could even form the thought to do it. His father reeled and then rushed him, only to be stopped by a second punch to the mouth. He laughed maniacally.

"*Yeah,*" *he said, spitting blood off to the side.* "*You're a real catch, son.*"

Caleb backed up, his heart racing so fast he was shaking. He'd never hit him before. Wanted to a thousand times, but never went there. It didn't feel as good as he imagined it would.

He picked up the backpack he'd dropped. The one he'd kept buried and hidden behind the field house for the last two months, that held a couple changes of clothes and three hundred and forty-six dollars.

"'*Bye, Dad,*" *he said.*

Another laugh, and another spit of blood. "*We'll see how long you last in the real world.*"

That was the last time he ever saw his father. He took off on his bike, around the block to give his dad time to leave, and then circled back and parked behind a grove of trees, hidden in the dark.

Hidden, because as usual his dad's words had hit their mark. He wasn't good enough for her. He was so angry, he couldn't pull in a full breath, and he was leaving finger marks in the grips, but he knew that part of what that asshole had said was true. She deserved better than him.

He had just decided to hit the road, when she walked around the corner. Her hopeful expression and the excitement in her face nearly took him down. Her nervous way of tucking her hair behind her ear . . . looking around her, waiting for him to walk up and pull her into his arms. To kiss her again. To kiss her all damn night. God, he'd wanted to. And for one second, he'd almost—almost changed his mind.

He'd always believed he made the right choice, but looking at her now—even more beautiful than he remembered, and ready to crucify him—he wasn't sure.

"I was told you'd be better off without me," he said, realizing how lame that sounded now.

Her jaw dropped. "So you hid like a coward and made my choice for me?" she yelled. "Screw this." She grabbed her door handle and pushed the door open.

"Where are you going?"

"Away from you," she said, stepping out and slamming the door.

"Shit," he grunted, palming his keys and getting out. "Sidney!"

"Which way to Crane's house?" she asked.

"Sid—"

"Which way!" she yelled.

Sawyer blew out a breath and pointed to his right.

"Thank you," she huffed, hobbling over some rocks in the road, one hand holding her hair out of her eyes.

"Sidney." She kept walking. Damn it, she was going to be the death of him. Again. "Sidney, please."

Nothing.

"You were the best thing that ever happened to me," he blurted.

She stopped.

Chapter 9

He didn't just say that. *He didn't. Just. Say. That.*

Sidney's feet felt like they melted right into the pavement, taking her lungs right along with them. Anger mixed with hurt mixed with a million reasons to just keep walking swirled around her head, making her head feel hot and dizzy. She didn't need hot and dizzy. She needed clear and focused. She needed the hardcore, irritating attorney with no people skills who pissed everyone off. That Sidney she could deal with.

You were the best thing that ever happened to me.

Hot and dizzy.

She turned around, shaking her head, trying like hell to pull up a mask of something. Anything that would disguise what was sure to be all over her face.

"Yeah. So damn good, you just left me there without another thought."

He chuckled silently but his eyes looked anything but joyous as he shook his head and looked off to his left. "Without a thought," he echoed incredulously.

"Well, what then, Sherlock?" she asked. "Oh no, I'm

sorry, wrong book. Sawyer. Were you kidnapped at gun-point? Abducted by aliens?" He continued to avert his eyes, and it only gave her more fuel to keep going. "Whisked away into the witness protection program?"

"Seriously?" he said finally.

"That's what I thought," she said, risking one step back the way she came. A step closer to him. "So you fill me full of pretty words and kiss me like your life depended on it, tell me to meet you, and then just disappear. Vanish from the earth. Without a note, a letter, a phone call—nothing. Just like your mom did to you."

His whole face tightened on that one, and Sidney feared she'd gone too far, but there was no going back now.

"So, what, you were just paying that forward?"

"That's a low blow," he said, his voice gruff.

"Well, that's what you shoveled out to me that night," she said. "And now—" Sidney laughed and raked her hair back. "Now I find out that before you ditched me, you actually watched me in probably my worst, most vulnerable moment ever. You watched me *cry* over you before you disappeared." She pointed at him. "You, sir, are a piece of work."

Sidney made to turn and head back down the road to see a man about a soda shop, but his words stopped her again.

"You ever make a mistake, Sidney?" he said. "Ever screw up, even once, in your perfect life?"

Looking back at him, sleeves still rolled up, arms crossed over his chest, standing in the middle of the road looking positively friggin' edible—God, he had no idea how riddled her life was with stupid choices and dumb mistakes.

"I was eighteen and scared shitless," he said. "I'd just

finally kissed the girl of my dreams and punched my father in the face in the same twenty minutes."

"What?" Sidney said, hearing the "*girl of my dreams*"
part but landing on the other. "Punched your dad—*he*
was the one who saw us? Who told you—"

"That you were too smart for me. That you'd find
someone better and I'd be holding you back or—I
think there was *ruining your life* alluded to in there, as
well."

There was no one better. In all the years since then,
there still had been no one to live up to or surpass him.
How sad was that?

"You punched him for that?" she asked, her voice
going a little breathless.

"I punched him for calling you a whore."

Sidney felt her eyebrows reach for the sky. "Come
again?"

"And then he left," he continued. "And you came.
And—" He stopped and closed his eyes as if he was remembering, then opened them right on her, taking two
steps closer. "It was enough. What he said. You know,
you hear that you're worthless enough times, you begin
to buy into it."

Sidney's hands were twitching with the want to comfort him, touch him, pull him in for a hug, and her
brain was screaming *no*.

"I might have made the wrong choice, but look at
you now. Fancy lawyer in a Boston office. You wouldn't
have gotten that staying in Derby." His eyes locked in
on hers. "Or with me. I was a mess."

I'm still a mess! She couldn't play that hand, though.
She couldn't play any hand, due to how he was looking
at her. She needed some distance from him, and the
two feet that were too easily spanned weren't enough.

Sidney walked around him, back to the truck, unfortunately losing her balance as her heel got caught on a rock.

"Oh, shi—" she exclaimed, the word clipped as her body slammed into Sawyer's and his arm caught her. Tightly.

The side effect was being close enough to kiss him. If she wanted to. Which she didn't. At all. Even with his mouth *right there.*

"Sorry," he said, as she laid her hands against his chest to push back, and yet she didn't push. And he didn't let go.

God bless America, she couldn't breathe. Everything in her wanted to run her hands right on up to his neck, his face, his hair, and wrap herself around this man with the hand burning a hole in her lower back.

"Let's, um—" she began, her gaze focused on his mouth solely because his eyes would have done her in.

"Get to Crane's," he said, nodding slightly.

"Yeah," she said, sliding her hands down his chest a little as he let her go. As unfair as that might have been, his hands did a drive-by down the side of her ass. So both of them stood there a little unsteadily.

"So," he said.

"I'm gonna get—back in the truck," she said, spurring her feet into motion. "Shit!" she whispered as she got in and shut the door. "Breathe. Grow up."

His door opening made her suck in a breath and cross her legs. Which showed more thigh. So she put her log back down and tugged her skirt down. In doing that, she noticed a button undone on her blouse, giving a nice little view. Jesus, she looked like she'd been making out in a backseat. And looking to her left, she caught Sawyer watching the whole show, a heat in his eyes that made the soles of her feet tingle.

"You done?" he asked.

Boy, was she. Done *for*. Things had changed in the last ten minutes. Her long-repressed anger had come out to dance and then was dampened with the news about his father. She couldn't really be mad anymore. And that was a problem. Mad had at least provided walls.

Sawyer couldn't remember the last time he'd spent most of a day so aroused. He couldn't remember another woman worthy of it, for that matter. But Sidney had his blood racing. She had him tweaked earlier, but now after holding her against him like that—feeling her softness against him. Her hands on him and her mouth just inches away, the sound of her breathing quickening and the look in her eyes that said she wanted him, too—all of it had his dick on standby.

They made it to Crane's just to find out he wasn't there. Went to the soccer fields but no one was playing.

And then it dawned on him.

"Aw, damn it," he said.

"What?" Sidney asked, tucking her hair behind her ear.

"It's the day after Halloween," he said, shaking his head as he made a quick right. "I forgot."

"Forgot what?" she asked.

"That no one in Moonbright passes up a chance to be cheesy."

Five minutes later, he pulled up to a large field, opposite of the WORLD'S LARGEST PUMPKIN PATCH sign.

"Is it really the largest?" Sidney asked.

"I just kind of take their word for it," he said.

"And Crane would be here, why?" Sidney asked as he got out. Just as a large orange sphere hurtled about twenty feet overhead. "Shit, what's that?"

Sawyer laughed. "That would be last night's decorations. Damn, I had a ton of this carnage I could have brought."

If he'd been thinking. Instead of chasing after Sidney Jensen.

Sidney looked back at him, the breeze lifting her hair, and damn if she couldn't still take his breath clean away.

"And Crane will be here?" she asked.

"Bet my paycheck on it," Sawyer said. "He owns the two biggest catapults."

"Fore!" bellowed a big booming voice off to the right.

"And there we go," Sawyer said. "Watch it!"

Sidney ducked instinctively and swayed backward as her heels sank into the soft sod, her ass landing right up against his crotch. His arms went around her and got a side grope of boob.

He wasn't going to make it through this day alive.

"We have to stop meeting like this," he said against her ear. She laughed, but not before he noticed the goose bumps on her arm and the quick intake of breath.

"I'll just carry them," she said, righting herself and pulling off her shoes.

"Good idea."

"Mr. Crane—" Sidney began, but her words were cut short by Sawyer's hand on her shoulder.

"Hold up there, Speedy," he said under his breath, stepping past her.

She tried not to be put off by being pushed aside, but to be honest, she was having a harder time dealing with all the touching. She had never been clumsy a day in her life, and yet now she'd stumbled into his arms twice within fifteen minutes. And the whisper against her ear, the heat from his hand that was damn close to her neck—it was like having foreplay all over town.

No. Not that. *Stop thinking like that.*

"Sawyer," the man said, peering down at the ground, then stepping down three steps of a ladder to reach it. An oddly insecure move for such a large, solid man.

And that he was. Sawyer was no small guy, and yet this man dwarfed him. In both stature and presence. He'd only uttered one word so far, and Sidney could tell he was commanding.

"Crane," Sawyer said, an easy smile on his face that was only given away at the eyes. *Damn it, she shouldn't know that.*

They shook hands and did that clap-of-the-shoulder thing that men do.

"Partying hard, I see," Sawyer said, looking out at the field.

"You know me," Crane said. "I'm a sucker for this shit—stuff," he amended, glancing at Sidney. "So how've you been?"

"Always good," Sawyer said. "You?"

"Well, you tell me," Crane said, leaning a meaty elbow back against the ladder. "I haven't seen you even accidentally for months, and now you show up and make a beeline for me. Somebody dying?"

Sawyer laughed. "Not to my knowledge."

"Not to yours. Your boss send you?"

Sawyer's eyes narrowed playfully. "Should she?" At Crane's uncomfortable expression, which Sidney didn't understand, Sawyer chuckled again. "No, I want you to meet someone," Sawyer said, reaching a hand back for Sidney. She felt that hand settle at the small of her back, and she tried not to focus on the placement of each and every finger.

"Hi, Mr. Crane," Sidney said, extending a hand. "I'm Sidney Jensen of—"

"She's staying at the cottage," Sawyer said, cutting her off, and squeezing two fingers gently against her spine. "And her car broke down in town. Needs her radiator fixed to even be drivable and she has to get back to Boston on—"

He stopped and dropped his gaze on her questioningly.

Oh, she could talk now?

"Sunday," she filled in. "Tomorrow."

"Ah," Crane said, nodding, a knowing smirk on his face. "You need me to call Oscar in."

"Afraid so?" she said, tilting her head, hoping to look cute and not like she'd just broken her neck.

"And yet Sawyer here could have called me with that request—"

"I did," Sawyer interjected. "You didn't answer."

"Yeah, the service tends to suck out here," Crane said, not even glancing down at his phone. "But you didn't have to bring her with you." He stopped and stared right into Sidney's eyes, and she was pretty sure her soul was draining as she stood there. "You need something besides your car fixed. What can I do for you?"

Oh, he was good.

Sidney held out a hand that he automatically took. "Sidney Jensen. I need to talk to you about Arthur Teasdale."

Crane dropped her hand like it was coated in dog shit.

Chapter 10

"You could have saved yourself the time," he said, climbing back up the ladder. "I have nothing to say."

"Sir, you can't force someone to stay in a rental agreement," Sidney said. "You can enforce penalties, early cancellation fees, deposit forfeiture—"

"You heard me," he bellowed, peering ahead like a general surveying the troops.

"But he can leave at any time," she finished. "Why are you fighting this? You could get another tenant with an actual running business."

"Nobody wants that place," Crane said. "I don't even want it. And when he leaves, I'll be stuck with it."

"That's not his problem!" Sawyer said through his teeth, stepping back forward. "The man lost his wife, for God's sake. Have a heart."

"I'm aware of that," Crane said, his tone going harsh.

"Sell it," Sidney said.

"It has a giant soda fountain in it," Crane said. "Layla had to have that installed, and it makes it a bit limited. I can't even turn it into a bar because that street's not zoned for it."

"Coffee shop, bakery, other things can work there," Sidney said. "Better than a closed business."

"I didn't tell him to close," Crane said.

"Quit being an asshole," Sawyer said, his voice raising. "He can't keep paying your inflated rent with no income." He paused. "And you owe me one."

Crane stepped back down and leaned back a little, looking down his nose at Sawyer as if he were looking through imaginary reading glasses. "Are you seriously comparing getting Marie a job to this?"

"A favor's a favor," Sawyer said.

"I thought that was what the car was about," Crane said. "Now you want a two-for-one?"

"Fixing her car is just being a good person, Crane," Sawyer said. "It's being a good businessman. This thing with Teasdale is—"

"None of your business," Crane finished.

"To hell with this," Sawyer muttered, turning around walking off.

Sidney, however, didn't move. She stood her ground looking up at the giant man with a pumpkin on a platform, crossing her arms over her chest and looking up at him patiently.

He kept his gaze on her, too, cockiness morphing into realization. Shit.

"Teasdale doesn't have money for an attorney," he said. "Especially one from Boston. Who are you, really?"

Sidney lifted her chin. "An attorney from Boston."

"You don't sound like it."

She lifted an eyebrow. "Like an attorney?"

He scoffed. "No, you have that droning drivel down. You don't sound *Boston*."

She shrugged. "I didn't start out there."

"You sound like Sawyer," he said with a nod toward wherever Sawyer had headed. She refused to turn around to find out.

"Well, I'm sure there are more than just two of us from—"

"You know him," Crane said, narrowing his eyes.

Sidney's tongue faltered, and she cleared her throat.

"You're from the same place, aren't you?" he asked. "The same little hick town."

"Because we both have an accent?" she asked, laughing, hoping it would cover up her lie.

"Because of how I just saw him look at you," Crane said, studying Sidney with a grin. "Like a lovesick schoolboy. Holy shit, you're *her*."

Sidney's breath felt trapped in her chest, unable to move in or out, just held captive there. Sawyer had a *her*? And she was it? "I—I'm who?"

"The girl he came to town all messed up over," Crane said, crossing his own arms. "A hundred years ago. Well, well, well."

All messed up over.

After punching out his own father.

Defending her.

Damn it if all her carefully constructed and ancient defenses weren't crumbling around her regarding him. The boy who shattered her already shaky confidence. The reason she bitterly swore off love and dove into work, into making herself a hard and formidable beast. A beast without people skills but still. And now . . .

"We were friends in high school, yes," Sidney managed to push out, her voice sounding decidedly wobbly. "That has no bearing on Mr. Teasdale's case."

"Which came to you how, again?" Crane asked.

Sidney smiled. "I'll ask the questions."

Crane winked, and she so much wanted to slug him. "Nice deflection. What firm are you with?"

"Finley and Blossom."

"Blossom?" he asked. And it wasn't about the name. It was recognition. Shit.

"Yes, sir."

"His damn niece," Crane said, slapping a big hand against the ladder. "I forgot she was a lawyer. Damn it. She sent you."

Oh, seven kinds of hell, now this wall was disintegrating, too. She needed a suit of armor.

"Everything okay?" said a voice from directly behind her. A voice that sent shock waves to all her nether regions, especially coupled with the hand that rested on the back of her neck. Crap, she needed more than armor. Sidney needed a force field.

"I work for her," Sidney said, ignoring Sawyer's question and fighting the urge to settle back against him.

"And you need to bring back the win," Crane said, chuckling.

God help her if she was ever up against this asshole in court. He could read her too easily. Or maybe she'd always been this easy. Sawyer's thumb moved a microcentimeter along her skin, and her heart slammed against her breastbone. Then again, maybe he was just her Kryptonite.

"Mr. Crane," Sidney said, moving one step forward so that Sawyer's hand would slip away. "Will you tell me why you are so hell-bent on keeping my client in this lease? Why you won't just charge the penalties and be done? Why you won't just take the *much* simpler route?"

Crane looked off as if studying the vast pumpkin battle plans before him.

"I can get your car in the shop and off the street," he said. "But if there are parts needed—"

"There are," Sawyer said behind her.

"Then Oscar won't be able to get them until Monday," he finished.

"Monday?" Sidney exclaimed.

"At the earliest," Crane said, climbing back up the ladder. "Best I can do, sorry. Guess you need to call in a few days' vacation to that stuck-up boss of yours."

Sawyer was about to crawl out of his damn skin. It was as if a switch was flipped back there. Ever since he touched her. Ever since he caught her and held her against him. Now he couldn't quit. He couldn't get enough. If Sidney was within touching distance, his hands had to find her.

Which was an easy enough fix. He just needed to get her out of his truck. Out of his day. Out of his town.

Out of his head.

That one would be harder. It took a long time the first go-around.

And now she wouldn't be leaving Sunday. Or Monday. Maybe Tuesday. Hell, he'd drive her to Boston personally by then.

He waited for the never-in-a-hurry Oscar to come with the tow truck, complaining about days off and wearing shoes and a multitude of other things. Waited for Sidney to update Teasdale on where they stood. Waited for her to slide those legs across his seat again, so he could drive around in a state of torture.

"Do you have enough clothes to make it that many days?" he asked once they were moving again.

Sidney sighed. "Well, I assume Amelia Rose has a washer and dryer?"

"Of course."

"Then I'll be okay," she said. "I always bring an extra casual outfit for the return home. Maybe I'll be the laid-back lawyer tomorrow."

"That might be better," Sawyer said, changing hands on the wheel so his right hand didn't go wandering.

"I was joking."

"I'm not," he said. "It might be more approachable. You could give Crane another shot tomorrow."

"You saying I look uptight?" Sidney asked, crossing a leg and making him do a double take. Again.

If uptight meant so hot that he wanted to shove that skirt up and do her right there in his truck, then *yes.* God, yes.

"I'm saying you looked like a million bucks, trying to reach a man on a ladder throwing pumpkins," he said.

"So I should have thrown a pumpkin?" she asked.

He grinned in her direction. "Might have been worth it."

The breathy little chuckle that accompanied the tug at her lips made his dick twitch. In that one second, she reminded him of the old days. Of the *them* they once were. He shook his head free of that. That was the last place he needed to go.

"Making a quick stop before going back to the cottage," he said.

"Where?"

"My place." The look she gave him was priceless, and he had to laugh. "To feed my dog," he said. "Relax. I forgot this morning and I'm probably working late tonight."

"Because of me," she said.

"That's what I'm telling Duke."

Not that every other reason hadn't crossed his mind

at least four hundred times, he thought as he pulled into the driveway and opened his garage.

"I'll be right back."

It only seemed a few minutes while he let Duke attack him, filled his bowls, and grabbed two bottles of water. But when he stepped back through the door to the garage, Sidney was out of the truck, in the garage, and peeling back a tarp. Her eyes going soft.

Sidney didn't know what drove her to step out and see if it was the same wheels peeking out from under that tarp. The same wheels that she'd watched all of senior year. The same wheels that almost carried her away graduation night.

But once it was in front of her, she had to see. And peeling the top back, her heart thudded in her ears as the faded black metal and cracked worn seat fell under the light. Sidney couldn't help but smile as she ran her fingers along the seams, back up to the handlebars—

"Oh—" Her breath hitched, her eyes burning with unexpected tears. "Oh my God," she whispered.

"It's been a lot of years since she saw the light of day," came Sawyer's voice from the doorway.

Sidney sucked in a breath that sounded like a hippopotamus snort, and backed up two steps. Wiping at her tears, she tried to read the troubled crease above his nose as he walked up to the other side of the bike and pulled the tarp back over it.

"I'm sorry," she said. "I didn't mean to—"

"Be nosy?" he finished.

A nervous laugh escaped her throat. "Yeah, I guess," he said. "I'm—I just saw the wheels and—I don't know." New heat filled her eyes. "My ring."

Sawyer's eyes locked on hers. "It's how I kept you with me for a while. Why I used the name you gave me."

If she could have scaled that bike gracefully to get to him, Sidney would have stripped bare and mounted him like a monkey.

He'd kept her class ring. Tied to the dashboard of his bike. He'd actually cared about her. It wasn't just a story. It wasn't just words. No one had ever done anything like that for her since. Or ever. And it was possibly the hottest thing she'd ever seen.

"Are you okay?" he asked.

Well, she was crying like a little girl. She laughed through her tears and nodded. "Just—very few things surprise me. And you keep doing that today."

He held out his arms and let them drop. "My special talent."

"Your dad," she began, unsure whether he'd want to know. "He was affected by you leaving. Just so you know."

Sawyer frowned. "What do you mean?"

"I mean, he may have been an asshole," she said, wiping two new tears away. "But after you left—after everyone pretty much knew you weren't coming back—he kind of *shrank*." Sidney watched his jaw work as he processed that. "He retired from the school early. And just sort of became—old. Before he was old."

Sawyer blinked fast and looked away, his brows knitting together like he was trying to push that image away.

"He still alive?"

"I don't really know," she said. "After Nana died, I left. There was no one there anymore to keep up with."

He nodded, blowing out a breath, physically clearing the trouble from his eyes. He peeled a corner of the tarp back instead, that being an easier subject. "You want it back?"

She shook her head. "Keep it." *Keep me.*

"Will do," he said, walking around the bike. Walking straight up to her without blinking. "Do you still have mine?"

"Of course," she said. "In a box. Inside another box."

His fingers came up to her face and wiped new tears away as she blinked them free.

"And if I wanted it back?" he said so softly she barely heard it.

"Not a chance in hell," she whispered.

A smile spread slowly across his lips. "That's my girl."

Sidney felt like a preteen, sneaking out of her room to the kitchen in her flannel pajamas. Socks on her feet, no bra, hair a mess. But she needed some of those cookies. It had been a *day*. A day followed by staring at the ceiling, totally awake for hours, thinking about too many things.

Finding the tin, she carefully removed the lid and felt her mouth water. The sense of calm and well-being and peace washed over her, just inhaling the aroma.

"I need to live on these cookies," she whispered, taking the tin and carefully sitting at the big wooden table. Closing her eyes, she took a bite. Dear God, it didn't get better than that.

A soft twinkle out the window told her it might. Moonlight. On a lake.

They had a lake?

Maybe it was just a pond. But who cared? Too many thoughts pinging around, that wasn't a good way to spend an evening. Not to mention the hijinks her libido was up to. The looks. The touches. The words. *The words.* And seeing her ring there. Tied to the handlebars like it was just yesterday that she'd pressed it into his hand. Oh God.

All the feels.

Sitting outside by the water with a brisk temperature to cool her jets? That was the ticket.

As long as there were cookies. And a blanket. Sidney grabbed the tin—she'd make some tomorrow to replace these, Lord knew she had the time—tiptoed back to her room for a warm blanket, and headed back through the kitchen to the back door. Only taking pause at a large pair of lined rain boots.

Judging from the size of them, either Amelia Rose had a man tucked away or they were Sawyer's. Sidney peered down at her stocking feet and got a little rush in her belly at the thought of wearing his boots.

That's my girl.

"Oh my God, how old are you?" she muttered under her breath, shoving her feet into them.

She wrapped the blanket around herself, tucked the tin under her arm, and opened the door, instantly glad for the blanket. The brisk night air chilled her cheeks and left clouds of vapor when she breathed. It wasn't likely to be a long sit. Grabbing a small flashlight that hung on a square-headed nail, she closed the door as quietly as she could and headed across the back patio.

Sawyer's boots clunked heavily on the wooden slats before going silent in the sod. Heading to the water's edge, Sidney started to wish she had something warmer on her body. Something under her favorite soft happy duck pajamas. But it was worth it, she thought, finding a high and dry spot to sit where the moon highlighted all the ripples on the water.

It was peaceful. Serene. So far removed from the busy chaos of Boston. Sidney could close her eyes and feel the sheer beauty of it. Only one thing could make it better. Maybe something with dirty blond hair and dark eyes, with a hard body and gentle hands and a lopsided smirk that could just about send her over the edge.

Yeah, that.

Okay, maybe two. She pulled the lid off the tin of cookies and inhaled. Oh, dear God, perfection. Selecting one and taking a bite, that feeling—the one from before, like warmth and happiness—poured over her.

This should be the first thing.

"Amelia Rose know you're out here scamming her cookies?"

Sidney yelped and dropped half the cookie when she jumped, but Sawyer scooped it right off the ground and blew on it, popping it into his mouth as he dropped down beside her.

Sidney just stared, mid-chew.

"Saw the light moving out here and thought I'd check it out," he said in explanation. "I didn't know it was just a cookie thief." He nudged at her foot with his. "Nice boots."

"You *saw?*" Sidney said around the cookie finally. "From where?"

Sawyer pointed to a warm glow coming from windows right around the curve of the water.

"My house."

"That's your house?" Sidney asked. "It didn't seem that close, earlier."

"It isn't by road," he said. "It's actually a whole separate subdivision. But our back yards are connected by a little bridge and walkway, so I keep an eye on things."

"Good thing I didn't decide to go skinny-dipping," she said.

"Well, I might have had to break out the binoculars for that," he said, nudging her with his shoulder.

Sidney laughed. "It would have been a short show, I'm afraid. That water's probably forty degrees."

"At least."

Sidney broke another cookie in half and handed it to him. Even being unexpected, this was nice. Shoulder to shoulder with him. It was easy. And real. Maybe her people skills were improving. Or maybe it was just him.

"So, I was thinking I might let you borrow my truck tomorrow," Sawyer said. "To go do whatever you need to do."

Sidney was hit with a ridiculous wave of disappointment. "Not up for the Crane tour again?"

"I just have a lot of work to do tomorrow," he said. "But I won't need Betsy."

"I'm sorry?"

"What?"

Sidney chuckled. "Who would Betsy be?"

"That's my truck," he said.

"You named it Betsy?" she asked. "For real?"

Sawyer waved what was left of his cookie at her. "You have ducks on your pj's, don't judge."

"And she was inspired by who?" Sidney said with a smirk, her eyes dropping to his lips when he turned to her. "Your first love?"

"If I would've done that," he said softly, "her name would have been Squeak."

Bam.

Sidney's heart felt like it reached out and slammed against every possible surface at once.

"Awfully pretty words again," she whispered, suddenly feeling how bare she was and pulling the blanket tighter.

He shook his head slowly. "Not just words." He looked out at the darkness on the water and rubbed at his face. "And something I've never felt again."

She couldn't breathe. And although she was almost sweating she was so infused with warmth, she started to shiver.

"Why didn't you tell me that?" she asked. "Back then?"

He smiled and shrugged. "Scared kid, I guess."

Sidney held his gaze, his eyes dark pools of black in the moonlight. Finally she nodded. "Yeah, me too," she whispered.

He blinked and narrowed his eyes questioningly. "Meaning?"

"Meaning, hello?" she said. "I was running off with you. Breaking all the rules." Sidney swallowed hard. "What did you think?"

Chapter 11

She was shivering in the cold and had just admitted that she once loved him. What did he think? That his damn head was spinning, that's what. But he could feel her arm shaking next to his, and physical he could deal with. It was tangible. She was cold. He could fix cold.

Pushing to his knees, he shrugged off his thick jacket.

"Here," he said, moving to face her, knees to knees. He tugged the blanket down and enveloped her shoulders in the jacket, warm from his body.

"I don't need—"

"Hush," he said, pulling it tight around her, closer to him, his knuckles resting against the softness of her breasts. The puffs of their breaths were mingling. "Just—" And then her lips parted slightly. And her eyes went impossibly shiny. And he was pulling her in. Or she was. All he knew was that his hands were on their own again, traveling up her neckline, feeling that silky skin, cupping her face, watching her eyes watch his mouth.

"Sidney."

"I know." Her voice was husky as their foreheads touched.

"I need you," he breathed, unsure where that thought came from. Since when did he need anyone? Since right that second, evidently, because closing that space between them was all that mattered in the whole damn world.

"I need you more," she said, her eyes fluttering closed, her face tilted as if her mouth was searching on its own.

He felt her hands moving up his chest, and knew it would be his undoing. He was wrong. Her lips brushing against his was.

Sawyer let his eyes close and his body take over. His mouth on hers, taking, giving, tasting, needing. Those lips he'd finally kissed one night twelve years ago. And compared to every woman since. That perfect mouth, better than any drug, as hungry for him as he was for her. Her head tilted perfectly so that each could dive into the other. One of his hands went up into her hair, pulling her deeper, as both of hers wrapped around his head, fingers in his hair, kissing him with her entire body.

Fuck, he couldn't remember a kiss ever being this hot. This complete. This everything. Until the little moaned sigh escaped her throat. And then all the switches turned on.

She couldn't stop.

The cold was forgotten. So many alarms going off in her head, and none of them mattered as much as kissing this man. Not just any man. This one. This one who stole her heart years ago, and made her skin tingle with every look, every touch, and now every taste. He kissed her with all he had, sliding her body to him so that she straddled his legs.

Oh God, she was toast. He felt amazing under her hands, against her body, it couldn't just be that—*shit*—his hands slid up her legs, grabbing her ass and tugging her tightly against him, making her wrap her legs around him and move on her own, kicking off the heavy boots behind his back so she could lock her ankles.

What was she doing?

She didn't know. All she knew was that she couldn't stop touching him. Stop kissing him. Stop moving like they were made to fit together, hands and mouths roaming, desperate to touch everything they could reach.

"God, Sidney," he growled against her mouth, his hands finding skin under her shirt, sliding up her back, moving to the front, cupping a full bare breast in one hand as he dragged his mouth from hers to taste all the way down her neck. All as she twisted her fingers in his hair and continued her leg vise around him, moving herself in a torturous rhythm that had her dizzy with desire. Then the buttons—they were gone—and his mouth was on her breast, hot and wet and—fuck, she was going to lose it.

"Caleb," she moaned.

"Sawyer," he corrected, sucking her nipple into his mouth.

"Fuck!" she cried, arching her back and grinding herself against something she desperately needed to be freed. "I don't care," she breathed. "Just, please, God, I need you."

In less than a second, he had her flipped onto her back, the cold ground seeping through her shirt but she didn't care.

"Are you okay?" he asked, his face looking strained

even in the low light. His hand brushed hair from her eyes as he quickly tucked the blanket under her head. "Baby, are you sure?"

She pulled his face down to hers, kissing him passionately. Was she supposed to be hard to get after all these years? If so, she wasn't there. She wanted him like she wanted to breathe. In fact, breathing wasn't all that important. Her breasts were open to the moonlight, each nipple getting a lick to chill them before he pulled her pajama pants down in one move and unfastened his jeans in the next.

"God, you're beautiful," he said through his teeth, pulling her left leg up over his shoulder at the same time that Sidney's hands pulled him free, stroking him in her need. "Jesus, God, baby, please," he growled, shuddering, moving the tiny strip of fabric aside.

Bucking under the flick of his fingers, Sidney cried out, pulling him inside her, taking him in as he thrust, groaning as he bottomed out and filled her up and she wrapped her other leg around him. Oh God, it wasn't going to be long. It wasn't going to be—*fuck*—the build started almost immediately as their bodies found the natural rhythm. His fingers digging in to her thigh as he pumped into her, one hand on her face, eyes burning into her.

She felt everything tense and begin to shake uncontrollably as the wave crescendo went barreling so hard and so fast she couldn't breathe.

"Sawyer," she gasped, her fingers fisted in his hair. She forced her eyes to stay on his as it hit her with all the subtlety of a freight train, pulling a sound from her that was pure primal ecstasy as his own roar of release nearly drowned it out.

* * *

Never in his life had a sexual encounter left Sawyer shaking and speechless. Never. He was a man. He typically got up and walked away. He'd had some intense experiences, and some damn crazy-hot antics, but this—this with Sidney was something else. This was his damn heart on a spigot.

And that was something he hadn't felt in a hell of a long time.

That was dangerous.

"Sidney," he said, finding his breath, finding his voice, coming back to her mouth, kissing her top lip and then her bottom one.

"Mmm," she said, her eyes still closed as if opening them would make it be over. "So, that just happened."

He gazed down at her, smoothing the hair back from her forehead. This was that girl. The one he always wanted. Miraculously lying beneath him in a state of post-orgasmic bliss. And somehow he knew he only had minutes. Seconds, maybe. Because even though he hadn't been around her in over a decade, he knew her. And reality was about to dawn in that head of hers.

"Yes, it did," he said.

"Oh my God, I'm not usually this easy," she whispered.

"And I'm not usually that fast," he said. A husky laugh bubbled up from her chest, warming him as she opened her eyes. He ran a finger down her cheek. "You called me Sawyer, too."

She chuckled, and it resonated through her body to him. Those eyes opened and focused on him, and the jab to the gut was like shooting back in time.

"Eventually."

"I gave you a pass on the first one," he said, resting his lips against her forehead. "You were distracted."

Another chuckle turned into a deeper laugh. "Dude,

you may have been Sawyer for twelve years, but I've known you that way for about twelve minutes, so the fact that I remembered anything in the heat of *that* is a miracle."

Sawyer was hit again by her smile, by the seriousness that took it over. By what he knew was coming. Especially the longer she just lay there, still, looking up at him. Each second that ticked by made him more and more hers. And that was going to hurt.

"What do you think would have happened?" she whispered finally. "Back then? If—"

Her words trailed off, but he didn't need the rest of the sentence.

"You would have fallen madly in love with me," he said, going for light.

Sidney's eyes welled up with tears, however, and she laughed to blink them free, sending them back into her hairline.

"I was already there," she said.

Bam.

Fuck, it was like a roundhouse kick to the chest. He closed his eyes for a couple of seconds to keep it together. "Then I would have screwed it up," he said, moving his thumb along her cheek. "I'm so sorry that I hurt you," he said, almost not getting the words out.

Sidney nodded, and her hands came up to his face. "I'm sorry he hurt *you*," she whispered, her words catching.

Everything inside him burned like someone stuck a fire poker right through his chest. Her eyes seared right through him as the quiet screamed. He couldn't do this. He *couldn't do this.*

"Okay," he said, kissing her hand softly. "Let's—"

"Yeah," she said quickly, wiping at her face. "We should probably—"

"Before we get arrested or something."

"Or your boss wakes up."

"Yeah, if that's not a mood killer, I don't know what is," Sawyer said, laughing lightly and feeling anything but light.

He helped her up as she held her shirt together—buttons scattered to the far corners of the earth. Found her pants about ten feet away and helped her back into them and back into his boots. It was clinical and polite and robotic and chilly in a way that had nothing to do with the frigid air, and it formed a sick pit in his stomach. She gathered up the blanket and the tin of cookies and turned back to him, her mouth open and poised to say something.

He wanted her to say something. Needed it. Because there was so much to say and he was suddenly struck mute and stupid.

Hold her. Kiss her. Do something.

Her mouth closed, and something in her eyes faded. He could see that even in the dark.

"Guess we got our night," she said softly, giving a little grin with a head tilt.

He smiled, feeling the frown behind it. Wondering if she could see it.

Don't agree. Tell her . . .

"Yeah," he said.

She nodded. "Good night," she whispered. And turned. Walked away. In his boots.

He stared after her, watching her silhouette get darker until the back door of the cottage opened to the tiny nightlight inside. He picked up the small flashlight she'd forgotten and walked it over to the back patio, leaving it by the door.

"I wanted forever."

Chapter 12

Sidney woke up to dawn making an appearance outside her window, something hard scratching her back, and her eyes the size of basketballs.

"Just shoot me," she moaned, holding her temples as she rolled over and the pounding started.

She couldn't cry before bedtime. Not like that. Not the full-out gut-destroying meltdown she'd had when she came in from—from him—and closed the door.

She hadn't even made it out of the kitchen. She'd slid down the door to the floor and wailed like a baby. The ugly, snot-inducing, chest-hurting, I'll-never-breathe-right-again kind. Like she'd only done one other time in her life.

Over the same damn person.

Something she swore would never take her down again. Ever. And yet here she was, with a cry hangover from hell and eyelids that felt like they'd been blown up into flotation devices.

And more than that. Her heart hurt.

Because that other thing she did last night? Sidney

couldn't do that, either. Sex just for sex didn't exist for her. That was why she hadn't gotten herself laid in so long. Because sex meant something. And it should. It didn't get more intimate than that. It didn't get more personal. It should be with someone you love, or at least have a feeling or two over.

What it should *not* be, at least in Sidney's case, was with someone you *once* loved. Who stole your heart, broke it, vanished, strode back in with said heart riding shotgun, and managed to claim it all over again. Sex and *that* situation should avoid each other at all costs.

Yeah.

This was not what Sidney came to this damn blink-and-you-miss-it town for. To fall back under the spell of the same damn guy. No matter how amazing it felt.

There might have been a misunderstanding the first time around, but there wasn't this time. They were different people now, living different lives. In different states. He had his—Sawyer Finn world, and she had hers. And the rest of reality. Their chemistry might still be off the charts, but they couldn't stay attached at the mouth 24/7 in order to have something in common.

The unmistakable aroma of coffee reached her, pulling her from pity to need, and she rolled back over, grimacing at whatever was digging into her spine and groping at her open shirt, mortified that the buttons were gone. Well, not gone, exactly. They were on the property if she really wanted to go looking, but—then again, Sawyer could just find them one day with the lawn mower.

And no, she wasn't that girl. The one who stayed in her sex clothes so she could fall asleep smelling him.

No. No way.

"Grow some ovaries, will you?" Sidney muttered, sitting up and shrugging off the pajama top. And stopping dead still with it in her hands.

Along the center back, scratching and annoying her, was a line of dried mud. Mud. From lying on her back.

A little burn hit her very tender eyes at the thought of that moment, and she tossed the shirt aside and stood. She would not be that pathetic woman.

Coffee was going to have to save her. Thank God Amelia Rose was an early riser.

Sawyer slung empty water bottles from his floorboard, and crushed an old hardware store list in his hand. Cleaning out his truck to lend it to Sidney.

In the dark.

He clenched his jaw as tightly as his fist was around that paper, closing his eyes against the memory of everything from last night. Her laugh, her taste, her body exposed for him under the moonlight. Her hands on him. The primal way she'd moaned his name. The way they fit. The way they moved.

And that was just the sex. That didn't even take into account all the *everything elses* that he always worked so hard to avoid. The magnetic fucking need to be around her. Chasing her through town. Making her business his. Walking over to the cottage last night—he knew damn good and well who that was, and there he had to go like a stupid kid. Because he could not leave well enough alone. He had to go sit by her and her idiotic duck pajamas that were so ugly they were hot. See those eyes that never failed to slay him. Looking at him like *that,* turning his whole world upside down in one night.

Who was he kidding? She'd uprooted everything the second he saw her sitting in Amelia Rose's kitchen.

Sawyer slammed his fist against the dashboard, sending tiny dust particles running for their lives. Damn it, he didn't have time for this. This *mooning* crap. Feelings. This was why he didn't do love.

And that was why he was dropping off his truck before she woke up. Because he was a chickenshit. Duke jumped in the truck and looked at him as if he agreed.

"We're just rolling up the road, buddy," Sawyer said.

Duke's tail thumped against the seat.

Amelia Rose looked exactly the same at five thirty in the morning as she did at five thirty in the afternoon. Perfectly put together, in her version of together. Hair still meticulously braided over one shoulder. Beads of every variety still dangling. Timeless smile still warming the room.

Pancakes and a fresh pot of coffee in her hands made her look even warmer.

"I might love you," Sidney said, taking the pot from her and pouring into both their mugs.

"I'll take it," Amelia Rose said, chuckling. "I don't normally have anyone to share morning coffee with, so I'm enjoying the company." She sat down across from her just as Sidney took a large bite of a pancake dipped in honey butter and homemade blueberry syrup. "I think Sawyer is, too, if last night is any indication."

Sidney nearly choked, slapping a hand over her mouth so she didn't blow pieces of pancake.

"He—um—we—" Sidney managed around her food, taking a swallow of coffee to push down what had become cardboard.

"Relax," Amelia Rose said. "A lot of couples come here, Sidney. It's not the first time. Won't be the last."

"Oh my God," Sidney mumbled, dropping her fork

and covering her face. She shook her head. "No. No. I am so—I have no words. He's your employee."

Amelia Rose started to laugh. "Sawyer is much more than that," she said. "He's like a son to me."

"Yeah, that's not better," Sidney said behind her fingers.

"And I suspect he's the reason you were up all night crying?" Okay, this day wasn't going uphill from yesterday. Just more bizarre. If that was possible. "I have some witch hazel for your eyes," she whispered.

"He didn't—" Sidney shook her head slightly, dropping her hands and her gaze. "He didn't do anything. It was just a bad idea. Too much history."

She took one of Sidney's hands in her own, and Sidney felt the instant change. There was no oil. No artificial anything. Just the elderly woman's cool skin against hers, and the overwhelming comforting aroma of butter. Again. Of course her plate did happen to be filled with it. But peace, and warmth, and an almost buzzing calm instantly rested her anxious core.

"You were the one," Amelia Rose said softly.

"That's what people keep telling me," Sidney said, her voice sounding sad to her own ears.

"And you're in love with him," Amelia Rose said.

The pierce to her heart somehow didn't destroy her calm, but it did bring tears to her swollen eyes.

"I—can't," Sidney said, laughing as she swiped at her eyes. "I know that sounds silly, and even sillier to have this discussion after seeing him for one day, but—"

"But you've worked hard to keep up this persona," she said. "To keep all your walls carefully maintained. To not let anyone hurt you again. To not feel anything."

Sidney's breath caught in her chest. "Something like that."

"Yeah, I know someone else with that same agenda,"

Amelia Rose said, patting her hand. "Here's a little news flash for both of you," she said, turning Sidney's hand over so that her palm faced up. She ran her fingers over Sidney's palm, and turned it back over. "Love doesn't work like that."

Sidney glanced down at her hand and back up to the old woman's gray eyes. "What did you just see?"

Amelia Rose's lips curved up at the corners. "I thought you didn't believe."

The back door opening broke the spell, carrying a certain Sawyer Finn and a large dog along with it. Sawyer was concentrating on hanging the flashlight back on the nail, and not looking up. The dog headed straight for Sidney.

"Hey, tell Sidney I dropped the truck off for her," he said. "Duke, get back—"

His words stopped cold when he turned and saw her sitting at the table.

Sidney felt the dog's head push under her hand, sniffing upward toward the food, but she couldn't look away from the weight of the dark eyes in front of her. She felt every inch of the maybe six feet between them, and was suddenly hyperaware of her homeless urchin appearance. The same pajama pants—the ones he'd stripped off of her—with a T-shirt that read *Do Boston*. Hair pulled back in a messy ponytail. No makeup to disguise the carnival-mirror facial features she had going on. Oh yeah. Just what she wanted him to see the day after they'd made love. Had sex. *Made love.*

"Well, this scene is familiar," Amelia Rose said.

Sidney rose to her feet, impulse driving her. Yesterday, she'd been slammed by seeing him again, and had reacted like a silly girl. She was a grown woman now, and could certainly fake her way through a post-sex greeting. Even though he was slowly walking toward her. Without blinking. Looking way better in his jeans and long-sleeved pullover than should be legal. She lifted her chin.

"Good morning," she said.

"Morning," he said, his voice sounding sleepy and sexy, like he hadn't had coffee yet. Sidney swallowed hard against that thought.

He reached for her hand and pressed his keys into it, the metal warm from his hand. "Try to bring her back in one piece."

Sidney smirked. "I might change her name."

One eyebrow raised, and she had the feeling she wasn't the only one glad for the brevity. "To what, may I ask?"

Sidney shrugged. "I don't know. Maybe I'll try out a 'Home, James,' and see if it responds," she said, playing on his last name.

"She's not a James," he said with a wink.

A wink that made her knees wiggle and caused her gaze to fall to his mouth. No, don't look there.

"She's not a *she*, either," Sidney whispered, leaning forward just a bit.

"Why is this dog in my house?" Amelia Rose asked, reaching down to scratch above his wagging tail.

"He—" Sawyer cleared his throat. "He wanted to ride," he said. "Probably smelled the pancakes all the way over here."

"Help yourself," Amelia Rose said, gesturing at the platter.

Sidney would give him hers, for all the good it was doing her. Nothing was going down her throat at this point. It was closed for business.

"No, I'm good," he said. He looked at her too long, too intently, like he was looking for some kind of answer. She needed to look away, but damn it if she could. "You okay?" he asked, his voice low.

She smiled and nodded and focused downward at the dog, blinking fast before all those damn feelings of hers decided to make a showing. "Perfect," she said, petting the animal's head. "I'll get it back to you as soon as I go see Crane."

Sawyer nodded and backed up a step.

"No rush," he said, snapping his fingers for the dog and making her jump. "Take your time." He glanced at Amelia Rose. "Cornucopia tomorrow, okay?"

She looked up at him sideways with amused eyes. "No rush."

Sidney saw him smirk before he walked toward the door. "Come on, Duke," he said. "Ladies."

And he was gone.

Sidney took a slow breath and rolled her head on her shoulders as she sank back down. "Okay, that's over," she breathed.

"Sweet girl, it's only just begun," Amelia Rose said, chuckling and pushing to her feet.

"What?"

"That man is just as head over heels as you are," she said. "And just as hardheaded."

Sidney's stomach flipped. "Why—why do you say that?"

"Because I know him, for one," she said. "He doesn't do this. This dance you two are doing. But second? He just handed you *Betsy*."

Sidney laughed, the first feel-good emotion she'd had since late last night. "True." She rubbed her face, wishing she could squeeze her eyes back to normal. "But there's too much—and I live in Boston." To her, that explained it all.

Amelia Rose went to the sink and turned around. "That's geography, Sidney. People are portable."

Sidney laughed again, feeling a scoff coming on that

weirdly faded as Amelia Rose walked closer. "And I don't—"

"Don't do small towns," she said, waving a hand dismissively. "I know." How did she know? Had Sidney mentioned that? "Tell me about Crane," the older woman said, cutting off Sidney's thought. "Why are you going to see Edmund Crane?"

"He's the one holding the lease over Mr. Teasdale's head," Sidney said. "He's playing hardball, and honestly, it makes no sense."

Amelia Rose sat back down, her eyes intense and amused. "Let me tell you about another love story," she said. "And then, if you don't mind, I'd like to tag along?"

Chapter 13

"Yes, Orchid," Sidney responded for the third time. "I'm working on it."

"I gave you the overnight stay," Orchid said over the speaker. Even with the phone sitting on the bed across the room, Sidney's boss's voice carried annoyingly well. "Honestly, I assumed you'd be heading back today. Now you're telling me it could be Tuesday?"

"Oh my God, stay with me," Sidney whispered to her reflection where she was trying to get ready.

"What was that?" came Orchid's grating voice.

"Nothing," Sidney said, twisting her hair into a professional bun, then remembering her casual look for the day and letting it fall in soft waves. "I told you, it's not about the case. I've got that under control," she lied. "My *car* broke down. I'm stuck here till it's fixed."

"Well, keep me in the loop on the wrap-up," Orchid said. "Fax me the resolution paperwork. And I'll pay for one more night there, but after that it's on you."

"Okay, thanks," Sidney said, saluting her. As soon as there was a dial tone, she made a face. Because waiting was logical. She blew out a breath, meeting her own eyes in the mirror. "You have to make this work. You have to make this happen. Because you don't like the mailroom people."

"Wouldn't have pictured you as a truck kind of girl," Amelia Rose said, sliding into the passenger seat as Sidney got behind the wheel of Sawyer's truck. "But you totally pull this off."

Sidney laughed, turning over the engine and kicking it into gear. "My nana drove a pickup, actually, and I learned to drive in that. Took me a while to settle into a smaller car, although I wish now I would have just kept her truck. That thing refused to die."

"Can't buy a new one?" Amelia Rose asked.

Sidney sighed. "I can. Technically. I have some money my nana left me, but I just don't want to spend it. I want there to be something special for that. Not something as ordinary as a car."

"You getting stranded isn't ordinary," she said. "I'll bet she'd want you to be safe and comfortable."

"I know," Sidney said. "It just hasn't felt right."

She might have looked at ease behind Sawyer's wheel, but it felt weird, seeing life where he normally did. Noting the gas receipt paper clipped to the visor. The fast food napkin folded in the cubby where an ashtray used to be. A scribbled note on a Post-it. A bottle of water tucked into the door pocket. Sidney was thinking entirely too much. It was just a truck. But it was little pieces of his life, and suddenly those pieces mattered.

Everything mattered. This town, these people, their stories.

Amelia Rose told her more than just a love story. She told her about the couple on the other side of the lake who met at a party, about the woman who owned the party shop in town who finally opened her heart, about Mrs. Duggar in the dress shop who found her soul mate after forty years, about a man at the local bank who authorized the loan for the couple across the lake to buy a house, coming to the cottage to sit down with them, and the Realtor, whom he ended up marrying four months later. And she told Sidney about Edmund Crane and Arthur Teasdale, and Layla, the woman they both loved.

Pulling in and knocking on Crane's door was the easy part. Sidney's people skills were going to have to rise and shine. Amelia Rose standing next to her on the porch was either going to help that or sink her where she stood.

"Smile, sweetheart," she said. "You look a dream in that pretty sweater, and Edmund Crane is a sucker for a pretty girl."

Sidney had taken Sawyer's advice and gone with her soft blue jeans, flats, and a white fuzzy fitted sweater that settled against her cleavage a little more than she liked. She didn't even know why she'd packed it, as her style was more conservative, but there it was. And she didn't really have a choice.

"He wasn't too suckered yesterday," Sidney said under her breath. "He basically called my bluff and informed me of the favor he was doing me, getting my car fixed."

The big wooden door opened, and Crane's large frame took up the open space.

"Imagine seeing you—" he began. Then he saw Amelia Rose, and one would think he'd been poked with a live wire. Stepping back and stretching to his full height, his whole head turned red. "What are you doing here?"

"Hello, Edmund," she said pleasantly. "How've you been?"

"Alive and well, thanks," he blustered, turning to a bemused Sidney. "Did your car not get towed?"

"Yes, it did," Sidney said, looking back and forth between them as Crane kept darting glances to Amelia Rose. "And Oscar said he'd order whatever parts on Monday, so I'm—basically here till it's done."

"Staying at the cottage," Amelia Rose chimed in. "You know, I get a little stir-crazy in there, Sidney, maybe I'll ride around with you while you're in town."

"Where are you from again?" Crane said quickly. "New York?"

"Boston," Sidney said.

"No problem," Crane said. "I'll get you a car to drive back. I have some inventory in my car lot in Portland, last year's models. I'll have one delivered by four this afternoon."

Sidney's mouth fell open. "What?"

"Sure," he said, holding out an arm like that had been on the table all along. "Keep it as long as you need."

"As—long as I need," Sidney echoed.

"Absolutely."

"Why, that's just princely of you, Edmund," Amelia Rose said. "Now she can go back to work and tell her boss the case is all settled."

His mouth opened and closed repeatedly like a fish.

"Unless it's not settled?" she asked, frowning. "Honestly, I haven't kept up."

"That's more complicated than just a car," he said.

"Actually, not really," Sidney said, miraculously finding her voice. "As I understand it, you're holding the contract—that was signed in good faith and kept up in good terms for almost ten years—over Mr. Teasdale's head as a personal vendetta?"

"As a *what?*" Crane bellowed.

"You heard me," Sidney said. "You rented that building to him and his wife as a way to stay in contact with Layla Teasdale," Sidney said.

"Layla *Barton*," Crane muttered. "She never should have become a Teasdale."

"Yep, keep making my case for me," Sidney said with a smile. "And then when she died, and her husband closed the shop, you refused to let him out. Out of spite."

"Out of respect for Layla," he said. "She loved that shop. It made her smile. Even after she got sick." Crane pushed through the door and walked to the end of the porch. "She'd be crushed to see it closed like that."

"She'd be crushed to see her husband go into financial ruin paying rent for nothing," Sidney said. "All so you can stick it to the man who got her?"

"You don't get it," he said, whirling around. "Have you ever been in love, little girl?"

Sidney's mouth went dry. "I hardly think—"

"It doesn't come again," he said. "You think it will, but it won't. You have to grab on before someone steals it from you." Sidney felt Amelia Rose's eyes on her. "I've been married and divorced four times. Because *he* got the love of my life. At one of *her* parties!" he finished, pointing at Amelia Rose.

Sidney looked at Amelia Rose. "Okay, this just got wonky," she said under her breath.

"Edmund, you've been blaming me, blaming Arthur, even blaming Layla and probably all your ex-wives for years. Blaming everyone for your unhappiness except for you," Amelia Rose said. "Take some ownership of your life, will you?"

"She and I were just fine till they hooked up at that cottage," he said. "With all your voodoo."

"Good Lord, Edmund," she said, laughing. "Voodoo?

Really? How about good old-fashioned chemistry and a man who didn't boss her around?" Amelia Rose stepped closer. "Forty years ago. Let it go."

"And then you took Sawyer," he growled.

"Who wasn't a child," Amelia Rose said gently. "I didn't win custody. I offered him a job. Didn't yell at him or make him do shady things."

"We aren't here to talk about Sawyer," Sidney said, trying to rope the conversation back in. This was what had happened with the Carson Foods account meeting, and she couldn't bear another one of those. "We're here to resolve this case. And I have to be honest with you, Mr. Crane," she said. "If you insist on this insane breach of ethics, you'll need to contact your own lawyer. Because we'll bleed you dry in court."

"Court?" he repeated.

Yes, and she prayed he wouldn't bite. Her case would win, but she didn't know whether she had the skills for court.

"Over this petty crap," Sidney added.

Crane's mouth worked again, his face went red again, and then his lips pressed in a hard line.

"Fine."

"Fine, what?" Sidney asked.

"He can have out," Crane muttered. "I'll sit with that elephant till I can sell it."

Sidney felt like her feet might leave the ground. She'd won. She'd fucking won. She'd won for Orchid's uncle! She wasn't a loser after all.

"Excellent choice," Sidney said, pulling a file from the bag on her shoulder. "If you'd just sign—here and here."

"Seriously, you brought it with you?"

"Wasn't a social call," Sidney said. "And thanks for the car, by the way!"

It was all she could do not to squeal on the way back to the truck, and even then she had to wait till she was out of the driveway.

"Oh my God!" she yelled, banging the steering wheel.

"Careful," Amelia Rose said. "Betsy might talk."

"That was—that was crazy," Sidney gushed. "Freaking crazy. I've never—just wow."

"You were impressive," Amelia Rose said.

Sidney's head jerked her way. "Me? No, no, no, that was you."

"No, ma'am," Amelia Rose said. "I might have flustered him, but you went in for the kill and took it," she said. "That was phenomenal to watch."

Sidney looked at her and blinked. "You think?"

"I know." Amelia Rose patted her arm, and Sidney felt warmth go to her toes. "And I think your nana would be proud."

Oh, there was a button to push. Sidney's eyes burned, and she sucked in a cold breath to stem it. No more crying. She'd done enough of that.

"Too bad you don't like small towns," Amelia Rose said, looking out her window. "We could use a people-lawyer like you around here."

Sidney almost choked. "People-lawyer?"

"Yes," Amelia Rose said. "Don't look so shocked. Someone to work for the little guy, like you just did."

Sidney chuckled. "There's something I've never been accused of. And operating out of my falling-apart car probably would be a little too much *little guy*."

"I don't know," Amelia Rose said. "I happen to know of an old soda shop going on the market." Sidney met her eyes as the older woman shrugged. "I'm betting you could get it for a steal. Could be a *worthy* investment."

Sidney faced forward again, the words bouncing

around the inside of the truck. She shook her head. "That would be crazy."

Amelia Rose smirked. "Boy, if I had a nickel." She slapped her knee. "But—you have to go where you're happiest. So. Going back to Boston tonight?"

All Sidney's happy vibes melted away into the vinyl seat. *Back to Boston. Where you're happiest.* Once upon a time, she would have said those two things went together, but not lately. Not job-wise. And not—not now.

"I suppose I am," Sidney said, hearing the disappointment in her own voice. "I guess the fun is over."

This was what she'd wanted since she'd arrived yesterday. Good grief, was that just yesterday? Since she'd laid eyes on *him,* all she had focused on was being able to get the hell out of there. To get back to normal.

Here you go, Sidney. Now you can leave.

"Well, you do know you can come back to visit any time, don't you?" Amelia Rose asked.

"Be careful," Sidney said, smiling. "I may take you up on that."

"I know someone else who might appreciate it, as well," Amelia Rose said, nodding her head sideways as they parked in front of the cottage.

Nodding in the direction of a man in worn jeans and a denim jacket over a black pullover shirt. Blowing a multitude of colored leaves with a leaf blower, corralling them into a big pile. Her chest tightened around her heart, watching him. She had to say good-bye. God, how was she going to do that?

How did a quick drive to Maine to get herself out of a pickle—get so pickled?

Chapter 14

Sawyer saw his truck pull up in front of the cottage, and he was both relieved and wary. They hadn't been gone long. Certainly not long enough to deal with Crane. His first concern was for Amelia Rose, but she got out laughing. Then out climbed Sidney. In soft jeans that hugged her ass and showed her every move, and a sweater that begged to be touched.

"Fuck me," he muttered under his breath.

He'd touched enough last night. Touched enough to make her cry and keep him up all night. And very little of that had to do with body parts.

"Walk away," he said under his breath, turning toward the shed.

It was lunchtime. A reasonable excuse to make himself scarce, head the back way home for a sandwich and some sanity. Keep some distance between himself and the woman he couldn't stop thinking about. He had two days or so left to pace that out, so he had to start now. He had no business falling for Sidney Jensen. Again.

He stowed the blower back in its place and turned in time for his gut to take a kick. Sidney was walking up to the doorway, looking like an angel. An angel who instantly had his dick hard with about fifteen different ideas, and his heart not hard enough.

"Hey," she said, crossing her arms.

"Hey."

"Just—bringing back your keys," she said, uncrossing her arms again and dangling the key ring from a finger.

"That was fast," he said, walking up to her, knowing he shouldn't. Knowing that nervous hair tuck and defiant lift of her chin meant that she was just as worked up as he was and that any contact between them would be combustible.

His feet weren't listening.

"Yeah, it went pretty quickly once—" Sidney gasped with a nervous little laugh when he took the keys and her hand in one move and didn't let go. He couldn't. Damn it. "Once—Amelia Rose got involved," she finished breathily.

"She's tricky like that," he said, using her hand to pull her closer. Inhaling the clean scent of her hair as their bodies touched and her free hand slid up his side to his chest. *Fuck.* "So he caved?"

He had no idea what words were falling from his mouth as his hands came up that magical sweater to her neck, her face. Her eyelashes fluttered a little as his thumb brushed her lips.

"Sawyer," she whispered.

"I'm gonna kiss you," he said, nearly there, the feel of her driving him mad. It didn't matter how bad an idea it was. Or how much he'd pay for it later. He couldn't not touch her as long as she was here. It wasn't possible.

"I'm going home," she said.

"I know."

"Today."

That word stopped his progression toward her mouth, just centimeters away, and his eyes locked on hers.

"Walking to Boston, are you?" he asked.

He felt her fingers curl into his shirt, another tell. She wanted him, regardless of her confusing words.

"Crane is sending me a car."

And that went past confusing, straight into delusional.

"Say *what?*" Sawyer asked, backing up an inch to see her eyes better.

"I know," she said. "But he's having it delivered here. A loaner till my car's fixed."

He had to back up another few inches, and dropped his hands to land on hers.

"He gave up the case with Teasdale, *and* lent you a car?" he asked.

Sidney bit her bottom lip. "Apparently."

"Because?"

"Because I think he wants me out of town and not to hang around Amelia Rose anymore," she said.

Sawyer laughed at that. "Gotta love that the one person he's afraid of in this town weighs maybe a hundred and ten soaking wet." He looked down at their hands. His on hers, against his chest. He nodded and squeezed as he let them go and backed away. All the way away, to a stool on the other side of the shed by the lawn mower. He sank onto it. Distance.

"I'm kind of on the hot seat at work, so getting back on time will be a plus with my boss," she said, looking at her empty hands like she didn't know what to do with them.

"Winning the case?" he said.

"Will just break me even."

He chuckled. "Well, then I'm glad it all worked out for you."

Her gaze dropped, and sadness draped her features as the silence stretched.

"Sawyer—" she began.

No. He wasn't going to do a painful good-bye with her. Hell, leaving without saying a word like he did last time would be better than that.

"I just want you to be happy, Sid," he said. "Where you are, what you're doing, who you are. Just tell me you're happy."

The troubled eyes that looked back at him told him anything but, and her slow stroll in his direction looked like something more final than an answer.

"I'm gonna miss you, Sawyer Finn," she said softly, sliding her arms around his neck. "I never thought I wanted to find you," she said, her voice giving way to emotion. "And now I can't imagine—"

Sawyer pulled her to him with a smile he didn't feel, everything inside him screaming not to let this end this way. Not to let her go. Not after all these years. It had been over a decade since he'd felt raw pain like this, and he wasn't a fan.

"Gonna miss you, too, Cinderella," he said against her neck, kissing the tender skin softly as she chuckled and pulled back.

Her hands moved to his face, her eyes brimming with tears, as she kissed him. Her lips were trembling, and when she pulled away and turned, Sawyer's chest felt like it cracked right down the center.

No.

"Wait," he said, grabbing her hand, not knowing what he was going to say but knowing something needed saying. The tears that were already falling from her eyes told him he was right. "Don't go."

"I have to," she said, her voice hoarse.

"One more night," he said, reaching. "Stay with me tonight."

Never in his life had he asked a woman to stay at his house. That was his haven, his privacy. And the thought of Sidney in it suddenly felt as natural as rain.

"You can leave as early as you need to in the morning," he said, rising to his feet and wiping her tears as fast as they came. "Please," he whispered.

"Sawyer, if I spend another night in—" She stopped and shut her eyes tight. *In his arms.* "I won't be able to walk away," she finished, the words cracking.

He pulled her as tightly to him as he could, holding her as she held him, with one sobering thought repeating itself over and over in his head. He didn't want her to walk away. Ever.

And when she finally did, she took his heart. Completely, this time.

Chapter 15

Sidney stood outside the building that housed Finley and Blossom, coffee in hand, studying the bricks that decorated the lower floor before it all gave way to glass. Like the bricks weren't good enough to continue on. Too earthy or too common. Not slick and shiny like the glass.

Then again, she could just be transferring a lot of emotional baggage to a building.

Still. She'd been standing outside for ten minutes, like some giant hand was holding her back from pushing open those doors, and there was no reason. She had nothing to fear from talking to Orchid, that would be a plus, and showing up today when she said she wouldn't be able to—well, that would be an ass-kisser, as well. Brownie points all around.

So, what was keeping her out there warming the sidewalk?

I just want you to be happy, Sid. Where you are, what you're doing, who you are. Just tell me you're happy.

Yeah, that. His voice in her head, while she waited

for the car, the whole drive home, the whole night in her cold, lonely bed after digging through storage boxes to find his ring. Wearing it on her forefinger like a teenager as she slept, instead of being skin-to-skin with him in his bed. Words that didn't make her question and doubt everything she was. Words that didn't bring to mind the look in his eyes and the feel of his arms around her and the sound of his plea for her to stay.

All the things. All the feels. All the shit that had her crying for another night, meaning that her eyelids had graduated to flying saucer level.

"Are you lost?" came a familiar voice behind her, making her jump.

"Orchid!" Sidney said, whirling around as her boss passed her by.

"Thought you were stuck in Mayberry today," Orchid said, breezing by on a wave of something that smelled expensive.

"I negotiated a car from a local dealer while mine is getting fixed," she said, crossing her fingers at the small twist of the truth. Her feet moved to catch up.

"I didn't see an e-mail come through with the lease documents," she said, pushing open the door.

"That's because I have it all with me right now," Sidney said.

"Signed?" Orchid asked, glancing over her shoulder.

"Yes, ma'am," Sidney said.

Orchid nodded as she pushed the elevator button. "I'm impressed."

Sidney felt the irritation twitch in her eyebrow. "Really? Because you told me if I couldn't do this—"

"I know what I told you," she said. "But I also thought that Mayberry would eat you up." She flashed a big smile. "You proved me wrong. If you can slice and dice in a sweet little town like that, maybe you have the heart of a cutthroat attorney after all."

. . . a cutthroat attorney . . .

We need a people-lawyer. . . .

The elevator opened, and Orchid strode in, her five-hundred-dollar heels clicking prettily on the hardwood. She turned and posed at the same time, looking at Sidney expectantly.

"Aren't you coming in?"

Sidney blinked. Last week, her biggest wish was to be successful like Orchid. It was like the colors had changed now. "Your uncle is doing okay, by the way. He's missing your aunt, but he's getting along. He'll be better now that he doesn't have to worry about her shop."

Orchid's perfectly carved brows drew together. "Okay." She punched the button to keep the doors open when they tried to close. "Whatever. Are you coming? I have a conference call in five minutes."

Goose bumps covered her entire body as she heard the words in her head before they ever came out of her mouth.

"I don't think so," she said, her voice sounding funny. "Have a good day, Miss Smith."

Orchid's eyes got huge. "*What* did you just say?"

Sidney smiled as the doors closed.

Sawyer was on a mission. Several, actually. He'd taken on three outside jobs in addition to his regular duties at the cottage, and had pretty much put himself on call for anything anyone needed doing, anywhere. Staying busy the past week was the only thing keeping him sane.

Amelia Rose kept wanting to talk about Sidney, but there was no *talking about Sidney*. There was thinking, there was dreaming, there was wishing, there was being really pissed off about Sidney, but talking? No. Sawyer was done with the subject of the one woman he ever let himself love and let go. Twice. The second time happening in one damn day.

Working around the clock was the way to go the first time, it got him through the rough patches, so he figured why the hell not. Two weeks in, he was a little tired and delirious, but his bank account would be happy.

The alert on his phone went off just as he was manhandling a dolly into the back of his truck. Next up was some furniture he'd been asked to go move around for Mr. Teasdale. Or for the new owner, actually. Crane had actually sold the place within days of letting go of the lease, and supposedly the new owner was wanting some stuff done, including moving out some of what was in there.

"Yeah, yeah, I know," he said to the phone. "No rest for the weary."

"Sawyer, can you pick up some of those wooden pallets behind the grocery store on your way back later?" Amelia Rose called from the front porch. "I have a project I want to do."

"Will do," he said. "How many do you need?"

"Six or seven," she said. "Whatever they have. But no rush."

"I won't be long," he said. "This is more a consultation than anything else," he said. "I don't know what all the new owner wants yet."

"Might be longer than you think," she said, an odd little grin on her face as she went back inside.

Okay, so Amelia Rose was having a weird day. That wasn't all that new, either.

Sawyer was hit with déjà vu as he pulled in front of the former soda shop. The last time he was there was when Sidney was there. When her car died and she actually had to speak to him, and the day began. He swallowed that back. He couldn't avoid everything in town just because Sidney had touched it.

Rubbing the back of his neck, Sawyer stepped out and closed the door with a louder squeak than normal. He didn't see Teasdale's SUV at first glance, but the avenue was busy with shoppers today. Lots of cars lined the spaces. He rolled up his sleeves to get busy, and opened the soda shop door.

First thing different was the temperature. As in, it was normal.

"One check mark in their favor," he mumbled to himself.

Second was that all the small tables and chairs were moved to one side of the soda fountain, and an impromptu office area was set up to the right of it. Complete with a desk and visitor chairs.

"Hello?" he called out. "Anybody here?" He hoped so, since it was unlocked. Surely the new owner didn't think just because this was a small town, that he could—

"I think so," came a voice behind him.

He turned on his heel, and very nearly tripped over it, as well.

"What the hell?" he said under his breath.

"Well, nice to see you, too," she said. *Sidney Jensen* said.

"What—how—what are you doing here?" he asked, his mind jumbling over itself.

She was standing maybe eight feet away, in jeans and a Snoopy sweatshirt, sneakers on her feet and a nervous smile tugging at her lips. She tucked a lock of hair behind her ear, and he thought his knees might give.

"Well, I kind of have to be here now that I've signed those pesky papers," she said, holding up her hands.

"So I drove in this morning and Mr. Teasdale and I have been going over the building—"

"What?" Sawyer said. "The building—what papers?"

"The kind that say 'Sidney Jensen, Owner,' " she said.

Chills traveled his skin, the kind that women get, and it probably made him a world-class wuss, but holy shit balls—she just said that.

"Are you serious?" he said, still not moving.

"Well, they also say 'Sidney Jensen, Attorney,' " she said. "But that's really more for the sign I'll hang. And I'm thinking of maybe something about cookies, too, but I need to talk to Amelia Rose about that."

"Don't fuck with me," Sawyer said, moving one foot forward.

Sidney started to laugh, and crossed her arms over her chest. "Um, no fucking going on."

"Don't play with me," he said, taking two more slow steps toward her, as she continued to laugh and backed up. "You're here? You're—moving here?"

"That's the plan," she said, stopping as she backed into the soda fountain bar. Her eyes—those eyes that drove him crazy with desire and love and frustration—grew large and dark and sexy as she realized she had nowhere to go. "I mean, I could commute from Boston, but you know my car kind of sucks, and—"

Two steps and his mouth was on hers, tasting her laugh, absorbing her following sigh of wanting and need. Her arms went around him as he dove into her mouth, taking everything he'd missed over the last two weeks. Kissing her till they were both breathless, till their hands were just as needy as their mouths.

Breaking away, he held her face in his hands, loving how her eyes were so dilated they were almost black.

"This is real?" he breathed.

"This is real," she said, her lips smiling against his.

"Why?" he asked. "Why would you give up—"

"I didn't give up anything," she said, her fingers working in his hair. "You made all that noise about being *happy*, so—" She stopped to take a breath and look at him, and fuck if it didn't take away his. "Happy was here," she whispered.

Sawyer shook his head slowly in disbelief, pressing a soft kiss to her lips and breathing her in. "I love you," he whispered against them. "I've always loved you."

"I love you, too," she whispered back, her voice shaking.

"So, what are you going to do with this bar?" he asked, needing to back up the emotion train before it ran him over.

She swiped under her eyes and laughed. "No idea," she said. "But it's staying. It's too cool not to stay."

"I have some ideas," he said.

"I'll bet you do," she said, kissing him once, twice, three times.

"But not until I make love to you in a bed," Sawyer said. "Slow. Thorough. No grass—"

"No mud?"

"No really large window," he said, pointing at the curtainless plate-glass window.

"I really think you shouldn't knock the grass and mud," Sidney said, moving up to a stool and wrapping her legs around him. "It was on the Rose Cottage property, after all."

"Oh," he said, laughing. "So you're saying you believe the legend?"

Sidney's eyes averted suddenly as if she had an epiphany. "Oh my God."

"What?"

" 'Your past will be your future,' " she mumbled, her chin trembling.

"What?" he repeated.

She shook her head, eyes misty, and smiled, looking at him the way she had in his mind for years. Except the girl in love was now the woman in love.

"Yeah," she said. "That's exactly what I'm saying."

Don't miss Kate Angell's newest Barefoot William novel, *No Time to Explain,* coming next month!

Chapter 1

"*Here comes the bride.*"

The wedding march echoed down the Barefoot William Boardwalk. The annual southwest Florida bridal event brought engaged and expectant women to the beach. It was a sea of sexy, sweet and everything in between. Joe 'Zoo' Zooker took it all in. Marriage made him sweat. It triggered his gag reflex. He could, however, admire the ladies planning their weddings, as long as they didn't involve him. He was a confirmed bachelor. For life.

"Does Crabby Abby's General Store sell condoms?" asked his Richmond Rogue teammate Jake Packer. Better known as Pax.

He and Pax presently leaned against the blue metallic railing that separated the boardwalk from the beach. Joe knew where the condoms were shelved. He'd stocked up earlier in the week. "They're back by the pharmacy, bottom shelf, next to douches and K-Y tubes."

"You need anything, bro?"

Joe shook his head. He had six Magnum XLs in his wallet to get him through the night.

"Be right back then." Pax pushed off the railing. He walked the short distance to purchase his protection. He planned to get lucky. So did Joe.

The team was in town for spring training, with a weekend to kill. Booze, babes, and sex would definitely come into play. Monday, and they'd turn serious. They'd live and breathe baseball. The entire team would assemble for workouts and scrimmages. Nine Roanoke Rebels would also hit the field. Affiliate Triple-A players, participating in preseason practices and an exhibition game. Showcasing their talent and hoping for the call to suit up in the majors.

Joe hated squad competition. Dean Jensen in particular got under his skin. The minor leaguer played left field. Joe's position. Joe had refused him, four years running. Under Rule 5 draft, Dean had one final year to either make the club's expanded forty-man roster or be passed over. The guy kept coming after Joe, harder and faster each season. He wouldn't let up. But then Joe wouldn't have either if the situation was reversed.

He rolled his shoulders now. Cracked his knuckles. It was too nice a day to dwell on the asshat. He turned and stared out over the Gulf. Clear skies. Turquoise water. White sugar sand. Sunbathers. Sand castles. Carnival rides, amusement arcade, and a long fishing pier stretched south. Paradise. He would retire here. Years from now. Following his last bat.

Joe waited patiently on Pax, for all of five minutes, before restlessness claimed him. He wasn't good at standing still. He was continuous motion. A few brave men mixed with the wedding-minded ladies. He tugged down the bill on his black baseball cap. His mirrored Maui Jim aviators allowed him to stare, and not be caught doing so. He stepped into the crowd. Pax would find him. Unless he found a hot babe first.

So many women. Blondes, brunettes, redheads. A chick with purple hair. The multicolored storefronts on the beachside shops were all open, welcoming the stirring breeze and aroma of salt air. The scent of freshly popped popcorn wafted, along with the aroma of chocolate fudge, cheesy nachos, cotton candy, and women's perfume.

Ladies came onto him. He was recognized by many. Flirted with by most. Inviting glances and promising smiles. His navy T-shirt scripted with *I've Broken All the Rules Today. So You'll Have to Make New Ones* drew whispered suggestions. Half naked women appealed. Kink tempted. He liked the attention. A lot.

Space was tight. Whether intentional or by accident, female bodies pressed him. Some snugged as close as skin. He didn't mind the touching. Although a few hands got downright personal. Arousal heightened his senses. He was looking for a weekend lover. No one fully caught his eye. So he kept walking with sex foremost on his mind.

Long decorated tables lined both sides of the boardwalk. Signs were visible. Bridal banners arced overhead. Women clustered, checking out the area's best photographers, florists, engraved invitations, caterers, bakers, wedding and reception venues, entertainment, hair stylists, makeup artists, prenuptial consultants, and other important services. Mannequins exhibited wedding gowns. Assorted accessories, from veils, crystal tiaras, rhinestone headbands, sashes, to jewelry came next. Along with the garters.

Garters. Worn on a bride's thigh. A total turn on. He scanned the ruffled, pearled, lacy, feathered, monogramed, broached, and rhinestoned collections. Foreplay. He might buy one for the pure pleasure of slipping it up his lady's leg, then slowly sliding it down. Sexy.

"Something blue," he heard a woman say, soft and wistful.

He glanced toward her voice. Stopped, and got an eyeful. A slender blonde stood in profile, alone at the end of the table, toying with a pale blue satin garter with a silver heart charm. He was a sucker for long hair. The sun had run its fingers through the strands, leaving them streaked and shiny. The ends touched her waist. He openly stared as she bent, her shoulders curving, her ass jutting out. Sweet cheeks outlined beneath her short skirt. Gently stretching the elastic, she worked the garter over a sandaled foot-her toenails painted silver-then up her calf, and onto her thigh. She had nice legs. Freckled knees. She straightened, admired the garter. She had yet to notice him. He appreciated her further.

Her smile came slowly, on a sigh. "Perfect, don't you think, Lori?"

He shifted his stance. Cast her in his shadow. Then removed his aviators for a better look. Twirled them by an arm. He wasn't Lori, but that didn't stop him from saying, "Hot, sweetheart."

Keep reading for a sneak peek at
HEAD OVER HEELS,
the latest in Jennifer Dawson's
Something New series,
coming soon from Zebra Books.

Back home Sophie had paid a college girl to clean her apartment. She'd worked so much she wasn't about to waste her weekends on housework. But she couldn't afford that now. Her six-month, contracted salary covered her rent, essentials, take out, the occasional shopping trip, and starting one of those mutual funds thingys she was supposed to have by now. Something had to go, and it wasn't like she was going to start cooking.

She frowned. Did Revival have delivery?

Panic sliced through her and she took a deep breath. She'd worry about it later. Her friends were watching her every move, she'd freak out when she was finally alone. She dusted her hands on her jean shorts, smoothed down her red tank top and squared her shoulders.

Time to get down to the business of becoming a country girl.

Just then a loud roar rumbled through the quiet streets, interrupting the tranquility of the neighborhood. A big, black motorcycle turned the corner. The motor was so loud it vibrated through her ears, and strummed through her blood, jolting the first signs of life from her.

Yes, of course motorcycles were dangerous, but Sophie had a tiny thing for danger and the Harley looked and sounded as dangerous as they came.

Sophie, Maddie, and Penelope all froze in the driveway, staring at the bike tearing a path through the street. She could tell the driver was a man by the breath of his shoulders but she couldn't make him out.

She waited for him to pass, but he pulled into the driveway next to hers and turned off the bike.

Sophie could only blink in shock. Her throat went dry. The driver wasn't just a man; he was *all* man.

Who in the hell was that?

The man didn't get off the motorcycle. Instead he sat there, watching her. At least she thought he watched her, but it was hard to tell behind his mirrored, aviator frames. He wore jeans, and the denim stretched over the powerful thighs that straddled the beast of a machine. He took his hands off the handlebars and the muscles in his forearms corded and flexed, before biceps filled out his black t-shirt. His shoulders went on for miles, stretching the confines of the cotton.

And that was just his body. But his face, holy crap his face. He had a strong jaw, hard features, and short dark brown hair. Sophie couldn't see his eyes, but he was ridiculously masculine and uncomfortably good-looking.

"Hey, Ryder," Maddie called out, before giving her a huge, sly smile. "This is Sophie."

Her friend clearly knew exactly who he was, but had failed to mention him.

She frowned as he nodded in her direction before swinging his leg off the bike.

He straightened to his full height and Sophie gulped. He was a giant. Tall and broad with lean tapered hips and a flat stomach. She'd bet every last dollar in her meager bank account that he had a six-pack under his shirt.

He walked across the grass.

Sophie scowled as her adrenalin kicked up and she had a sudden urge to flee.

Maddie waved a hand between them. "Sophie Kincaid, meet Ryder Moore."

He came to stand in front of her, tilting his strong jaw before raising his sunglasses to peer down at her. His eyes were like nothing she'd ever seen before. They were gray, light and almost eerie.

He smiled and her heart skipped a beat. "Sophie, I've heard a lot about you."

She crossed her arms over her chest. She didn't like this man. She didn't know what he was doing here, but she wanted him gone. "Why's that?"

He jerked a thumb over his shoulder. "I'm your neighbor."

Oh no. Why, god, why?

He grinned down at her. "And your landlord."

Oh crap.

This wasn't going to do at all.

Don't miss the first novel in Sharla Lovelace's
Charmed in Texas series, available now from
Lyrical Shine!

A Charmed Little Lie

Lanie Barrett's life didn't turn out quite the way she had hoped, or has led everyone from the town of Charmed Texas, to believe. As her beloved aunt got sicker, Lanie wove a fairytale story even her aunt apparently found questionable. Now, Aunt Ruby has died, and in her will she's challenging Lane to prove that her stories are true. If Lanie is to receive the house she grew up in, the only place that ever felt like home, she must live there for three months and prove to everyone that she and her husband are as happily in love as she told her aunt they were. The only problem is that Lanie doesn't have a husband. Not even close.

Until she meets Nick McKane. Nick is everything Lanie's husband was described to be. Even better, he's just lost his job and needs money to pay for his daughter's art school dreams. With an agreement in hand that will give them both what they want, the two move into Aunt Ruby's house and set out to pretend to live Lanie's fantasy. The only problem is that it isn't long before fantasy is starting to feel more like reality . . .